"Every historical mystery tr[...]
moment in time. Anthon[...]
novel."   —M[...]

"Few literary depictions of the 1906 San Francisco earthquake match the intensity and visceral power of those in Flacco's gripping first novel. . . . Dickens meets Hannibal Lecter. Brace yourself."   —*Booklist*

"Screenwriter Flacco nicely evokes the aftermath of San Francisco's 1906 earthquake in his fiction debut."   —*Publishers Weekly*

"Loaded with suspense."   —*Mysteries Galore*

"A winning debut."   —*Alfred Hitchcock's Mystery Magazine*

"A marvelous page-turner of a thriller set against the fascinating aftermath of the great 1906 earthquake and fire."
            —JAMES DALESSANDRO, author of *1906*

"A fast-moving tale. . . . Where Flacco especially shines is his depiction of the two children, newly orphaned Shane Nightingale and the plucky girl who calls herself Vignette in order to give herself a more mysterious air. . . . It's clearly deserving of a very wide audience."
            —SARAH WEINMAN, author of *Confessions of an Idiosyncratic Mind*

"From its opening pages—when we are plunged headlong into the terrifying chaos of the great San Francisco earthquake of 1906—to its riveting climax, *The Last Nightingale* offers an abundance of those page-turning pleasures readers seek in historical thrillers."
            —HAROLD SCHECHTER, author of *The Devil's Gentleman*

"Atmospheric, chilling, and with more twists and turns than crooked Lombard Street, *The Last Nightingale* has it all. I couldn't put it down."
            —CARA BLACK, author of *Murder on the Ile Saint-Louis*

"Set in a world on the edge of Armageddon, this gripping and completely original thriller that will raise the hair on the back of your neck."
            —WILLIAM BERNHARDT, author of
            Capitol Conspiracy and *Strip Search*

THE LAST NIGHTINGALE

ALSO BY ANTHONY FLACCO

THE LAST NIGHTINGALE
TINY DANCER
A CHECKLIST FOR MURDER

THE
HIDDEN
MAN

THE HIDDEN MAN

A NOVEL OF SUSPENSE

ANTHONY FLACCO

BALLANTINE BOOKS

NEW YORK

The Hidden Man is a work of fiction. Names, characters, places, and incidents
are the products of the author's imagination or are used fictitiously.
Any resemblance to actual events, locales, or persons,
living or dead, is entirely coincidental.

A Ballantine Books Trade Paperback Original

Published in the United States by Ballantine Books, an imprint of The Random
House Publishing Group, a division of Random House, Inc., New York.

BALLANTINE and colophon are registered trademarks of Random House, Inc.
MORTALIS and colophon are trademarks of Random House, Inc.

The design on the title page features an incorporation of a photograph
from the Panama-Pacific International Exposition, courtesy of
San Francisco Memories (www.sanfranciscomemories.com).

LIBRARY OF CONGRESS CATALOGING-IN-PUBLICATION DATA
Flacco, Anthony.
The hidden man : a novel of suspense / Anthony Flacco.
p. cm.
ISBN 978-0-8129-7758-5 (trade pbk.)
1. Police—California—San Francisco—Fiction.   2. Panama-Pacific International
Exposition (1915 : San Francisco, Calif.)—Fiction.   3. San Francisco—Fiction.
I. Title.
PS3606.L33H53 2008
813'.6—dc22   2008005202

Printed in the United States of America

www.mortalis-books.com

2 4 6 8 9 7 5 3 1

Book design by Simon M. Sullivan

TO SHARLY
for the magic of believing

AND TO RU
for loving me back

ACKNOWLEDGMENTS

I gladly offer well-deserved thanks to Jane von Mehren and editor Paul Taunton. To Paul for his excellent editorial input, and to Jane for running Mortalis Books with integrity and soul. This is a publication group any writer would be proud to join. I am grateful to be among them.

Equal gratitude to all readers of *The Last Nightingale*, my first book with Mortalis, for your generous enthusiasm and support. In the end, dear reader, all of us are here for you.

I must not forget my loyal graduate interns, who work so tirelessly up here at my hilltop literary bunker for no more reward than their daily composition drills and the Day-Glo "Graduate Intern" vests provided for onsite use. Why, when I think of the thankless jobs they cheerfully do, every single day: manning the guard posts down at the gates, patting down visitors for handheld electronic entertainment devices and then turning them over to the head intern. (He has asked to be credited as "Flashmaster" D. O. Widdit. In the famous *Literary Bunker Group Shot* making its rounds on the Internet, D. O. is the huge one with the sledgehammer.) Also high praise for my onsite visitors' counselor here at the bunker, Maryann Francois, M.BS., who so expertly defuses the visitors' reactions when D.O. grinds up their devices in his big wooden bin at the end of the driveway.

... The millions of fans of young nephews Matthew and Daniel may rest assured, it appears that nothing can be done to stop the lads, who will loudly sing into your face whenever the urge strikes. On the other side of town, nephews Drasko and

Nikola remain forces to be dealt with and admired, while solitary niece Nicole enters adulthood with lovely strength and poise, and her brother Jordan greets the world as a young officer in the U.S. Navy. Up in Seattle, Jill emerges as a freshly minted young adult with a quick mind and gentle humor, while her brother Scott is hard at work on, if I have it right, some sort of mind-meld technology back-engineered from the Roswell crash, or—it's complex. My brother Dino is actually learning Mandarin and traveling alone all around China, brother Nick is holed up in a think tank figuring out how to make things to defend people from other things, and brother Dominic has become so scary good with Photoshop that all bow before him, lest a *perfectly convincing* photograph should just happen to appear on the Internet, showing . . .

THE
HIDDEN
MAN

CHAPTER ONE

THE FAMED MESMERIST James "J.D." Duncan paced backstage, practicing his *And Now You Are Hypnotized!* glare, the one that people recognized from his posters and always wanted to see in person. Each time he passed over the thin crack in the floor that ran across the backstage area, he carefully adjusted his stride to hit it on the middle of his boot sole. At a moment when his confidence needed to be at its peak, it reinforced his faith in himself to tempt the stage gods with an arrogant disregard for stepping on cracks.

At least the boys in the stage crew had followed their strict instructions, this time: clear the backstage floor of any obstacles, then leave the "Master of the Secret Powers of Mesmerism" alone to pace and concentrate, prior to the show.

J.D. sipped away on his customary preshow tea, to warm up the old throat. But he still felt thirsty, dried out even, while he strode back and forth in the darkness.

He paused to listen in on the announcer, who was busily warming up the crowd like a man in love with his own voice. The house was packed with over a thousand of the city's most elite residents, so the silver-tongued devil out there was taking forever to get around to the introduction. J.D. hated it whenever some local blowhard master of ceremonies sapped the energy out of the folks before the star of the evening arrived onstage. It sometimes forced him to use up half his show on audience humiliation gags, just to get them stoked back up to a workable energy level.

It occurred to him then that he was feeling *extremely* annoyed over tonight's delay. His fingernails dug into his clenched fists. He could sense the urge to action, deep in his muscles, and he thought what a welcome relief it would be to feel the announcer's cheek-bones crush beneath his knuckles.

Then, abruptly, as if with the flick of an electric light switch, he found himself full of strange sensations. His skin began crawling with anxiety, ready to break out in a heat rash. This was odd, on a winter evening, backstage—where no heaters were permitted.

An unpleasant vibration came from somewhere deep in his skull; he was grinding his teeth, biting down hard. He forced his jaw muscles to relax, but within seconds his teeth were clenched again.

When a slight movement caught the far corner of one eye, he whipped around in reflex and found himself facing the backstage fire door. The exit led to the back alley, next to the trash bins. It seemed as if the door clicked back into place just as he turned around to face it.

But someone leaving? Unlikely. Civilians were not allowed back there. And who in the crew would leave by the backstage fire door when a show was under way, and risk being heard out in the house? Nobody who wanted to keep his job.

So he had believed. Now his heartbeat boomed inside his chest. Duncan told himself to relax. But before he completed the thought, another bit of motion caught at the corner of his eye, from the other side. This time, there was nothing there.

That made him wonder if he had just imagined the first one, whatever it was. He could not be certain now.

His sense of anxiety grew worse. His body was an electric motor fed with a steadily increasing flow of current. He had no way to turn it down. His skin broke into a hot sweat and a second flash of body heat took him by surprise.

This never happened before a show. James "J.D." Duncan was always cucumber cool under pressure; it was how he kept ahead of the folks.

He took the last quaff of the tepid tea, but instead of calming him, it burned him inside. The feeling of heat radiated through his gut and gathered in his bones. His body seemed to gain ten degrees of temperature in that single swallow. He felt as if he must be glowing in the dark.

Only then did he realize that he was pacing in a furious circle, with his footsteps barely covered by the droning announcer on-stage. The man cruelly pontificated about the evening's cause for celebration: *"San Francisco's First Intercontinental Telephone Line—All the Way to New York!"*

Still, J.D. knew that the folks out there, born high or low, were all waiting for *him,* right where he wanted them, needed them to be. Every single one of them had come hoping to be amazed by this new American phenomenon of public hypnosis. Despite any worldly poses that an individual audience member might strike, he knew that every one of them hoped that ol' J.D. really would deliver just as it was promised in the advance ballyhoo—and that his spells would truly *Give Strength to the Weak!*

Thus the folks came primed to expect hypnotic spells with the power to tap each individual's essential life force and *"open it like a valve in a pipeline!"* Tonight—as on every performance night— J.D.'s bubble of a reputation would only survive to the extent that he successfully walked the tightrope between what people would barely tolerate and what they would reject outright.

At least the tightrope was wide. After all, the new century was promising that the 1900s would bring an age of scientific miracles. Such things seemed to be emerging in every direction. Why, in less than a month, the entire world would be focused upon the city of

San Francisco, freshly reborn after the devastating Great Earth-quake and fires of 1906. Soon, because of the coming world's fair, the Pan-Pacific International Exposition, the new city would be ablaze with all the fanciest wonders of the technological era.

Everybody in the audience had arrived at the theatre with their disbelief already surrendered, primed to witness unusual things. They all knew that their young century was entering a time of great expectations. To mesmerize such people did not involve any penny-ante sleight of hand; the skill probed much deeper than that. J.D. knew that good mesmerism was truly sleight of mind.

Even the hardnoses in the audience lived in the same world as everybody else, and each one carried his own expectations of en-countering the next man-made eyepopper on any given day. The power of that very sense of expectation was the raw clay of J.D.'s work. How fine it was to be up there on that stage, invisibly sculpt-ing the folks' sense of social inhibition, then standing back and watching their bodies happily dance along, released.

He jerked—startled—as another bit of motion caught his atten-tion. It was as if a shadow darted past. He whipped around to con-front the source but again found nothing. This time the sense of frustration made him cringe.

J.D. searched for a reason to remain calm, assuring himself that these sensations did not necessarily mean he was coming down with some sudden illness. They even seemed suspiciously familiar, an exaggerated version of those slight visual anomalies and odd sensations that he had experienced on a few rare occasions.

It only happened back in the beginning, when he got careless in his measurements and took a bit too much of the elixir. Experience soon taught him that a few extra grains could be enough to make the dose feel excessive.

But tonight, an overdose of the elixir, even a pinch, was impos-sible. He had never taken it before a show. Never.

J.D. checked the announcer's patter again. Finally, the man was nearing the point of calling out his introduction. But now it was a different sense of urgency that overwhelmed him; he had to know what was happening to him before he faced a crowd of a thousand of the city's elite.

He fled to his dressing room, just a few yards down the hall, but he stopped cold in the doorway. He stood staring into the room, toward his dressing table, where there was a dire message spelled out by the objects placed there. Its meaning was as threatening as a graffito scrawled in blood.

His fine leather pouch, the one filled with the precious powdered elixir—it was sitting out. Right there in the open. The godforsaken thing was smack in the middle of the tabletop, in front of his makeup mirror!

This was also an impossibility. He never left the elixir sitting out, anywhere.

Worse: A little of the powder had been spilled about the bag itself and onto the table. Who on earth would spill it like that, wasting it? And why had they expected him to have it, in the first place?

Is it the Germans? Do they want it back?

His stomach lurched; somebody had found out about his secret hiding place. Not only that, they had been foolish enough to get their hands on a medicinal substance like this one, only to abandon their big find. This was no casual robbery. He had been invaded by someone who realized on some level that J.D. could not pursue the matter with the police—that would compromise his need for secrecy regarding the elixir. More importantly, it could reveal the condition that made it necessary for him. His image would become a joke.

Whoever had done this, he felt certain that they understood little or nothing about the substance. They would have stolen it, otherwise. *And if they didn't know what it was, why would they load my tea with it? What could they gain by any of it?*

With that grim question, J.D.'s own logic confronted him. He felt his spirits plummet. The conclusion was terrible but true, like his mirror reflection on a hungover morning, and it left him with a single, ugly conclusion.

Nobody could have done this except for him.

It was self-evident. The problem was the stubborn fact that he had never once taken his elixir before a performance. He had a healthy fear of its power. It had to be used with great care, each dose trimmed to the minimum for effectively clearing his fogged brainpan and reacquiring his powers of recent memory. That was all.

Even under the proper dosage, he sometimes succumbed to overpowering urges to jump and dance, or to fall into spontaneous bursts of giddy laughter. These things, in front of the public, in front of an *audience,* could do more than threaten his respectability; they could ruin his legacy—precisely the opposite of the elixir's purpose in his life.

The crystalline powder saved his life every day by allowing him to hide the terrible symptoms, but the stuff was not entirely controllable. He had always known that it was unsafe for performance situations.

So why did the open bag sit there, mocking him?

He hurried over to it, retied it, and relocked it into the false bottom of his makeup kit. He decided that this time he would carry the entire kit with him and leave it offstage, just outside the audience's view, so he could keep his eye on it throughout the show.

He snapped down the lid and stood up, ready to return to the stage area, but he was moving too fast. The blood rushed down and out of his brain, and seemed to swirl away through his feet. The walls swayed like window curtains. He fought to regain his balance.

Ever the professional, J.D. also took advantage of that moment of inactivity to listen for his cue . . . and noticed to his horror that everything was silent. The idiot announcer had just called out his introduction while he stood there too stunned to hear it.

Fear of failure sent a helpful blast of adrenaline through him that steadied his balance and cleared his vision. Habit overtook him. He rushed out through the stage wings, automatically straightening his coat and tie.

But things began to happen too fast. Everything that he looked at seemed to be extra shiny, as if somebody had put a coating of wax over life itself and then buffed it to a high gloss. His eyeballs felt a size too big; there was a slight tickle in his eye sockets whenever he shifted his gaze.

J.D. felt a wad of dread hit him. "Elixir" or not, there was far too much of the stuff in his system, much more than anything he had ever experienced. He was in no condition to get onto a stage. He could hardly predict his own reactions.

He had no business being out in public at all. In his present state, he belonged in his private hotel suite, or perhaps even a hospital bed, but certainly not downstage center.

Some of the audience members were even on the very board that held his contract for nearly a year's worth of employment. It included his luxury suite at the Fairmont Hotel and his generous per diem.

How many doses is this, all at once?

It struck him that it made no difference. The fact remained that J.D. was committed to giving this performance, in this time and in this place. It simply could not be allowed to matter that he might very well be reduced to incoherence by the overdose, or that, as his opening number, he might suffer a seizure and die onstage.

He dropped the makeup case where he would be able to see it, just barely offstage, then paused in the last bit of shadow before stepping out into the glare. Habit carried him through his last-moment ritual. He went over his very first line and simultaneously checked his fly. Then he steeled himself with the reminder that the elixir was made very far away, in Germany, and that it was only a couple of years old. There was no danger that the audience knew it even existed, let alone had any idea what its effects might be.

Therefore, he reminded himself, *they will only decide that some-*

thing is amiss if you fail to deliver the entertainment. Whether or not anybody was aware of a new chemical substance named *methylene-dioxymethamphetamine,* everybody knew when they were bored.

That's the secret, he reminded himself while he took that first step out onto the stage. *Just don't let them get bored. They will forgive anything else.*

The strong spotlight swung toward him while he stepped into view. Its beam was generated by the theatre's brand-new, all-electric direct current illumination system, and after the light was concentrated through the powerful Fresnel lens, it hit him so hard that it sent a rush of golden sparkles swirling through him.

A sudden wave of ecstasy pounded into him. It was all he could do to remain on his feet. No matter that he was already in full view; nothing could stop such powerful waves from washing through him. He planted his feet and doubled over, writhing with the irresistible sensations.

Everything good so far, J.D. reassured himself. He knew that during the first moments of any show, the audience was so ready for entertainment that they would play along with practically anything. He called that time period the Golden Moment, and the secret of its forgiving magic lay in understanding that the Golden Moment was always short. You could get away with all kinds of slips and false starts, but whatever it was that you asked the audience to play along with during the Golden Moment, you had damned well better be able to tie it all up before the end of the show.

If you do, they will love you.

If you don't, they will mock you out of town.

J.D.'s time-leash tended to be a bit longer than those of other performers, because his audiences were always primed for weird experiences in the mysteries of hypnotic trances. He had to hope that during tonight's Golden Moment, the audience would interpret any odd behavior on his part as being some kind of exotic preparation ritual.

It worked, to an extent. Everyone fell silent in fascination while he gyrated and jerked in response to the overwhelming physical sensations storming through him.

A little luck arrived; the social scale of that particular audience was such that no rude noises came from the house, in spite of his unique behavior. No unkind observations were spoken in that special sotto voce style of the theatre world, that false display of discretion intended to be overheard. Throughout the packed house, dignity trumped common impulse. Except for some confused muttering, the respectful silence held—for the moment.

By the time J.D. regained enough control to proceed to the podium, he knew that he was still inside the Golden Moment, but just barely. He gazed out over the audience with an equal mix of elation and terror.

Still there was no other course but to press straight ahead. He knew his routine well enough to hope that if he let himself run on sheer experience—and did not put too much thought into anything—he might somehow fake his way through the evening without stumbling so badly that no recovery was possible.

That small hope consoled him well enough that once he began calling out his customary opening lines to the rapt audience, his fear at finding himself in this situation was not as bad as the realization that he still had no memory of taking the elixir. Certainly not mixing it into his tea. Or of forgetting, unforgivably, to put the bag away.

No. He realized in that instant that he had been wrong to doubt himself. If the elixir had been in his tea, somebody else had to have put it there. Someone else did it, despite the fact that he had never met anyone on the American continent who was even aware of its existence.

J.D. knew the elixir's effects well enough, but the knowledge did little to protect him from it. After being exposed to such an amount, he felt his trademark sharp mental skills turning to dust.

One last, semicoherent thought ran through his head before he surrendered to the situation and attempted to run through his show under a combination of ingrained memory and force of habit. The thought was that as soon as the performance was over, he should be sure not to forget about something. Backstage, seeing a door closing from the corner of his eye.

But by this point, his vision was filled with tiny heat waves. The faces in the audience appeared to be painted on balloons.

And yet the Golden Moment carried him. His standard opening run of hypnosis jokes came out of his mouth as easily as his breath. Their sole purpose was to relax and disarm the audience, to get them synchronized. And during the familiar introduction, he was able to sit back inside himself and let the long years of practice guide his performance while the hidden man ruminated behind the mask.

Something about a door backstage, but what? Did someone sneak in just to slip this massive dose into his tea? Why would anyone know about this incredible elixir, and not steal *it?*

But before he could expend any energy on the mystery, he had to demonstrate the color of his smoke and the glint of his mirrors to the movers and shakers of San Francisco. He had to give the folks a solid sample of what they had bought from James "J.D." Duncan for the full duration of their Panama-Pacific International Exposition.

If he failed to give them a show, an entire year's worth of steady work would be lost. Worse: The gossip factor would be unendurable.

Now that he was in his sixth decade among a population who frequently lived no longer than that, any sort of sullied reputation— say, a story about an aging performer who might be losing his special powers—would be a kiss from the Grim Reaper. James "J.D." Duncan could not afford to take any backward steps at this late point, or backward might well become the only direction that the folks allowed him to travel in.

So he kept his mouth moving with the familiar words, tried not to listen to himself too hard—and hoped like hell that he was making sense to the folks out there in the house.

CHAPTER TWO

SIMULTANEOUSLY
**THE PACIFIC MAJESTIC THEATRE—
SAN FRANCISCO'S FINEST**

DETECTIVE RANDALL BLACKBURN WAS in a dark mood. He was a damned *homicide* investigator, far too valuable to be wasted on an evening of private guard duty for some show business bigwig. He tried to remember when he had ever suffered through such an idiotic waste of his time, even back during his days of walking a beat. Nothing came to mind.

Blackburn stared out through the hallway window on the theatre's second floor, but the late evening darkness was thickened by an inbound fog. There was little to look at. Along the upper reaches of Market Street, where the streetlamps were still only powered by fragile gas lines, the best that the lamps could do was to provide glowing place markers in the featureless night. He could see the faltering yellow-orange gaslights for no more than two blocks in the distance, and between them only flat darkness littered with charcoal shadows.

"Crime weather," Blackburn muttered under his breath. He pushed his gaze a little harder into the night.

Pitch-black. One of the two ways that criminals like it best. Pitch-black, or sunny and clear. Rain keeps them home.

He pulled the silver watch from the inside chest pocket of his coat. The open face showed nine-twenty. The silver plating was rubbed through in some places, right where the fingers go. He had also replaced the crystal face six times, so far, courtesy of half a dozen of the countless petty crooks and vicious killers over the years who forced him to take them down with brute force. He pocketed the watch again, protecting it out of long habit.

At the age of forty-one, Blackburn knew that he could still dominate most men in their twenties. But he also felt the speed leaving his legs, felt the knees giving in to frequent snaps of pain that came out of nowhere. On some of the worst mornings, he awoke with knuckles too swollen to make a solid fist or to hold his nightstick with any real grip. He could work the fingers back into action, but it sometimes took a few minutes of vigorous rubbing.

And now he was a detective, by God. Entitled to thrill and amaze his superior officers by sniffing out criminals while leaving the eager up-and-comers to vie for the endless honors of flushing perpetrators from the shadows. Let them take the victory lumps and earn the useless purple hearts.

Yet tonight, the department brass in their immortal wisdom had him on the sort of honorary "body guard" duty that made a great training exercise for a wet-eared rookie. Naturally, then, the department was going to waste the services of a detective on such an assignment. No advance instructions, just "show up at the theatre and be prepared to work."

The runner with the orders had warned Blackburn that the captain was meeting with Police Chief White about him, at that very moment. "Under no circumstances" was Blackburn to leave the second-floor hallway before Captain Merced arrived.

But once he got up there, he was left to wait while the rest of the audience filed in, gradually finding their seats. Eventually, the heavy doorway curtains were pulled shut and the show began. Blackburn heard the strains of patriotic theme music, an announcer booming on and on about the *Glorious Achievement of Instantaneous Communication by Voice, from One Side of the Country to the Other!*

The renowned mesmerist, James Duncan, then took over the

audience. Duncan immediately began to shout and bellow from the stage, strangely forceful in his delivery. Blackburn casually wondered if this trait was part of the man's usual act. He could not make out the words from his position, but the showman's voice remained filled with bursts of fiery passion. He sounded like a half-crazed evangelist. The man's emotional tone was unusual enough to tickle at Blackburn's investigative sense, even though he could not see the stage.

Since he was under orders to play the role of personal escort to this showman, he tossed the question of onstage emotional levels into his mental "could be something" bin, just in case. It was an old habit. The bin was large.

Forty-five minutes of the mesmerist's one-hour show went by. Frustration compressed his head, but under orders from his captain, he could only wait and quietly pace in a slow loop.

His boot heel lightly nicked something on the floor. He had just done the same thing moments before. This time he looked down and saw that there was a hairline crack running all the way across the floor. It extended as far as he could see from that point. His heel had briefly caught on it because the floor on one side had taken a slight vertical drop—maybe an eighth of an inch. He had never studied masonry, but he knew that this was a fairly new building, brick and stone over a steel frame. It was built atop the ruins of the theatre that was demolished by the Great Earthquake, and billed as a solemn testament to the need for worthy construction in this unstable part of the world. Here, of all places, it seemed odd for such a long split to run through a new building's floor. The fact that he noticed it at all was a grim marker of his level of boredom, but he made a mental note to report the crack to somebody back at the City Hall Station.

At that point, his train of thought was finally derailed by the appearance of Captain Christian Merced. The man puffed his short and portly body up the stairs, swiveling a domed head in all directions until he spotted Blackburn. When he did, he immediately locked on to Blackburn's eyes. Merced was not imposing as a physical figure, but his momentary anger amplified his permanent sense of rank and made him a formidable presence.

Blackburn felt the same cold chill that he sometimes caught during card games. Nothing good ever followed it.

The captain stepped toward the nearest curtained alcove, and without so much as a glance back at Blackburn, he flicked a silent gesture of commandment to join him. Blackburn's cold chill deepened while he stepped over to him.

The moment that they were both inside the temporary alcove formed by the thick velvet sound curtains, Captain Merced stared straight up at Blackburn. His expression seemed to insist that Blackburn's greater size would do nothing to protect him.

"Detective Blackburn," Merced began, but he stopped and swallowed, making a visible effort to quell his emotions.

After a brief pause, he went on. "Tonight, Chief White was so upset and angry with *me* . . . that he actually questioned *my* competence. Do you hear me? *Four years,* he's been in that position, and I have never heard one peep out of him. Not against me or my command!"

"I'm, ah . . ."

"Sorry! You're sorry." Merced took a deep pull at his cigar. He blew a long, tight exhale straight against Blackburn's uniform.

"Of course you're not *really* sorry, though, are you?"

"Excuse me, sir?"

"But we're about to take care of that. Because it's all downhill for you after this, Detective."

"For me."

"Maybe I shouldn't even be addressing you as 'Detective.' "

"What?" Blackburn did not mean to yell. The word barked out of him in a burst of shock.

"Hold your voice down, damn it!" Merced's words hissed like a steam pipe. "Or I will make good on that threat!"

"Sir, I have *no* idea what—"

"I know that you have no idea, Sergeant. I'm here to tell you! It's that damned half-breed family or whatever kind of group you've got going on over at your house!"

Blackburn lost all sense of self-control and grabbed Captain Merced by the lapels, then whispered down onto his eyeballs, "My *family*, Captain. That's all you have to say, if you want to refer to them. My *family*. That's enough said."

Abruptly, Blackburn regretted his choice of reactions and a sense of foolishness flashed through him. Along with the certainty that he had allowed himself to be baited and trapped.

But to his astonishment, the captain's expression shifted and he gave out a small laugh of delight. "No! Oh, no! There's a *whole lot more* to be said, Detective. Because nobody really minded when your young ward or whatever he—"

"My son," Blackburn corrected. "I adopted both of them, Captain."

"Neither one uses your name."

"They already had one." He slowly released his grip on the captain's lapels, wondering where in the hell things were going to go after this.

Merced ignored that and continued, "Shane Nightingale was entitled to quit officer school. So he's the 'artistic type.' Fair enough. No harm in trying."

"He was mostly worried that I would be embarrassed because of it." Blackburn could scarcely believe that they were talking this way, after he had just assaulted his superior officer.

"Exactly!" Merced replied with gusto. "He worried that he might have humiliated you by dropping out! But *now*, he won't have that burden anymore! Gone!"

Merced was frighteningly delighted. He gave a fake gasp. "Poof! Is it a trick by the Great Mesmerist down there, James Duncan? No! I'll tell you what it is: The low-water mark has just dropped by half a mile. Because at least your 'son' only failed after making an honest try."

Blackburn did not dare to say a word, to move.

Merced kept talking, but his grin turned malevolent. "I suppose you call Vignette Nightingale your 'daughter,' then?"

Merced was far too happy for any of this. Blackburn did not bother to reply.

"Your 'daughter' is nineteen years old. Same age as Shane was, when he tried. But do you want to tell me how in God's name she got the idea that she was going to be the one in your 'family' to make it through police training? Everybody knows the department doesn't put women in uniform. *Everybody.* If they don't know it— say, they're new in town?—we tell them. Right off."

"Are you saying that Vignette tried to sign up for—"

"No, no! What I am *telling* you is, that beanpole of a young woman looks quite a bit like a young man when she cuts her hair off. *That* is what I'm telling you."

By now Blackburn was completely at a loss. He had seen Vignette earlier that morning and she had plenty of hair. She was wearing it in a different style, but it was not a man's haircut by any means.

"Captain, did she actually go down to the station and try to fool someone, so she could go through police training?"

"No, Sergeant. She did *that* two weeks ago, when she applied. Last week, her incoming class of candidates began their first day, and for all of that week, your 'daughter' lagged behind on physical strength tests, but scored right up near the top on most of the others. I'm told that the instructors went home on Friday looking forward to seeing how this new recruit was going to come off in the days to come."

" . . . Vignette?"

"She was exposed by somebody, just today. Two of our officers brought in a note that explained it all. Otherwise, come Monday, she would have been back there, I suppose. With the other recruits! Outshooting everybody at the gun range, for all I know!"

"Sir . . . Vignette has been attending police training . . . as a man?"

"A skinny one who doesn't talk much. Half those recruits look like girls to me, anyway. Lot of soft young bastards."

"And getting away with it?"

"You are *not* hearing this the way you ought to! Yes. She pulled it off for a few days. But she's been ratted out now. Good joke, right? Uh-huh, until tonight, when Chief White got wind of it and *I* got to eat a horseshit sandwich for dinner. My humor is very bad, Detective. That's why I am giving you this news myself."

"Does Vignette know she's been found out?"

"Vign—*Forget* her for just one minute! Mister James Duncan down there on the stage is the one who requested you as a body guard tonight. That's why you're here. And you could have gotten away with just hustling him around for a bit after the performance, then going on home, all finished, none the worse for wear.

"But no. One of your 'family' has embarrassed me, Detective Blackburn. And I find that the only way I can impress my unhappiness upon her is to make you so miserable that you go back home and do it for me."

"Sir, if you could just talk to her."

"We are far past the talking point. Here is what I will do. I am going to grant Mr. Duncan's *other* request, which was for you to be supplied to him throughout the duration of the exposition, for personal guard duty."

"What is this? I'm a homicide detect—"

"Exactly! I would never have so much as mentioned it to you otherwise. You would have kissed his arrogant ass for a while tonight, and tonight only, and then you would have been done with it. Now, you are going to be his personal, on-call bodyguard for the entire affair."

"Ten *months?*"

Captain Merced's only reply was to smooth his lapels back into place.

"Captain, if you want to bring me up on charges for grabbing you—"

"Forget that. Not interested."

"You would throw away nearly a year of my—"

"Now you're starting to get it, Detective! You are going to be my messenger to your 'daughter,' who wouldn't be trying such nonsense if *you* had raised her right. And for the next year, the frustrations will go home with you every night."

"Sir, any personal grievance you feel toward her is—"

"*You* will pay on her behalf, every day, and at night when you go home, I believe that you will eventually make *her* pay. Isn't that perfect? It will appear to her as if she got away with her little game, just because the department wants to avoid publicity. But she will eventually feel the consequences. And you have been elected to bring them back to her."

"Captain. You were deliberately goading me over my family."

The captain spurted another short and nasty laugh. "What the hell do you do over in that house of yours? And what have you been telling those young people? Who told her it was all right to behave that way?"

"Does she know the game is over?"

"*You* are going to tell her it's over. And also that she will never show up around a precinct house in this city again, or we will arrest her on every horseshit charge that the boys in booking can dream up. Beyond that, let her think she's getting away with this, if you want to indulge her. Personally, I think she ought to have to sleep out on the porch for a few months."

"I don't treat her like that."

"That much is obvious. Possibly the main problem. So you go right ahead and give her a pat on the back for fooling the department. I'm gonna bet that after you spend a couple weeks following around some stage performer, you'll be filling her life with the kind of misery she deserves."

"But she didn't do any harm, right? She didn't damage anything?"

"Goddamn it, Blackburn, the department's reputation is something! We don't need to have it tarnished."

"I'm sure she'd be willing to offer an apology," Blackburn said, not at all certain that Vignette would do any such thing.

"Here's what you do," Merced countered. "As soon as the show ends, report to Mr. Duncan and remain with him until he dismisses you tonight. He'll give you your schedule for the rest of the week."

"Sir, there's got to be a better way to—"

"*I'm* not going to be the one to punish her, Detective." Captain Merced fired up a large wooden match. He put a fresh cigar in his mouth and lit it, then tossed the match to the floor and ground it out with his heel. He finally permitted all his outrage and contempt to flash out in a feral grin.

"You are." This time he exhaled a thick cloud that filled the alcove. He left it behind him when he walked out.

Blackburn stood motionless, stunned. He refused to allow himself to react. *If you begin moving—a single move—your legs will take over, and in ten seconds you will catch him and your hands will be around his throat.*

He was helpless against his protective instincts toward Shane and Vignette. The sound of anyone speaking a word against either of them cut him to the bone. Now it was clear that Merced had showed up tonight already determined to pull this trick, whether Blackburn had been stupid enough to let the captain bait him or not.

In which case, Blackburn realized that he probably could have gotten away with punching the little gnome, as long as it didn't leave a mark. Maybe in the stomach.

He stood for a few more seconds, fearing that Merced might pop back into the alcove to dig in one last word. But when Blackburn finally allowed himself to step outside, the hallway was empty.

He sighed. This news about Vignette was too much. There was more here than he could sort out anytime soon. He had to push her out of his thoughts until he could get home and find out what had actually happened.

Until then, he would have to deliberately keep himself busy

with the job at hand. The first thing to do after the show would be to take issue with the lauded personage of James "J.D." Duncan about this job as a grown man's nanny.

In a burst of optimism, he wondered whether he might meet with this Duncan fellow and simply convince him that a homicide detective was not really the optimum choice for an entertainer's personal body guard. After all, there was no reason for a stranger to request Blackburn, specifically. Maybe the man just wanted to be assured that he would be coddled by somebody who was really good at it, and since he had the city forces on his side, he requested a detective. With a little luck, the man might be made to understand that this was an improper use of Blackburn's skills.

One thing at a time.

And then, if he could do a solid job of unraveling this ball of knots with Duncan, perhaps he might clear his head enough to go home and deal with Vignette. He tried to visualize himself asking her what the hell happened over at the cop school, and doing it some way that would not cause her to react by folding herself up into a silent box. She was capable of staying there for days, for weeks.

One thing at a time.

The most important thing was to avoid chasing down Captain Merced and throttling the arrogant bastard for casting such contempt onto Blackburn's family. He was incredulous that the man would think that just because Blackburn was thrown into a ridiculous assignment, he would react by doing Merced's dirty work for him, that he would blame Vignette for the miserable duty and take out his job frustrations on her.

One thing at a time.

He made a conscious effort to bolster himself with a deep breath, then headed downstairs to look for an usher to show him backstage. There, he could grab this Duncan fellow as soon as he finished his performance, and calmly—oh, so calmly—set him straight.

CHAPTER THREE

THE TALL YOUNG MAN OF twenty-one with the dark hair and slight build stood in the darkness along the side wall of the theatre. His position was down close to the front of the stage, and he stared up at James "J.D." Duncan with a smile of fascination.

Shane Nightingale had spent the first few minutes of the show feeling too worried over what might be going on with Randall upstairs to be able to pay much attention to the stage show. But then at some early point, this Duncan fellow abruptly stopped his stage patter and took a long pause . . . before stepping to the front. It was odd enough to grab Shane's attention.

From there, Duncan began to speak over the footlights and out to the audience. He moved his penetrating gaze over them all, as if each and every one of them was a beloved member of his closest family. That increased Shane's attention right away; until that moment, the showman had struck Shane as being reluctant even to look at the audience. And from that moment onward, Shane's interest was rewarded. The entire performance somehow tilted off center.

It was a subtle shift, but something suddenly felt dangerously out of place to Shane. The sensation was so potent that it rattled his body with a shiver.

Duncan had captured Shane's attention by this point. The showman owned it altogether once he opened his mouth.

"My dear ladies—my gentle men: I must reveal to you the absolute truth!"

The legendary mesmerist held up his hands, palms out: a liar no more.

"I have just this instant realized that the best way to honor the forthcoming opening day of the Panama-Pacific International Exposition is for me to cease this common performance of things. Hah—'things.' Things anyone will be able to see throughout the exposition. Not unworthy things, to be sure. Nonetheless, matters perhaps best left to another day. The healing sessions? Well and good, but not tonight. The large-scale demonstrations? I am always eager to do them, but they too must wait. Because I understand that what *this* august gathering truly deserves tonight, truly cries out for tonight in the depths of your spirits, is to *See the Veil Lifted!* Look behind the ordinary illusions and learn how to work with them yourselves!"

The audience released a collective gasp of delight and a roll of excited applause. He waited for them to get it all out before he continued.

"Tonight, I will not merely open up the energy that resides inside us all; I will show you how to do it yourselves! Not to eat a fish, but to catch a fish! This audience deserves a *one time only* opportunity to witness *secret exercises* such as I *personally perform* prior to my greatest and most challenging undertakings in the Mesmeric Arts!"

Another roll of thrilled applause rose up from the house. Shane felt waves of anticipation run through the theatre like a sudden strong breeze. He had to stop himself from laughing out loud. Here was this James Duncan, who for all the world struck Shane as a glorified carnival act, yet he was being revered by an audience of the city's top social register—all on nothing more than the combination of advance publicity and strange onstage behavior.

Whenever Shane glanced over at the faces of the audience, it was plain that the man up there on the stage was doing a thorough job of getting away with all of it. But then, for the next several minutes, Duncan did little more than make odd singing and breathing noises while demonstrating all sorts of stretching exercises. He seemed to be flexible and was capable of some unusual contortions, which he repeatedly invited the audience to remember and copy in the privacy of their own homes. From their beaming faces and nodding heads, the audience gave Shane the impression that later at home, yes indeed, they would all be sticking their heads under at least one leg.

But before long, Shane found himself feeling troubled that Duncan's "explanations" for his bizarre physicality did not seem to connect to anything. All Shane heard were what sounded like the products of an ungoverned stream of consciousness.

Nevertheless, whenever he turned back to look at the faces in the house, every one of them watched Duncan, enraptured. They all appeared to be convinced that they were truly learning "secrets of the universe" and demonstrations of mesmerism.

Meanwhile, Duncan was up there, sweating like a fever victim, wild-eyed, face flushed. The inside of his upper lip continually stuck to his top front teeth, while he talked in what seemed to be a long stream of instructions: how to make this particular move, or how to breathe in this particular pattern, in order to create some particular effect in his secret work.

Shane could not suppress a wide grin. This evening was turning out to be a lot more fun than he had expected. While the audience listened to Duncan's ranting, each person was clearly hearing his or her own variations of "inspirational" content.

Shane doubted that any two members of the audience would tell the same story about what they "learned" at this special presentation, but they were all primed to go home satisfied. He had never seen a clearer example of crowd hypnosis. Even though Duncan claimed that he was giving up his planned demonstrations of group hypnosis in order to reveal his methods and exercises, the audience was unwittingly acting along in perfect group hypnosis itself, supplying their own meanings to his jumbled patter. Duncan had them mesmerized, after all.

Shane could hardly believe his luck. All he had expected to do was accompany Blackburn to the theatre, then join him for whatever remained of the show. He had seen the posters plastered around the city in recent days, and had a vague idea of what James Duncan's show would be like, but he never expected to be treated to such a potent demonstration of one man's mental control over a large crowd of strangers.

He could only stare in admiring wonder. In the slow years since Shane's terrible final night in the Nightingale house, he had managed to develop enough of a social veneer that he could function in most adult environments, if for short periods of time. But no matter how well he did it, he was never more than a visiting stranger, anywhere he went. He marveled at the amount of power that someone like James Duncan could hold in such abundance, when Shane himself had so little.

However, he also could not help wondering if that man up on the stage had the faintest inkling of what he was actually talking about. Duncan was continuing to rattle through his thoughts on all sorts of arcane subjects—always behaving as if he were formulating deep pronouncements. But at no point did he ever actually come out and say much of anything.

Shane had never seen anybody do this so well, or imagined anyone being so blatant about it. It reminded him of watching one of the martial arts masters down in Chinatown; everything was mixed into a flurry of spinning and thrusting. False starts, digressions, interjections—the man never paused long enough for any of it to settle. He blew past meaning through sheer emotional power. The intensity of his delivery was especially remarkable; he reminded Shane of a man pleading for his life.

Shane may have been ignorant of Duncan's method, but he loved observing his skill and he was enthralled by the showman's rambling double-talk. He decided that if Randall didn't show up by the time Duncan's show ended, he would just wait around for him backstage and look for an excuse to meet Duncan early.

Meanwhile, he felt like a field biologist who has just discovered an entirely new species. In his experience, anyone who could be so open and friendly and smooth in front of a crowd usually turned out to be quiet and withdrawn in private company, even somewhat cranky. But with the level of onstage energy that Duncan possessed, who could predict how high his flame would burn, offstage?

After witnessing James Duncan's public persona and watching him herd a crowd of sophisticates with fancy invisible whips, Shane was eager to observe the man himself. Possibly even learn something that would allow him to experience more of his own social strengths and fewer of his weaknesses.

CHAPTER FOUR

PEOPLE FREQUENTLY DISCOVERED THAT it took more than they were prepared to offer to put a scare into Vignette Nightingale. She insisted on choosing her own causes, fighting her own battles, and, most importantly, choosing the time and place for the conflicts herself. *Allowing the opposition to call the field is stupid.* She and Shane had discussed that very idea a few times over the years, and she was reasonably certain that they were united on that.

At the age of nineteen, Vignette's full adult strength was finally with her. She felt it all the time. Even in dreams, she understood that if she could make it to clear ground, she could outrun anything that a nightmare threw at her. Her legs always had more energy than they needed: walking, running, even leaping over tall bushes along the sidewalk on blasts of pure exhilaration—sometimes with the frequent added bonus of irritating grouchy pedestrians. And while her arms were not all that strong compared to those of a young man her age, they were just as fast as her legs. Meaning that Vignette could slap a face six ways from Sunday before the recipient got a clear impression of having been struck the first time. A few men knew that already.

But even a spirit as strong as hers could be snagged and held captive by a strong enough adversary. On this unfortunate day, she was stranded in the manipulative grip of Randall's brand-new fiancée, better known in Vignette's private thoughts as "the Eastern Whore." And at the moment, she was trapped in a little maneuver that Vignette called the Snap Bean Ritual.

The rules of the Snap Bean Ritual were simple: She got captured by the Eastern Whore and sent into forced labor. They toiled over a giant bowl of snap beans together, and this part mattered: *moving at a pace controlled entirely by the Eastern Whore,* they set about plucking ends off each string bean before tossing them one by one into the big receiving bowl.

The task could take half an hour. During that time Vignette remained nailed to the floor by the task and helpless against the real point of the exercise, which was an onslaught of polite verbal dissection that would gradually pull her intestines out, yard by yard, while the Eastern Whore disdainfully commented upon each and every inch, until—

"Ahem," Miss Janine Freshell politely cleared her throat. "You won't leave all the plucking to me, will you, dear?"

Vignette forced herself to meet Miss Freshell's probing gaze. The world might look at the woman standing before her and see a famous author from New York City, but Vignette saw only the face of the Eastern Whore who was out to steal Randall.

"Sorry."

"They don't pluck themselves," Miss Freshell said with a mock-pouty face.

"It's just a lot to take in. And he could be home for supper anytime."

"Oh, if I know our Randall—"

Vignette ground her teeth.

"—he won't bring Shane home until after the performance tonight. If that telephone works like it's supposed to, he's going to be able to call and tell us if he's coming home late. Think of that!"

She plucked two beans together for emphasis, and tossed them into the receiving bowl in a single no-nonsense motion. "They're likely to be hungry once we all get back late tonight, though."

"I just can't believe that the unit commander isn't saying anything to me about it."

"Embarrassment, dear. We all try to avoid it. You know how Randall always—"

"Oh God in heaven, yes, I know *this* about Randall, and I know *that* about Randall, because I've lived here for the last nine years! So really, I should be the one telling *you* Randall this and Randall that!"

Vignette picked up a fistful of snap beans, forgot what she was supposed to do with them, and threw them back into the pot.

"That's just your nerves, dear, taking in the blow. I know it's hard for you to receive this sort of news. The men were here early, and I was only able to let them in because I came over early myself, just to make sure someone was at the door. I knew you'd be here alone. Randall told me how they're making him get this new telephone for his work, and I know how soundly you sleep. We wouldn't have wanted the men to be forced to return later, would we, dear?"

"Miz Freshell, I really wish you would stop calling me 'dear.' I like my name just fine."

"Fair enough. I know about the orphanage and about you changing your name, and all."

"That's *not* what I meant," Vignette snapped.

"Your loud tone of voice tells us that you need to put together a plan and not act out of panic. If you have things you need to confess to Randall about yourself, about needing a change in your living situation, now is the perfect—"

"I'm not *panicking*. I just don't understand why the police use their telephone men for messengers, instead of just grabbing me when I show up!"

Miss Freshell already realized that this part of her story was tricky, the lie of how the policemen had told her about Vignette. She quickly moved past it.

"I told you: avoiding embarrassment. Besides, the messengers were policemen themselves. They just happened to know now how to install the thing."

She lowered her voice and spoke as if this were a delightful secret: "It's for police work, but they say you can call anywhere at all with it! Anybody else who has a telephone. I don't know anyone who does, right off, but some people must. The best ones, actually. Think of it—a private little circle of influential people who are among the privileged few to have such a device of their own! We can speak back and forth to each other!"

When Vignette failed to ignite over that, Miss Freshell shrugged and added, "So I think the captain just used them as messenger boys. Now, listen—I asked them if anybody had informed Detective Blackburn yet, but the men were just regular cops, you know. Doing what they were told."

"I just—" Vignette stopped and forcefully exhaled.

"Can you work the beans while we talk, Vignette? If we have dinner ready for everybody when we're all here, it might make it easier for you to tell him, you know, your reason. Or your excuse. Or whatever you have to say."

"Oh, damn it to hell!" Vignette slapped the table in frustration.

"Certainly, you can use that language if you have no other way to express yourself, dear."

"You really think he might not know already? God! You think I might have to tell him myself tonight?"

"Men are so sensitive about having their territory invaded by a female." She pinched just the tiniest bit off the end of a bean, and flicked it away. "And from their point of view, it's much worse that you fooled them for so long."

"Do you . . . Do you think that maybe this is so embarrassing for the department that they'll keep it a secret even inside the department? In that case, Randall would never hear about it!"

Miss Freshell did not scoff at the idea. She just gave Vignette one of her porcelain smiles, the same smile that had snagged Randall like a deep-sea fishhook. She did, however, pick up one of the longer beans and wiggle it at Vignette to remind her to get back to the Ritual.

This time Vignette let her hands do the repetitive work on their own while she worked at convincing herself that all of this could simply go away. Pinch one end, pinch the other end, toss the bean. Pinch one end, pinch the other end, toss the bean.

It would be so wonderful if she never had to search for an explanation to offer to Randall—the "real reason" why she had elected to endure the police department's all-male training regimen. She would not have minded knowing, herself. Pinch one end, pinch the other end, toss the bean.

It just had to be done. Like the tall shrubs along a sidewalk that dared her to leap them, regardless of what kind of clothing she had on. Like the endless long walks that went late into the night and sent her through neighborhoods that no unaccompanied female ought to dare enter. It had to be done. Pinch one end, pinch the other end, toss the bean.

Plenty of times in recent years she had plainly seen that if she put her hair up under a hat and wore overalls and boots with a long-sleeved shirt, everybody treated her like a young man. All she had to do was walk and move in a very plain fashion, and try not to talk too much. Keep the voice low, never yell.

Back when Shane had to quit police training, her heart broke for him, but she never had any thoughts about personally "righting the wrong" on his behalf. It would be so convenient to offer that to Randall, but the lie would stick in her throat.

The whole truth? Randall, being a man, had taken no notice when she cut off her hair two weeks earlier, because she covered herself with a wig that he must have written off as a new hairstyle. Miss Freshell noticed the wig, of course, but only made a few remarks indicating that she assumed Vignette was just playing with her appearance.

None of it explained what compelled her to invade police training. Such a thing was not only forbidden, it was dangerous. She had been doomed by Nature to fail there, since someone had to catch on sooner or later. The thought of being caught later, however, had always been much less daunting to her than getting caught early on. At least later in the program she would have already proved the point.

She had also counted on the fact that she was legally an adult, at nineteen, and also had a different last name than Randall did. It seemed clear to her that her actions should be regarded apart from his. It was only fair. And it had seemed so apparent to her that if she did well enough in the program before something tripped her up, then whatever "embarrassment" might go around would hardly have any reason to fall onto him.

But she still needed something to tell him. *This is why I did it, this is what I wanted to achieve. I wanted to beat them at their own game because I hate it when they open doors for me. Where in Hell do men get the idea that just because you are female, they have to open a door for you? The man saves you from the awful fate of opening a door for yourself exactly as you do when nobody's around to make an issue of it in the first place.*

On the rare occasion that one stares at me in a disrespectful way, I want to stab my fingertips into his eyes.

I'll settle for showing the tough guys at the police training school whether or not I'm too dainty to open the damned door for myself.

But that was more than she could ever expect Randall to understand. No matter how much you love someone, no matter what gratitude you feel, people's reactions can be unpredictable. You think you know them, then they prove you wrong.

So what *would* Randall do? Perhaps he would show her tolerance, but then maybe not. There was no way to know until it was too late to back away from it.

He was consistently kind to her, but she had never told him things like this about herself. It always seemed that he somehow understood and accepted her true nature. But she had also deliberately avoided testing him on it and dreaded being wrong. Dark anticipations rolled through her on waves of nausea.

She knew that certain things cannot be put back once they get out, such as any public knowledge of Vignette's true nature, where an inexplicable bonfire forever roared inside her chest. The power of it forced her to dance away the excess energy, all across the walls of her life. To her it was stillness and routine that tasted of danger. The exercises, the rituals of conventional tradition made her feel as if she were being force-walked toward her own open grave. The sensation of it hit her the same way that a tight space hits someone with claustrophobia.

Maybe that's what I can tell him. Make him see that it's just my nature, and that's all. It's nothing against anybody else. It's just something I need, like those miners up in Alaska who go crazy if they don't get enough sunshine.

Vignette had come to see her ongoing dilemma as simply this: She was born with a warrior's heart packed inside a beanpole female body. She could run in blazing sprints for two or three blocks, or drop into a dog trot that she could keep up for miles. But in a world overrun by large male strangers who were occasionally crazy and hostile, her physical speed and mental skills were all she had to protect her.

So her battles had to be carried out in the safer, invisible arena of deception and trickery. The particular area of personal expertise that she had developed over much of her life was a refined set of manipulative skills that Vignette simply thought of as *moving things around.*

Things, people, lives. She engaged in battle only at moments of her own choosing, and danced circles around attackers with her speedy legs, a quick mind, and lightning-fast reactions. It was there, in the art and craft of moving things around, that Vignette's considerable skills served her.

At least, that had been her plan at the all-male police training school, where her ruse of passing herself off as a young male recruit worked perfectly for that first week.

Pinch one end, pinch the other end, toss the bean.

CHAPTER FIVE

J.D. HAD LONG SINCE lost control of the performance. The extreme dose of elixir bit random holes in his ability to sustain his stage technique. Now, as the hour-long show was nearing time to end, the evening's Golden Moment was distant history. His uncontrolled babbling had only worked to buy time. That time, too, was now expended.

If he was going to brass his way out of this, he needed to bring some kind of big finish to the proceedings. *Make 'em think they've seen a goddamned* show!

He was stalling the crowd by placing verbal implants under the cover of physical distraction. It was a basic skill. He could sustain it even in this distorted hour. Habit was protecting him, up to a point.

At least the audience members were having a good time guffawing at the test subjects, whom J.D. had lined up at center stage, all facing forward, separated by an arm's length.

He had taken them through the entire setup, using a mix of praise drawn from the audience on the volunteers' behalf. He boosted the technique by raising the individual stakes for each one, asking them each a few personal interview questions. That fastened the experience to their sense of manhood as well as to their ideas of social propriety, creating an effective leash that they did not even realize was there.

As always, the young men were willing to serve as guinea pigs, but determined not to let anyone get the best of them. Everyone in the audience could see that in them. The implied credibility that these boys represented was actually his ace in the hole.

But that much only took care of the setup. For the twist, he had each one demonstrate a few basic bends or stretches "to prove they were fit for the task," but which actually served to reduce their physical inhibition. While each one did the moves he asked of them, J.D. still remembered what he was doing well enough to praise their movements as if they each showed real talent.

As always, while each subject bent and twisted his way through the requested physical movements, J.D. whispered their priming instructions to them under the guise of giving individual encouragements.

Tonight, at that very moment, he assumed that he had done so. But to save his life, he could not actually recall doing it.

He guessed, from the young men's demeanor, that he had done his job as expected and that all were successfully primed. More than anything, it was his sense of balance that told him he still had a few seconds to bring this disaster to some sort of a closing. If only he could remember tonight's trigger phrase while the audience still laughed at the young men, who were dutifully holding the poses that J.D. had molded each one into while he spoke to them.

The man on the audience's left side, downstage right, had been bent into a capital C.

The next man was bent straight over, arm out touching the floor with the other arm bent to connect the two lines, to make a capital A. The others were all bent into the letters to form C-A-L-I-F-O-R-N-I-A out of their ten bodies.

The men would hold it for as long as J.D. wanted them to, with little or no sense of pain from the exertion. Not one of them realized what he was doing. Each one's mind was relaxed and filled with pleasant images of what a fine fellow he was, cued up by J.D.'s combination of physical touch, public instruction, audience pressure, and whispered indoctrination.

But the trigger—what was the damned *trigger*? He had milked this elementary bit for all the juice it had; now it was time to send these quietly prepared young men back into the audience. They were primed to end his show for him, living proof of his abilities, surefire in assuring that the folks would come back to see another performance, and another after that, always trying to figure out how ol' J.D. made things happen.

He stalled by letting them go back to their seats and by whipping everyone up to applaud the boys off the stage. It only bought him a few moments. Soon they were in the process of sitting back down and everything was all stacked up to set off, upon his command.

Of course he had given each man a trigger. You always give them a trigger. He did it in the same way he tied his shoes, without having to think about it. Habit had protected him, but memory was failing him, one tiny piece at a time. The loss of the trigger phrase was about to leave him with one fat turkey egg, broken and running down his face.

Now he was flailing away, stealing time by loudly praising the cooperative young rubes while he goaded the house into a few more rounds of applause for them. He noted the young men's dizzy smiles of embarrassed gratification. He could see that each one of them felt as if he had really taken part in something. The young men threw grins to one another across the audience rows, now bonded like a wolf pack.

So the prime was set and everything was ready.

But already he could see the first traces of confusion rising up on the folks' faces. Some of them—the damned quick ones—sensed that this thing was running out of steam. He could feel the floor beginning to tilt.

A flash of prickly frustration and hot anger rushed through him.

He wanted to scream, tear open the top of his skull, pull out his brain, and shake it like wet laundry until the trigger phrase fell out. The magic of the elixir lay in its ability to keep his head clearer and his memory sharper, to prevent his spirits from falling into that awful abyss that always waited for him. But in the wrong dosage, it was like riding a wild beast.

Now there was nothing left but to say a few words of thanks, blah-blah-blah, and *pull the trigger.* Then while they're still laughing and applauding, gesture to the mayor and his wife, wave to all, exit stage right. No curtain call. Nothing.

Never was there a better night to leave 'em wanting more.

But the trigger. Maybe the name of a local bigwig? No, not with all the other bigwigs there, to feel left out. Save that one for the small rooms.

And with that, as if by magic, the topic for the trigger phrase hit him: promotion. *Promotion!* He took a deep breath.

"And in closing," he called out in a well-projected voice that was instantly stronger, steadier, "I thank you all for sharing in the secrets I have revealed tonight. Of course, there is much more to come. Please return again and again, to join me while *I appear throughout the fairground, at . . .*

And with that, all ten of the young men simultaneously popped up to attention and bellowed in unison at the absolute tops of their voices, *"The Panama-Pacific International Exposition!"*

In the audience there was the initial reaction of surprise and confusion. Meanwhile, there stood the ten young men, sheepish at their own unexpected outburst . . . and still there was the audience, slowly realizing that the men did not *know* that they were going to do that . . . followed by the collective realization that their entire group had just witnessed a successful demonstration of group hypnosis . . . and then the big payoff—when they broke into the thunder-rolling applause of mass surprise and delight.

J.D. was already off the stage before the applause even peaked. He snatched up his makeup kit in one hand and headed back toward the commode. Passing a water pitcher near the stage manager's booth, he picked it up with his free hand and carried it along without slowing down, quaffing it down while he strode through the backstage area.

Even back there in the wings, applause continued to wash over him. *And so they bought it,* he thought in gratitude, *every one of them.* The old magic had actually worked once again, tonight. Thousands of hours of practice served to lock him inside a protective cocoon of habit, at a time when his conscious mind could do little more than misfire and shoot off sparks of fear.

For so many years, he had been the servant of his own discipline. Tonight it had saved him.

Everything around him still had that odd, shiny gloss. But at least that awful sensation was fading, that of his head being a lantern with the gas turned up so high that his skull could burst into flames. It was impossible to look anyone in the eye and believe that they did not see it.

He gratefully made it to the commode. It felt good to allow himself to fall silent, deep in thought. Now all he needed was to get away from the public eye and to be safely alone. His fogged brain told him that he needed to sleep this off, more than anything else, even though sleep was unlikely for hours to come.

His legs felt as though they were packed with millions of tiny stars, and that the stars were twinkling, twinkling, twinkling, as hard as they could, poking away at the inside of his skin. *What is the word?* . . . Asleep. *You say "my leg is asleep." Why do you say that?*

The leg hurt like hell and there was nothing sleepy about it.

He felt it then, the slippage. The damned brain slippage became more pronounced once he was off the stage. On the heels of the energy he expended in bluffing his way through an entire performance—possibly the most important performance he would give that year—fatigue quickly enveloped him.

That always happened after a show these days, but tonight the effect was worse. *The dose. Where did it come from? Nobody in San*

Francisco knows I have the elixir . . . The backstage door. Something
about . . .

If only he could sleep. Clear his head. He would be better once
he got some decent rest. His body felt like an empty tank. The sustained level of near panic that gripped him throughout the show
seemed to have burned off the strongest effects of the elixir.

Even though his heart still raced, the fog of his fatigue was already thickening. It was welcome, at this point. Anything for the
chance to rest and think things through. With a little luck, J.D. decided, he might even be able to close his eyes sometime before the
sun came up.

On his way back out of the commode, he absently stepped on
the long crack in the floor. In the back of his mind, where the rem-
nants of his photographic memory resided, he noticed that the
crack appeared to have grown a bit during this single performance.
But he was so powerfully distracted that the detail escaped his conscious attention, and there was nobody else around to take notice.

Except for the two tall men standing next to the backstage entrance. It took J.D. a frozen moment to figure out why there were
suddenly strangers in the backstage area. Then it hit him: this man
was that Blackburn fellow, the police detective he had requested
for the duration of the exposition. A stage hand had pointed out the
big cop while he was waiting around before the show.

Duncan's mouth went dry in an instant of panic. His mind was
racing too fast for the molasses drip of conversation, but he realized
that the detective had no other reason to be backstage except to
talk to him. There was no way to avoid it. Blackburn appeared to
have brought along another one, some young fellow, and God what
a night—the pair had just started in his direction.

CHAPTER SIX

EVEN THOUGH THE SHOW had not been over for long, Randall Blackburn was astounded by how badly things were already going in Duncan's dressing room. The showman seemed all worked up, showing a remarkable amount of after-show nerves. He continually paced up and down the length of the narrow room.

Duncan had just swatted aside Blackburn's early attempt to point out that a homicide detective was not likely to be the best choice for a personal bodyguard. He stopped him cold.

"Once again, I am sorry if the assignment is not to your liking. The fact is, I asked specifically for you, Detective."

"Me."

"Oh yes."

"Why is that?"

Duncan exhaled in exasperation. "Because of your investigative skills, of course."

"In homicide?"

"Yes, again. Homicide. You don't think so? You think I would make it all up? You will eventually change your mind, but I would like to still be alive when you do. You see, I don't just want you to protect me at public appearances like a simple body guard. Rather,

I will rely upon your trained eye to intercept potential problems from the crowd, guests up onstage, et cetera."

"Any trained officer can watch over a crowd for you."

"But in between, your most important job, your real job . . ." he stopped pacing just long enough to complete the thought. "Your real job will be to investigate my murder."

Blackburn felt his patience beginning to dissolve. He glanced over to Shane, who was keeping a quiet watch from the dressing room sofa.

"A future murder? Mr. Duncan, maybe I should explain that my job begins *after* a homicide. The law can be a funny thing. I hope to prevent other murders, but it takes that first one, at least, to get the ball rolling."

"Yes indeed! Thus my strong preference that you should investigate my murder *before* it happens. Pick the potential assassin out of the crowd and follow him home and investigate him."

"It's a him?"

"What else?"

"You never know."

"Find out what kind of intersection the event of my death and the intention of my killer have in common. Then come up with a way to deflect it. The crime. If you fail . . ." He decided to leave it at that.

"Mr. Duncan, I—"

"So! You understand? Keep it from happening." He stopped pacing for another moment to call into the shadows, "May we please get some more water back here, someone?" He smiled apologetically to Blackburn.

"Mr. Duncan, is somebody after you?"

"Oh yes. Jealousy, you know, it can drive a murderous heart."

"Do you have a rival?"

"In my field? I have nothing *but* rivals. It takes that kind of envy to put murder into play."

"Or fear of the unknown," came Shane's voice from over on the sofa.

Duncan looked over at him with obvious annoyance. "Are you still here, Mister . . . ?"

"Nightingale."

"Yes. I believe I told you that your presence is not necessary."

"He's with me, Mr. Duncan."

"I only sent for you, Detective."

"You are the lucky winner of a package deal, sir. That's just the way it is."

Duncan rubbed his face furiously for a moment, then abruptly stopped, inhaled, and demanded, "What can this young fellow do that is so impor—"

"Fear of the unknown makes more sense," Shane piped up again, "for a motive." He smiled and shrugged. "A rival who wants to personally eliminate you has to be willing to risk losing all chance of ever having any success, for himself, if he is caught. He has to be willing to give up his hope. It takes something very powerful to drive someone to that point. What better than the fear of an unknown future, one that is unknown because of the damage that this man thinks you have done to him?"

"As you say. And that's why one of my rivals is going to try to kill me."

"Except that fear of the unknown can strike anybody," Shane replied, "from any walk of life. That means that a potential assassin has an advantage on you, right off. Think of it: To some of the people in your audience, your work looks like black magic or something like that."

"I don't discourage my audience from speculating as to where I get my—"

"And once some of them start to get the idea in their heads that what you do is something of the occult world, then it's only a matter of time before one of them decides that it is the Devil's work and that he doesn't mind dying, just to get rid of you."

Duncan looked over to Blackburn, puzzled. Blackburn could not keep the wide grin off his face. "You can see how he comes in handy," he said.

"Oh that is magnificent, gentlemen! You have now opened up the field of potential suspects to include practically—"

"Everybody," Shane topped him. "Anyone who's ever seen your show or come into contact with your work."

"Ah-hah. Thank you so much, Mister . . . I'm sorry, but I've forgotten—"

"Nightingale," Shane reminded him again. He was still standing among the checkered shadows with his hands in his pockets, making no move to come forward to Duncan. "Shane Nightingale, Mr. Duncan."

"And," Blackburn interrupted, turning to Duncan with an expression that dared him to disagree, "what Mr. Nightingale has just done for you is to allow you a realistic assessment of your source of potential attackers. It's grim news, but without it, there's not a thing that I can do, or that anybody else can do for that matter, that will keep you safe. You have to begin by knowing what to guard against. In this case, your very line of work puts you out in full view of anybody with the price of admission."

Shane added, "The theatre is where John Wilkes Booth got President Lincoln."

"I know that! Why do you think I called you? That's why you have to stop it now!" Duncan shouted, suddenly wild-eyed.

Blackburn and Shane silently regarded him, waiting to see if there was more to come. Instead, Duncan clapped one hand over his mouth and took several deep breaths while he furiously polished his face with the other. Eventually, he removed both hands and continued.

"I apologize. Of course. It's the strain."

"What strain would that be, sir?"

"Somebody keeps taking things!" Duncan shouted. "Right from the bottom of my . . ."

Duncan blanched and fled from the room, with Blackburn and Shane close behind. But he only ran to the backstage commode, where he seized a small wooden box from the floor, and gasped with relief.

"Here it is! It's still here!" Duncan hugged the box to his chest.

Blackburn turned to Shane, who merely rolled his eyes and looked away.

"Someone took that chest from you, Mr. Duncan?"

"This? Oh no, it just . . . Somebody got into the . . . Nothing! I'm tired, that's all. Very tired, gentlemen. Detective. Mister, ah . . ."

"Sir, you're not giving me anything at all to go on. I'm still not sure what you actually expect me to—"

"Yes! I know! Confusing! But sleep. Some rest. We'll all feel so much better, yes? Give me a day. Two days. Give me two days, and we'll meet here. Right at noon. Eh?"

"Mr. Duncan, let me just come out and say it. I don't see any call for you to have a homicide detective to follow you around, when what you really need is a couple of young patrolmen. Young guys dying for a perpetrator to come along."

"I know what I need, Detective! Right now, give me two days. We'll meet here at the theatre."

"Crack of noon," Shane added.

"Yes!" Duncan nearly bellowed in relief. "I just need to go now, that's all. In two days, we will, uh . . ."

"Form a plan," Shane said.

"Exactly!"

"Figure out how to find a killer who hasn't done anything yet," Shane added, "before he does whatever it is that he's possibly planning to do."

"I am not joking."

"Neither am I. Right now, at least, they don't know that we are watching you. So we start there, at their point of ignorance. We may suffer from a lack of details about your potential assassin, but for the moment, the fact is that this person doesn't know that you are taking protective measures. That can move the advantage back toward you."

Duncan stared at him for a moment, then turned to Blackburn. "All right. You can bring him along with you."

Then he clutched his wooden box tighter and walked out of the theatre, leaving through the rear fire escape. A moment later, he stepped back in through the door, quickly examined the door frame, the door itself, swung the door back and forth a couple of times, then shook his head and disappeared again.

He did it without once looking over in their direction. It was as if he had forgotten about them already.

In a late-night tavern not far from the theatre, the nondescript man swallowed steady rounds of inexpensive bar gin until his pocket cash started growing thin. Then he staggered away from the tavern in a display of willpower before he spent it all. He spent the rest of the night in a nearby church's open chapel without knowing what kind of church it was. Theology made no difference to him. He only wanted to be alone with God.

He was proud that his personal character contained more than just the mere ability to walk away from the temptations of Demon Rum. He was also able to maintain the rigid control of a true supplicant while in this holy place. Example: Despite the alcohol and the silence of the chapel, he did not allow himself to fall asleep there. He remained awake and alert throughout his long prayer vigil.

There was much to contemplate. And with his long-familiar rage satisfied at last on this beautiful night, he now found himself able to feel remorse for certain things that he had to do, to make it happen. He had to admit that he had acted in a sneaky and vengeful way—perhaps even a lethal way. He could feel how unfortunate it was, that he had been provoked into such behavior.

So the nondescript man remained on his knees for hours, allowing the growing pain and stiffness to punish him. And still, the bodily pain was assuaged by his sense of great relief from the prison of his poisonous rage and the torment of unrelenting hateful thoughts. He had freed himself from them by taking action. It was so fine to feel cleansed and at peace with himself at long last. Gratitude filled him.

Overflowing with spiritual generosity, he prayed for everyone he knew, as well as for the entire, struggling world, that mercy might be shown to them even as it had just been shown to him—yes, one as humble as he, who had been Divinely guided through the process of bringing down an unforgiven bit of filth like James "J.D." Duncan. It mattered not that he did not know precisely what form the disaster would take. He trusted that it was a thing of poetry because God was on his side.

And because of that, he had rock-solid faith that by now Duncan was either dead of poisoning from his massive dose of "secret" elixir, or he had made a fatal fool of himself onstage and ruined his credibility in front of the city authorities. Either outcome would be fine.

The glow of peace filled him.

Shane drove Blackburn home in their newly purchased Ford Model T. The car was already three years old, but perfectly reliable. It even still looked good. The years since the Great Earthquake had seen a large increase in the number of automobiles on the city's roads, but there were still plenty of horse-drawn wagons and carriages in everyday use. So Shane made an absentminded game out of weaving to avoid the horse flop. With the car's springy suspension, the ride remained smooth enough that each man still rode along lost in his thoughts. They were halfway home before Shane broke out with a small laugh.

Blackburn glanced over at him. "What."

"Nothing. Thinking about Mr. Duncan, I guess. Did you see the part where he fooled the whole crowd into thinking that they were hearing all of these ex . . . ex . . ." He exhaled through his lips in this brief visit from his old stutter, then repeated, "exotic secrets?"

"I missed it."

"I wish you had seen it. Everybody went in for it! All of them!"

"You didn't."

There was a brief pause, then Shane grinned.

Blackburn went on. "So why didn't he have the same effect on you?

"Don't know. I was watching him close up, because I wanted to learn something about how a man like that can be so at ease. You know, in front of a crowd like that. To always know what to say, what to do. Amazing."

"You're telling me that that's why he couldn't fool you? Because you were watching him closely? Come on, everybody watches a guy like him as close as they can."

"Yeah. It's just . . ."

Blackburn smiled. "It's *just* a perfect example of why I want you tailing me on some of these cases."

Shane smiled. He considered it for a moment and finally said, "I thought you were just getting me away from my daily restaurant work to relieve the boredom of waiting on tables. Act of mercy or whatnot."

"That, too," Blackburn solemnly agreed. "Act of mercy. Any guy who has enough money to go to college but chooses to wait on tables instead needs all the mercy he can get."

Shane grinned, unfazed. Blackburn decided that this opportunity was about as good as he would find. "Listen, Shane, before we get back home, I need to talk to you about your experience with, you know, with police training."

"My 'experience'?"

"Not the training itself. But can you think of anything that you and Vignette might have ever discussed about it? Anything that might cause her to . . ." He stopped and sighed.

"All right. You have my attention now," Shane quietly said. He glanced over at Blackburn for an instant before turning back to the road.

"I guess what I am trying to ask you is whether you can think of where she might have gotten any strange ideas about it. About your leaving."

"About my being asked not to come back?"

"I know they were wrong, but—"

"They weren't. I didn't belong there, that's all."

"But is that what you told her? Because I don't know, she seems to think—"

"I told her that I just wanted to impress you." He let that one hang there for a second, then grinned and added, "That was before I realized that you would be so much more impressed if I got a job as a waiter in a fancy restaurant."

"I'm the last man in the world you need to impress."

"Ha! Mmm. Sorry to disagree again, but you're probably the only person either of us feels much called upon to impress at all. Anyway, what about Vignette?" Shane grinned in anticipation. "All right, tell me. What did she do now?"

CHAPTER SEVEN

VIGNETTE OPENED HER BEDROOM DOOR in response to Shane's knock. Her hair was wrapped in a towel; she wore a long bathrobe and was holding a copy of Jack London's *Call of the Wild*.

"Sorry," she said. "I'm getting ready for—"

Shane pushed past her and walked into her room without a word. He sat down on a straight-backed chair at the foot of her bed.

Vignette sighed, closed the door, and then spoke while her back was still to him. "All right, Shane, the only time you come in here and flop down like that is when you've got a bone to pick."

She turned to face him. "So let's hear it, because this is still my room and I'm not leaving."

She waited. He said nothing.

". . . I'm supposed to guess? That is just lovely, Shane."

He still said nothing, but he finally turned to face her. When he did, he held her gaze.

Vignette sighed and shook her head. "You know it's really very late for you to be like this with me. I ought to be asleep at this hour. Why don't you spare us a lot of wasted time and just say whatever it is that you came here to say?"

Shane fixed her with an expectant look, but he still said nothing.

"Oh, come on, now. Is it really so bad? What could be so bad? I'm tired, Shane. Tell me what's on your—"

She stopped and went pale.

"Oh wait. Is it . . . Did you hear something? Is that it? It is? That's it? . . . What did you hear? Who told you?"

She spun toward the door in alarm, then back to Shane. "Was it from Randall? Did you hear it from him? Just *tell* me, Shane, damn it!

"It was Randall, wasn't it? Isn't that right? The point is, where did he hear it, though? You know what I mean? How many other people know?

"Damn it, Shane! You know I hate it when you stare at me like that! If you don't stop I'm going to make you get out of here. I mean it. How much does he know?"

Shane looked away from her and slowly shook his head.

She took in a deep breath. "Everything? He knows everything? How is that possible? Who told him?"

Vignette whirled and began nervously pacing the room. "I was only going to go back for another day or two. Maybe a week. I knew it had to stop. I just, I just wanted to show that I could do it. To prove it can be done!"

Vignette kneeled next to his chair and took both his hands. "Shane, you have to believe me. I didn't do it as some sort of reaction because you left that place. I know you didn't belong there. Didn't I tell you that you didn't belong there? Hell, I don't belong there either. But nobody *expects* me to be there, you understand? That's the thing. You see that, right? That's why I had to go! You do see that. Right?"

Shane regarded her for a long moment with a wary smile, before he finally exhaled and shook his head again. He nodded at her, stood up with a great sigh, then embraced her in a bear hug and did not say anything at all.

"All right, look," she said. "I don't think that we need to mention this again. As far as I'm concerned, anyway. You know how some people always have to go back over things and back over things? As if they could just drill them into your head? Not us. Because it's settled. That's what I think."

Shane held her and gently patted her back. She tightened her grip on him the way that she liked to do, one of the only two men in the world that it was safe to hug like that. It was a quick test to see if things were all right. She knew within a few heartbeats that they were. Shane's hug was deep and strong and did not hold back any of his love for her. It was a brother's love, with the erotic component safely missing. She had no idea how he accomplished that, any more than she could imagine how Randall did, either. It struck her that these were the only two men on the planet who did not represent a threat to her.

As far as experience had taught her, any man who was given the chance would lunge for her on any pretext, hands grabbing for her face and body. They sometimes descended like flies, either because she was pretty and petite, or because she was a youthful-looking nineteen and appeared to be easy prey.

So much of her love for Shane and Randall was heightened by her gratitude and amazement that after nine years together, both men had always accepted her story about her shared lineage with Shane. She *said* that she was his sister, so that was enough for them. And from that moment on, they treated her accordingly in every way.

It was a mystery to her; Vignette had no other experience for comparison. Her own sexual innocence was gone long before her body had matured. She was forced to learn about feminine wiles and male gratification as a matter of her survival, back when the so-called friars at the orphanage still got away with things like that because she was only "Mary Kathleen," and that little girl lacked the skills to *move things around* well enough to keep herself protected.

By the time she renamed herself and fled for the streets, her innocence had melted within the corrosive atmosphere of the place. The authority figures who did it to her had always carefully explained why their actions were all her own fault, for arousing their desire.

Nine years earlier, the first time it hit her that she and Shane and Randall were actually going to move in together, she felt the beginnings of a slow panic. How was it possible to survive being alone in the close company of two males? The question burned in the pit of her stomach, a sort of vigil fire, while she waited for the betrayal that was sure to follow. She never went so far as to sleep with a knife under her pillow, but it took the first couple of years for the one in the back of her mind to dissolve away.

She had no idea what particular part of their brains these two men were using that she had never witnessed anywhere else, but she had seen its effect. Her knowledge of it was thicker than water. That knowledge also presented the main quandary of her life, because it did not permit her to loathe and despise men. Otherwise that would have come to her as naturally as breathing.

And then there it was: another example, right there, when Shane released her, stepped back, and grabbed her by the jawline. He playfully squeezed her face. Then he pushed her away with a gentle shove, turned around, and walked out without having said a word.

It took another hour or so before Randall Blackburn peeked around the door frame to the living room and spotted Vignette sitting in a darkened corner. He walked on in and stepped over to the gas fireplace.

"Hi. Why don't you come on over and have a seat by the fire?"

"I like it in the shadows, right now."

"Good enough, if you're happy there. I'll just sit here where I can poke up the flames." He smiled at the little joke while he scooted closer to the gas fireplace. Vignette did not react. "Shane went to bed?"

She spoke up from her place in the shadows, without looking up. "Yes."

He pantomimed poking at the fire with a stick, smiled at her, then stopped poking and stopped smiling. "Well then, uh, I'm glad you waited up."

"It's not as if I had a choice or something."

"What?"

"Stop it, Randall! I can tell she said something. I know she did. She's like that. She broke the news to me that they had found me out, because the police told her when they came to put in that damned telephone thing. She wanted me to be the one to tell you, at least that's what she said. Except she had to go and do it herself. *I* was supposed to tell you!"

"Vignette, Miss Freshell hasn't told me anything. And the police didn't tell her anything, either."

"And you still call her 'Miss Freshell,' Randall, putting her up on a pedestal!"

"Just because I show her respect—this conversation is not about her."

"Who?"

"Miss Freshell."

"Ah.

"Who is still not the topic."

"No, right now, the topic is who told you."

"Captain Merced told me. Tonight, at the theatre, during the show. Not that it matters."

" . . . oh."

He sat still after that, staring into the fireplace, waiting for her. Eventually, she found her voice.

"You can think it through all you want. Doesn't matter. Nothing changes. And nothing changes because it's so simple."

"What's simple?"

"That there's nothing out there for me, Randall. There never was and it never changes."

"All right. I know you say that, Vignette, but—"

"There's nothing out there for me! And so there's nothing wrong with me staying here and not being in any hurry to go be a spinster somewhere."

"Don't use that stupid word. You're far too young for it. Even if you were twice your age, it would still be a stupid word."

"And I am sure as hell not anybody's wife, not anybody's mother. How do words like that fit me? Can you see me doing that?"

"Not right now, maybe, but you're still young."

"So how long does it take until you know?"

" . . . Don't ask me. But you don't want to wait as long as I did, Vignette. I mean, I've been single ever since I lost . . . that was too many years ago. You can look at me and see that, can't you?"

"No I can't, in fact. What's wrong with it? Our lives are good, just like they are. Far as I'm concerned."

"Yes. But things change. In life." He groaned to himself. *Things change in life?* If he had already reduced himself to saying something like that, he was in cold, deep water.

He tried again. "You understand, though, right? After a while . . . I think, whoever you are, after a while, you don't want to be alone."

She took a deep breath, then shook her head. "You, maybe. I think that it's about the only thing that will work for me."

"Vignette, here it is: You can't go into any of the precinct houses. You can't go into the City Hall Station, anymore. Not for a year or so, anyway. Maybe longer. It depends on how long it takes for this to be forgotten. And the men who run an organization like this, the thing they fear the most is looking weak. In their minds, for a young woman to beat them at their own game by fooling them like you did, it makes them look ridiculous."

"I don't even know those particular fellows, and I can't see how they can take personal offense."

"I just told you how. And what you think, what I think, it just doesn't matter. They react automatically to something like this, like swatting a fly. The important thing now is for us to make sure that these men don't notice you for a while. We don't want them to think about you at all."

"I swear, Randall, if I had to stay home and keep house for some man just because he stuck a ring on my finger, I'd go insane. How do the wives avoid suicide?"

"The *police,* Vignette, I'm talking to you about the police. Now the thing that you have going for you in this is the fact that they want to hush it all up. Women aren't supposed to be able to do what you were doing, and apparently doing quite well. And right now, the city is so conscious of its civic image that they just want it all to go away. You're in luck."

"I didn't know a city could feel things."

"I mean the people I work for."

"They're not going to take this out on you, are they?"

"What, on me? Why would they do that?"

"Right. I know. So they won't do it then?"

"Don't you worry about me. Let's talk about what you're going to do with yourself, with your life."

"Oh. Well, I can get married. Or be a spinster schoolteacher. Or a spinster librarian. Or maybe even a spinster retail clerk! Isn't that wonderful?"

"Vignette!" he was loud, nearly shouting. Randall never shouted at her. It immediately got her attention. When she finally raised her eyes to meet his gaze, she was surprised to see more pain in him than she felt herself.

"I have to be able to trust you, Vignette."

"But . . . You can, though. You still can. Regardless."

"Police training?"

"Sometimes I could explode, Randall! I swear I could! None of the roads ahead of me are going to anywhere that I need to be. Not even anywhere I can stand to think of being."

"Regardless. The three of us only have each other as long as there is that trust."

"You and Shane can trust me."

"We can. Except when you decide that you need to do something like this."

Vignette sighed, dropped her head into her hands, and silently rocked from side to side.

"I know you have to live on your own terms. But I hate to see you rely on your money like that."

"Randall, if I keep my life simple, I can live off of that investment for years and years. And all of that time, I won't have to cram myself into somebody else's little world."

"That's good. But what I'm afraid of is that at some point the money runs out or the investment goes bad, and if that happens, you'll be stuck out there on your own without any decent skills."

"I can do all kinds of things, as far as working at a job, Randall. I just can't stomach the way that they'll treat me. And I don't care if it's the same way that they treat the other women. Those damned women seem like a herd of cows to me."

"So it's not a pointless job that you're afraid of having to endure?"

"Hell no. It's that I'll be expected to endure it without getting into fights with morons. How am I supposed to do that?"

He chuckled. "Yeah, well, when you put it that way . . ."

"How much did they tell you about me?"

"Just whatever they found out when the tip came in. They only got it late this morning. What did you do about your hair?"

Vignette removed the wig. Her hair was shorter than Shane's. Still, he could hardly believe that this face had deceived so many men through several days of testing. It seemed to him that her pixie features were accented by the short hair. She must have clinched the male illusion with sheer attitude.

Blackburn had not lived with this person for the past nine years without learning something about how to coexist with a young female. This one was an actress, first of all. He knew the proper response.

"Well I don't believe I've ever seen a woman wear her hair that short, but you know, you really make it look good."

She stared at him with a faint smile. Finally, she stood up and walked over to him, put her arms around him, and then just stayed there.

"I'm sorry, Randall," she finally said, her voice muffled by his shoulder. "I never thought it through. I was in it before I knew it. And then it just seemed like I had to keep it up. It was like being caught in fast water."

"All right, then. I'm thankful you didn't get hurt."

"Hurt somebody else, you mean." She gave him a tiny grin.

He laughed. "Just let me trust you. From now on, Vignette. Please."

She looked up and squarely met his gaze, then hugged him again, nodding. Suddenly it frightened her to think how close she had come to setting off a real disaster for both of them. A wave of guilt overwhelmed her. She was glad that Shane was not there to see this.

"I'm sorry."

They stood hugging for another quiet moment, before Vignette stiffened slightly and pulled back to look at him. "When did you say they found out?"

"Late this morning. Somebody had a couple of officers deliver a note to Chief White. I guess it wasn't too long before he had my captain summoned to a meeting and really chewed him out."

"No, that can't be right," Vignette said. "They already knew, early this morning. The officers came to put in the telephone, first thing. They told the Eastern . . . Miss Freshell. She waited around until I got up, just so she could tell me that I'd been caught. She's so sweet, mmm?"

"You're saying that the officers who installed the telephone were also messengers, and they had a message for you about all this, but they left the message with her instead?"

"Yes."

"I don't think so."

"Early this morning."

He sighed and shook his head, rubbing both hands over his face. "I'm tired. Why don't you go on ahead to bed? I'm going to have a brandy before I turn in."

She quietly agreed and left the room, chastised. But he called out to her, "You sure it was this morning? When they told her?"

Vignette stuck her head back in the doorway. "Told you, I wasn't even up yet."

"Okay," he replied with a tired smile.

After she left again, Blackburn sat for a long time, staring into the gas flames. His mood was darker than usual. The gas fire and concrete logs reminded him of the flaming leaks that burned in the broken rubble after the Great Earthquake.

He still hoped that there would turn out to be a plausible explanation for why Miss Freshell already knew about Vignette early that morning, before the department found out. He needed time to think it through, but first he had to get some sleep. A faint sensation of dread was just beginning to throb beneath his stomach.

CHAPTER EIGHT

THE LATE AFTERNOON LIGHT from a cloudless sky made for perfect visibility; there was no way for the nondescript man to keep any potential mistakes from being seen. Even though he was more filled with rage now than he had ever been back when he thought God was on his side, he remained alert enough to wisely avoid passing in front of the Japanese Pavilion. It would be too easy to attract notice from there. The place was already surrounded by watchful guards because the damn industrious Japanese had to go and make the other construction teams look bad by being the first to complete their hall.

The shopgirl walked stiffly beside him, an arm linked through his. She trembled in fear, with his pistol surreptitiously tucked into her ribs. He could sense the weakness in her knees and feared that if he allowed her to stop or even to slow down, her legs might give out, drawing attention.

All six hundred and twenty-five acres of the exposition site were alive with last-minute construction. Any of the workers would sound an alarm if they saw a young lady collapse, perhaps even heard an attempt to scream.

The tension of his situation was so high that it briefly penetrated his sense of purpose. At first, the awful danger of snatching up this charming girl and forcibly walking her across the fairgrounds filled him with an erotic sensation.

Halfway to their destination, that feeling had decomposed into a more pragmatic state of fear. Caution kept him moving briskly along. He bruised her ribs with the pistol barrel to make sure that she followed like a good girl. It took all his concentration, because even though he had no desire to be caught, her growing terror and confusion warmed him inside.

The simple goal was to keep moving, giving the impression that they were a couple leaving work together. Nobody would pay any attention. His presence made it almost certain, because he had always moved within a curious sort of empty space. It traveled everywhere with him. The empty space cloaked him so well—whether he liked it or not—that in most situations he could arrive, stay, eventually leave, and as far as most other people knew, he had never been there at all.

The anonymity was neither entirely reliable nor as good as actual invisibility. Because there were always those occasional *noticers,* coming out of nowhere and having to *notice* every damned thing. They provided the risk element. Just one noticer could be enough to set off a whole chain of them—busy little noticers forming a promenade leading him straight to prison.

Unacceptable. If things went wrong, he was genuinely terrified of the consequences. But the wave of pleasure that accompanied the danger was so strong that now his legs were becoming as weak as those of personal Revenge girl, if for different reasons. The similarities between an assailant and his victim were beautiful to him.

"Step along," he whispered through a fake smile. He pushed the barrel into her ribs again, just to remind her.

Luck kicked in for him at that point; everyone else passing by was too busy to notice anything. Revenge girl managed to keep her feet under her, no doubt hoping to buy good treatment from him with her cooperation.

At any other time, she might have been able to do just that. But God had made a mockery of the nondescript man. The same God to whom he had been so grateful, one day earlier, had abandoned their partnership in the mission to bring down a man whose arrogance cried out for destruction.

The Divine betrayal was even worse than it would have been for him to discover that God did not exist at all, because the betrayal was personal proof that God not only existed, but was the type of Heavenly entity who was willing to fill a desperate man's hungry soul with the impression that guidance was at hand every step of the way . . . only to turn his back upon his nondescript servant at the most crucial moment.

Oh no. No, no, no.

His rage was a boiling black tar, clinging to anything that it touched, burning away. He guided the terrified shopworker into the Hall of Science, down to the completed "Cave Dwellers" area where his workers had been given time off for finishing ahead of schedule. He checked to see that all was clear, then quickly pulled her back through his concealed door and into the large dead space behind the imitation cliff.

He had fixed the trick door and added some more insulation to the inner "cave." With nothing left for him to do but finish the display's last few touch-ups himself, he had spent his free time behind the fake rock cliff, readying a private little area that God, as it turned out, may not have picked out for him after all—but which He really should have.

He made the place ready without knowing how it would play into his need for revenge, working purely on faith. *Plans are for atheists,* he reminded himself. And who could tell about that? The exposition was set to last for ten months.

Questions for tomorrow. He had failed at Duncan, the genuine article, and the scalding rage drove him like lashes of a whip. He could not wait. Once she was properly tied and muffled back inside the hidden cave, he finally admitted to himself that he was not going to be fulfilling her hope of letting her go.

He did not have a catch-and-release policy.

At that same moment, in the kitchen of the Blackburn-Nightingale residence, Vignette stood between Randall and the Eastern Whore and tried not to drop the dish that she was rinsing and flee the room. Miss Freshell had her trapped in another one of her domestic rituals. Vignette called this one the Wash-Rinse-Dry ceremony, which left her stranded in the middle rinsing position and handing each dish to Randall. She did it without looking at him.

Miss Freshell, in all her evil glory, controlled the pace of the ceremony because she did the washing. You could never go any faster than she wanted you to. This meant that nothing was ever over, in this little ceremony, until Miss Freshell damn well said it was. And now with poor Randall still so besotted, he no longer seemed capable of anything more than parroting Freshell's proclamations and glaring in disapproval whenever Vignette or Shane put up any friction over the new set of opinions in their lives.

Vignette felt like a worm under the beak of the Eastern Whore. This woman was able to shred her quarry and speak at the same time.

"—not that the Ladies' Hospitality League needs any recommendation from me. I *know* that you will find them to be the same stimulating mix of interesting women that I do."

"Yes. Yes."

"Vignette . . ." Randall muttered under his breath to her.

"What, Randall?" Vignette snapped. "What? She said it, she's said it before, I acknowledged that she said it. So what is it?"

"No, dear, Randall and I both agree that the very best thing for you now is the stimulating company of women who make an art out of graciously serving others. We are having our third orientation meeting on Saturday, but I'm sure I can convince them to take you as a late arrival." Freshell beamed a withering smile at Vignette, then moved it over to Randall and held it there for several seconds while Vignette fought the sensation of bursting into flame.

Instead she focused on simply holding still and nodding . . . rinsing each dish carefully . . . not dropping it . . . not looking up at Randall . . . not smashing a dish over Freshell's coiffed curls . . . not screaming and screaming and screaming until Randall woke up out of his unbelievable sleepwalking stupor.

"It's only for ten months, dear. I'll guide you through it. And since you'll be there while I'm gathering material for my next book, you can always return the favor by working as my assistant! Fair as the day is long, wouldn't you say?"

And of course, while she asked the question of Vignette, her eyes and her smile were reserved for Randall. It struck Vignette that it felt just like this when she got herself caught in that tremendous riptide while swimming around the Golden Gate. She had been swept along by that overpowering force with no one to help her, even though she could see people on the shore. Now here was Randall standing right next to her, and he would never be able to hear her scream.

"Vignette," Randall quietly said, "in light of things, you know, this is fair for you to try. And to really give an honest effort to it."

"How can I—"

"*Also*—as a personal favor to me—because you would be giving me something to tell my captain that might convince him that I'm not running an asylum here, and he does not need to continue with his bad jokes."

"Randall, you don't—"

"Not that his bad jokes would be enough of a reason in themselves, but as long as we have this opportunity to send you to a sort of finishing school, it's a nice bonus for me. It's something good that I can tell him about you."

He smiled at her and touched her face so that she met his gaze. "For me, Vignette. Please. Do this for me. Do it because I want good things for you in life and I can't do enough to help you get them. I want you to know how to get the best out of your own life, and this can help you.

He grinned. "And besides, aside from getting bored once in a while, what's the worst that could happen?"

Vignette handed him the next dish, but he was the one who dropped it. It hit the floor, breaking into clean halves. And in the quick moment when he bent down to pick up the pieces, Vignette slipped and allowed her eyes to turn toward Miss Freshell.

The Eastern Whore flashed her the briefest moment of a sneer, glaring in angry triumph. Vignette did not know the exact reasoning behind it but she felt an instinctive revulsion.

She found herself stuck in a web newly spun across a familiar spot, where there had always been clear air before.

Shane was just finishing up the first day of his new work schedule at The Sea Mist, a Market Street restaurant so unusually posh that there was no food, only cuisine. He was now working strictly the lunch and afternoon hours, leaving him free to accompany Blackburn at Duncan's evening performances. But after his first day on the early shift, it was already clear that he would be paying for the excitement with a drop in wages.

Just as he leaned over his last table to polish down the top, he felt a strong hand grip his upper arm and pull him upright. He turned to see James "J.D." Duncan peering at him like a man who has just caught a spy. Duncan pulled Shane into a high-backed booth and lowered his voice to a harsh whisper.

"Nightingale! I thought that was you. What are you doing here?" he demanded.

"Finishing up my afternoon shift," Shane replied, puzzled, trying to figure out the cause for the older man's alarmed expression.

" . . . This is what you actually do?" Duncan looked at him as if he smelled bad.

"No, Mr. Duncan. This is how I actually pay my bills. There are other things that I actually do."

"I specifically requested Detective Blackburn and I'm sure I never said anything about a restaurant waiter accompanying him!"

"Mr. Duncan, The Sea Mist is one of the best restaurants in town. It took me months to get a job here. I'm not ashamed of this work."

"Fine, but you're not a policeman!"

"No. I've already established that I'm not cut out of policeman material. Even so, Detective Blackburn believes that I can help him." He sighed. "Look, I have these . . . sometimes I see . . ." Shane stopped, wondering how far to take the explanation.

Duncan ignored it. "You two are related, yes? I've been asking around. People tell me anything I want to know. You may as well just—"

"He adopted us. It's no secret, Mr. Duncan. My sister and I have lived with him for the last nine years."

"All very touching. Except when it's at the expense of my security."

"Mr. Duncan . . . First, it is just not in him to put you at risk like that. Second, he asked me to come because there are specific ways that I can help him."

Duncan still did not react. He simply stared with a darkening expression. When he finally spoke, the words came out drenched in venom.

"I only stopped in here today because the theatre is so close by. But now that prompts the question: When was the first time you were ever backstage there?"

"The other night, when we came back to see you after your show."

"*Only* then?" Duncan asked, using the vocal tone of a man who already knows that he will hear nothing but lies.

"Yes."

"*That* was your first time?"

"Yes. It was."

"Maybe your first time was on that same day, but . . . a bit ear-lier?"

"No, by the time we got to the theatre, the show was about to begin. I didn't even get a seat."

"I'm not talking about the performance! I'm talking about your activities backstage."

"Mr. Duncan, we should go outside if you want to talk more. I'm not supposed to stay around here after my shift is over."

"Has Detective Blackburn shown you any special techniques? Police procedures for doing things like, oh, finding hidden com-partments in things? Picking open the locks?"

"No, Mr. Duncan. He has not." Shane leaned across the table and spoke with deliberate gentleness, realizing that he could never get away with offending this powder keg of a man.

"Mr. Duncan, sir, I just help him a little sometimes, that's all. Sometimes I can give him a different view of things. In your case, I also came along backstage mostly because I looked forward to meeting you, after that performance. Sir, I was very impressed by your ways with the crowd!"

Duncan stared at him for another long moment, then his shoul-ders slumped and he exhaled heavily. "Oh, all right. All right, then. Our world has entered the Age of Nonsense, so why should this arrangement be different? My body guard will bring along his fa-vorite waiter."

He stood up, shaking his head. "And if we get hungry, why, the energetic young fellow can always . . ." Duncan sighed and walked away without looking back.

Shane turned and bent to finish polishing the table, but he felt the familiar grip on the back of his arm. Duncan leaned in again, so close that Shane smelled his coffee-soured breath. It was strong, as if the man drank gallons of the stuff.

"People find it difficult to deceive me for any length of time, Mr.

Nightingale. Perhaps for a passing moment, or maybe they slip through some convenient little lie, but not over the long haul."

Shane decided to forget cleaning the table and to go. He left the tip cash there for the next man, then straightened up and walked directly out of The Sea Mist without bothering to see if Duncan was following.

Once out on Market Street, when he sensed Duncan's footsteps behind him, he continued the conversation where they had dropped it, without bothering to look over at him. "Yes, sir. You are hard to fool. That's good to know."

"Save the humor for another time, young man. I have realized that the thing to do is not just *allow* you to attend with Detective Blackburn. Instead I'll be calling the captain to *insist* on your presence with him at all times!"

"Well, that is good news for me, then. But what purpose does that serve? You already agreed that I could be there."

"It has to do with the precision of language, Mr. Nightingale. Before, you were allowed to come. Now, I insist that you be in my sight, whenever Detective Blackburn is with me. And I will see to it that both the theatre and my hotel each notify me immediately, if you are ever seen in the vicinity of the theatre *or* my belongings!"

With that, Shane stopped in his tracks. He was barely more than half of Duncan's weight, but nearly as tall. He ignored their respective masses and leveled his gaze straight into Duncan's eyes. "Mr. Duncan, would you like to tell me what it is that you're afraid of? Because whatever it happens to be, I tell you respectfully, sir, I should not be on the list."

Duncan's face was like rock. "Fear? You underestimate me, Mr. Nightingale. Precaution is not the same as fear. There will be no more backstage visits for you, no visits anywhere, without plenty of other people knowing where you are. I have enough pull with the City Council to see to it that all of this occurs."

"I realize that."

Duncan gave up a begrudging smile. "And of course you understand exactly what I am doing."

"Taking precautions."

"Beyond that! You were surprised, weren't you? Why don't you just come out and say so? You never expected me to ride out a dose as heavy as that one, to give a complete performance and then walk away?"

"I don't know anything about that. I just admired the way that you handled the crowd."

"You weren't even the tiniest bit disappointed that the dose didn't make me go insane in front of the most important people in the city?"

"Now wait, Mr. Duncan! If you think that I'm some kind of a threat to you, why do you want to 'insist' on having me around so much?"

"I am keeping you close. No slinking around in shadows, for you. If you are, perhaps, a man who wants to do me harm, you will not do it in secret. You will carry out the act in front of others."

Duncan straightened up with a look of triumph, the face of a man who has just outsmarted a tough adversary. He took a step back, forced a showman's smile, and opened his arms in that famed welcoming gesture that was so loved by audiences everywhere.

"Friendly warning."

He turned and walked away again, this time without coming back.

CHAPTER NINE

DAYS LATER
IN THE DEAD SPACE

By the time the nondescript man dragged his captive young woman into the dead area behind the false cliff, he had already spent an entire day alone in there, testing, doing his research. And so he knew that as long as he kept a gag on his victim, nobody outside would hear a thing. On rare occasions, he could feel the vibrations from passing footsteps, falling on the same floor as his floor, not so far away. To any sane mind, they were a last feeble warning, a cautionary tale.

His experiences in working with the Boss had whet his taste for high-tension excitement, way back when. Now he needed it just as much as Duncan did. Thus every hour of suffering that he inflicted upon the Revenge girl allowed him to squeeze out a little more of the poisonous rage. It helped even more, when he made her apologize for everything over the years, and got her to say the kinds of things that should have been said to him all along.

And he loved the romantic, orangey-red light of the single candle flame, loved the way his hulking shadow moved around at all angles on the inner walls of the artificial cliff, while the shadow of her bound form remained motionless. He was so drunk on romance that the scene could not have seemed more perfect unless a violin player stepped in.

He constricted her throat with his thumbs until she woke up, gasping, uselessly struggling against her padded restraints. Not only could she not move a single inch, the special bindings would not leave marks. Gentle chains, he forced her to call them.

"Start from the beginning. We're not going to do anything this time. I just want to hear it. You can use the practice."

He pulled loose the knot binding her mouth gag and removed the cloth. When she coughed, licking dry lips, he gave her a sip of water from his personal canteen, tenderly. He even pulled back for a few seconds to give her the opportunity to compose herself and prepare.

Then he pressed both thumbs into her windpipe again and repeated, gently, "Start from the beginning."

Her voice came out in a dry hiss, but he could hear her words well enough. They drizzled over him like cool water on burning coals. Never enough to put out the fire, but a relief nonetheless, a most welcome relief from the pain of the endless burn.

He grabbed her hair and pulled so hard that her words came out between clenched teeth. "You do it so I don't need it from any other man! Nobody else!"

He let go of her hair, let go of her altogether, then backed away a few steps to let the poor thing get some rest. She was clearly exhausted now, after days of this. What an experience it had been. What a learning process! The nondescript man had discovered that if he obtained enough gratification, he could manage to see past his usual sexual compulsions long enough to get some idea of what the other person in the room might be experiencing.

And now, sated as he was, it hurt him to see this innocent working girl bound up in such a fashion, even though his method of padding her bindings was a stroke of inspiration. He reminded himself that it was far more comfortable than the ropes or chains that any other man would have used.

He could appreciate that her offense against him was nothing

more than that of being on her way home from work at the fairgrounds, some girl toiling away at getting a gift shop ready for the
big opening. She just got herself caught out there at the wrong time
of day; he could have grabbed any desirable female. Either way, it
was going to happen. He was self-hypnotized, primed, set, and
ready to spring. It was no longer a matter of choice. He would risk
it all for the chance to get one of those women back to his insulated
dead space, back where he could safely lose himself in the abyss of
her suffering.

How odd, he marveled, the way one thing leads to another. The
long gray ordeal of the nondescript man's pointless life was quite
unexpectedly interrupted, when the dead space behind the cliff
was first revealed to him. It cost him a hundred dollars to switch
areas with the foreman who was originally assigned to it, by claim-
ing that it was closer to his rooming house.

But as sated as he was feeling just then, there were moments
when he realized that he never should have kidnapped an innocent
shopgirl, no matter the temptation. He glanced over at his victim,
who was either shivering or convulsing against her bindings. What
did she ever do to him? he asked himself, other than commit the
crime of being delicious and unavailable to such a man as he?

By now she had already been a guest in his dead space for so
long that there were certainly family, friends, possibly co-workers,
all asking about this girl. *Did she meet a man and elope?*

In that moment, he felt a cold rush of envy when he realized that
a better brain than his would visualize the problem clearly enough
to find a better solution. He saw no solution but one, but since the
nondescript man was quite painfully aware of his middling intel-
lect, he expected nothing more of it now.

Someone with a mind like Duncan's, however, would likely find
some other opportunity buried in all this. A man with the ability
to manipulate whole groups of people and convince them that
they loved to function as puppets—a man who is anything but

nondescript—such a man would *somehow* sniff out legitimate opportunity here, where the nondescript man possessed nothing but a mental fog.

He hated to admit it, but the great James "J.D." Duncan would probably even know, or magically guess, how many people were active in this woman's daily life—people who might actually be upset that she had turned up missing. Thus Duncan would be able to predict how hard they would search for her.

The nondescript man grappled with that notion. What would Duncan expect people to do in reaction to her disappearance?

They will walk the fairgrounds, most likely. Six hundred and twenty-five acres of flat land is not that hard to search. They will come inside the pavilions, including here at the Hall of Science. They will look around, maybe call out for her, maybe not. Possibly ask him questions, as foreman.

He racked his brain for more and got nothing, so he tried bargaining with himself: That was likely to be the extent of it, wasn't it? Whatever sort of search that they mounted for her, they would never be so aggressive as to start tearing into completed scenic effects like this one, would they? Not for a mere shopgirl. If she was that important, why would she have such a job? Would they rip up their own property just because some girl doesn't show up for work?

But then, he had to wonder if they might decide to tear up the place just for the publicity, so the press would see that the exposition's leaders were pulling out all the stops to find the missing girl.

Tell us, wise Mr. Duncan, he thought, *would they do that for the publicity?*

They might. Maybe he should station himself outside, doing make-work? Then when they showed up, he could deflect any potential interest in the dead space. He could point out to them that the entire caveman set had been completed before the poor girl went missing. They didn't know about any dead space, so they might listen to him. He might be able to stop them right there.

He reached the end of his thoughts on it. No matter how many more ideas a finer blade might be able to might carve out of the situation, he had nothing left beyond the bleak knowledge that the same God who had abandoned him had also given James "J.D." Duncan his undeserved abilities. The whole thing had taken on the aura of a cosmic setup, with him at the center.

He consoled himself with the reminder that it was all only information now, nothing more. God may have abandoned him, but since then, everything had gone so smoothly that somebody out there had to be on his side. He could never have come up with a space like this *and* successfully put it to use, all on his own. Somebody down there liked him. He grinned and nearly laughed out loud at himself. The fact that the experience was definitely not Divine in origin did nothing to dampen his enthusiasm for it.

It could not be allowed to matter, anymore.

There was just too much rage for it to go unreleased. The stuff accumulated quickly and came over him with compelling force. Relieving it was slow work, and how long could this one girl last? The smell inside the dead space was already heavy. Once she died . . .

After all, she was only a stopgap measure. The rage would continue to swell until James "J.D." Duncan had at last been professionally destroyed. Beyond that, he hardly cared if he himself died in the process, so long as Duncan's public humiliation came first.

His thoughts were interrupted when the girl whimpered a bit, just enough to catch his attention. He automatically shifted his gaze to her. At that instant, inspiration struck him like an arrow.

What to do with her body.

CHAPTER TEN

THE COMMITTEE OF FIFTY elected to hold a preopening ceremony on February 19th, one day ahead of the exposition's official opening day. This way, they reasoned, the city could celebrate on its own for one brief instant. After that, this great exposition would belong to the rest of the world. The new transatlantic and transcontinental telephone cables guaranteed that visitors to San Francisco would telephone their individual reports from the great exposition in many different languages, all over the planet.

Until that year, the phenomenon of instantaneous global reach was a thing unknown to history. With that in mind, the city's "private" celebration was tastefully held away from the fairgrounds, back on Market Street, at the Pacific Majestic Theatre. Thus the committee was careful not to steal any of their own well-crafted thunder from the exposition's grand opening up at the newly made fairgrounds on the northern end of the peninsula.

The same committee that employed James "J.D." Duncan and contracted his services for the entire fair had also noticed that he was making himself publicly scarce since his single pre-exposition performance. It struck them as unseemly, a touch arrogant. Perhaps more than a touch. The rare coinage of arrogance was re-

served for the Committee of Fifty and for those they deemed suffi-
cient to wield it. That list did not include a theatre showman.

When written notice arrived at J.D.'s hotel to inform him of the
show that he was to present on the 19th, two weeks hence, he decided that it was probably time to sober up and emerge from his
room anyway. He was agreeable even though on the day of the 19th
he would still be twenty-four hours away from officially beginning
his contract. Since he had already given them his one free "demonstration" show, he did not really owe them anything at all.

Of course, he reminded himself, there was always the issue of
good working relations, proper mingling with the money mongers,
whatnot. Private vacations were refreshing, but probably best not
overextended.

In recent weeks he had been making do without the clarity of
the powder in favor of the oblivion of the bottle. After a lifetime as
a teetotaler, he had come to find that the sensation of utter inebri-
ation was deeply seductive. Within drunkenness he expected little
from his rational abilities or his powers of memory—and so felt no
disappointment when they betrayed him as they were doing, step
by step, in the manner that Dr. Alzheimer had so terribly described.

But all of that was for another day. It was time for a bath, a
shave, and some sunlight, not too much. The call to arms had been
sounded. And so after the overly cheerful messenger departed,
Duncan stood before his full-length mirror with the committee's
note still in his hand. He pulled open his robe, dropped his
trousers, and stood in his silk shorts to survey the damage . . .

He looked like something that had just been expelled from a
particularly nasty mountain beast.

He tested himself a bit. "Good evening—" his voice broke.

He cleared his throat. "I say, good evening, ladies and—" His
voice broke again.

He cleared his throat once again. "Good evening, ladies and—"
He collapsed into a coughing fit that doubled him over until both

his hands were on his knees. The force of his hacking was such that all he could do was stagger in a tiny circle.

After a long minute, he was able to get the coughing under control, but by then gravity was feeling very wavy and his head throbbed. His ears rang in time with his heartbeat.

He decided to go ahead and just sit right down on the floor. Maybe for a minute or so. Just to get his wind back.

At that unfortunate moment, and entirely without intending to do so, he glanced up at his reflection in the mirror. The sight froze him for a moment; a whiskery evaporite with sallow skin and sunken eyes seemed to be wearing his bathrobe.

So, the thought struck him. *Two weeks until showtime, then.*

At the same moment, Vignette stood silent as a shadow inside of the front room coat closet. She was close enough to the slatted door to hear the chatty women in the next room, even though she was hidden back in the corner behind Randall's heavy winter coat. Nobody had any reason to touch that coat, so she felt safe enough. Her dark clothing helped her to remain in the shadows whenever anyone opened the door to put a jacket in or take one out. Her top was a simple blouse that allowed free movement, as did her lightweight trousers.

Her shoes were the softest men's shoes that she could find. She could run fast in them, all that she wanted to, and practically forget that she had them on. Either her leg muscles or her wind would give out on her before her feet would blister. That fact always gave her special confidence during high-acceleration situations.

She had already endured two and a half hours in there, just to make sure that she avoided being spotted around the house and drafted into the occasion. She needed to be free to perform this reconnaissance work.

Now they were all there: all six leaders of the Ladies' Hospitality League. Just them and Miss Freshell, who was brashly using their family home to host the ladies. Of course she convinced Randall that she could not possibly entertain them at her hotel.

She had also astonished Vignette by telling Randall that she intended to use the meeting to introduce Vignette to these women, so that Vignette could "experience the social company of women of that caliber."

And of course she said nothing to Vignette about it beforehand. She had taken over Randall's brain and now she seemed to think that she was taking over Vignette's life.

The Eastern Whore's behavior tempered Vignette's resolve to the point that it no longer mattered to her if she had to do something that might make Randall mad—not if it helped him to open his eyes to this woman. He would eventually get over being mad. He always had before, hadn't he? And once he got far enough away from Miss Freshell to get his vision back, he would see that they were all better off without her in their lives. He had to.

Meanwhile, the nattering continued and there was no way for her to avoid it. These nattering ladies seemed to do nothing else in life other than natter at other nattering ladies until they sounded like a flock of squawking birds. Vignette's hidden place held her in the path of every tedious word, while the women cheerfully one-upped each other with passing references to gifts, vacations, property, and the remarkable successes of various children, many of whom seemed to be already grown.

Vignette sighed and shook her head. Over the course of her time in the closet, she had begun to experience the nattering as if every word were a single tooth on a heavy saw blade being slowly dragged across the top of her head. For an instant she thought about pulling Randall aside at the first opportunity and trying to tell him about the nattering (perhaps skipping the closet part), strictly as a way of using it to help explain why she could never live like one of these creatures, why she had to sneak into police training, why she *needed* to succeed at it.

The thought faded. She could not imagine being able to get the concept across.

She noticed that a painful stiffness was really starting to settle into her legs and her back. It was a relief to hear Miss Freshell raise her voice to get things started. Her tone clearly indicated that it was time to stop the informal nattering and begin the official nattering.

Vignette had to hand it to Miss Freshell; she knew nothing if not how to natter. The six ruling Ladies' Leaguers lowered their individual natters by a couple of notches in response. It was enough to indicate polite cooperation with her but not so much as to give the impression that any of these ladies took orders from Janine Freshell, just because she had written a few little romance books.

"Well, ladies, I am so disappointed that Randall's stepdaughter, Vignette, has missed our refreshments. I can't imagine what has detained her, as she was so eager for the opportunity to meet all of you. I'll hope she arrives soon.

"In the meantime, I promised you a charitable donation to the Ladies' Hospitality League, to help you to continue your fine work, and I'll come directly to the point. I am hereby formally offering to you—as the officers of the league—ten percent of all of the proceeds from my next novel!"

Vignette heard delighted squeals from the excellent ladies. Miss Freshell tastelessly allowed the squealing to go on for an uncomfortably long time while she soaked up their gratitude.

With this financial gift for their underfunded organization, along with the prestige of having a book as the source of the funds, Vignette decided that these killer birds disguised as society ladies were as happy as if they had just found a pile of money worms.

"It's going to take place right here in San Francisco, set in our present time, and use the exposition as the backdrop!" That set off a round of squeals so intense that it was hard to believe nobody passed out for lack of air.

Vignette was still locked in surprise. Generosity was not in Miss Freshell's nature; Vignette was sure of that much. She had never seen the woman do anything without a damned good reason, and it always had to do with Miss Janine Freshell first.

The nattering increased. It was more intense now that it was fueled by the rumor of money. Flattery flowed. The women, it now seemed, had all read Miss Freshell's last book. They *loved* it. Vignette thought that Miss Freshell sounded so grateful to be among such company that she wanted to slather them in butter and lick them all clean.

From that point on, her patience in the closet was finally rewarded. She could not doubt that what she overheard was far more blunt and truthful than what Miss Freshell would have presented, if she had known that Vignette was there. The Eastern Whore explained to the others that there was this one little, polite "condition" on the money offer. She needed their collective signatures upon a letter of support from the league, and she needed it to be addressed to her publisher. In it, she wanted them to remind the publisher that they would also be at the exposition for the entire ten months, and thus would be very interested in reading the book.

With their contacts at the exposition, they could even boost sales right there, if the publisher got it into print soon enough. Miss Freshell assured them that she could complete it in three months. She gave a pretty giggle and confided to the women that Detective Randall Blackburn was turning out to be an even better protagonist that she had hoped he would be, when she first arrived in this provincial little seaport. She assured them all that by the time she was finished with him, he would have no choice but to be her full-time escort, because he would be "too famous for police work!" Everyone laughed and nattered.

When it was all over at last and the women began to retrieve their coats, Vignette huddled back in the shadows with a much clearer idea of what the afternoon had been all about. The Eastern Whore had just used Randall's house to host a meeting to bribe local power-women into boosting her career, while making a joke about the disastrous effect it would have on Randall himself.

Now all Vignette had to do was wait for the house to get quiet and for Miss Freshell to wander off somewhere. She could slip out of the closet and leave out the back way, then return through the front door in a couple of hours with some story about why she missed out on the lovely opportunity.

CHAPTER ELEVEN

J.D. PACED BACK AND FORTH on the sidewalk across from The Sea Mist restaurant, even though it was only a few hours before curtain time. He kept his eyes on the front door. He was expected inside, and had called the meeting himself. The only thing to do was to go on in and get to it.

But he had taken all of the elixir that he dared to that morning, since there was an evening show—he was reluctant to try pulling off another onstage miracle like that last one—and the beneficial effect was not strong enough. Was he getting worse? He could not tell, not really. At times when he felt depressed, his mind seemed to be coming apart. But when his spirits were back up again, then all his symptoms seemed like things that he could overcome, if he just summoned enough willpower.

The only thing he remained certain of today was that this time, the elixir had failed to clear the cobwebs or to give him back his reliable memory. He could feel the powder coursing through his system, rushing his heartbeat, but the positive effect on his abilities was nil.

Because he could not remember what he intended to tell them at the meeting. Why did he call the damn thing?

Focus, he ordered himself. *Breathe deeply. It's just a security meet-*

ing of some kind. Detective Blackburn is going to meet you here. It's close to the theatre, and the young Nightingale fellow works there. You told them to meet you there, but that you wanted to have the actual meeting while walking along the sidewalk, to avoid eavesdroppers.

But why were they meeting in the first place? Something about security, yes, but what?

It was time. He crossed the street hoping that it would come to him, once he was in there with the other two. He could usually manage a smooth stream of small talk in such situations, until his memory clicked back in.

So when he arrived at the front of The Sea Mist, in spite of his trepidation he pulled open the heavy brass door and walked in holding his posture straight and his chin high. Experience had long since taught him that every once in a while, sheer force of attitude can save the day when all else around you is failing, provided that you remain utterly committed.

He prepared himself with a reminder straight out of his personal toolbox: *You may meet with resistance—you already know that. And since it is expected, you will show no surprise if you encounter it. Half of an opponent's confidence can be stomped out in that very first second, if you don't flinch. If you can stare them down. If you can smile . . .*

The nondescript man followed Duncan from his hotel at a safe distance, then hung back while the showman stopped outside The Sea Mist restaurant and paced the sidewalk for a while. His presence was well camouflaged by the clang of the Market Street trolley and the clopping draft horses that competed for space with backfiring automobiles and trucks.

Once Duncan finally disappeared inside the place, the nondescript man moseyed over close enough to the restaurant's front window to take an elaborately casual look inside. He got a glimpse of Duncan seated at a table, talking to the tall young waiter. It did not tell him enough. Was Duncan about to walk back out and head toward the nearby theatre, or would he dig in and stay awhile?

To buy time, the nondescript man bent and made an elaborate ritual out of finding a pebble in his shoe and getting it out. By the time he was finished and stole another peek, he saw Duncan being joined by a big man in an inexpensive three-piece suit. This was a grown man in the full sense, quite fit looking. A soldier, maybe, or a cop of some kind.

The nondescript man was almost at the end of his time-wasting routine when the door opened and Duncan came out, accompanied by both the big man and the young waiter.

A cop, then, judging by the way he moves.

The three slowly walked away, engrossed in their conversation. He could not make out a word of it at that distance.

Still, he made no attempt to follow. There was no further need. His reconnaissance was a success because he now knew that Duncan was safely occupied with these two, and thus the coast was clear over at the theatre. It would remain so for a while yet, driving a nice little wedge under this window of opportunity, holding it open. For how long? Say thirty minutes, at the least? Half an hour was several times more than enough.

With the frenzy of last-minute preparations going on at the fairgrounds, he had encountered no trouble in remaining nondescript while he posed as a deliveryman and wheeled a dolly with a crate strapped to it straight out of the Hall of Science and across the fairgrounds. The situation had called for moving unnoticed across an area filled with workers. For a man of his natural anonymity, it was a casting call from Fate.

Once he reached the main gate, whatever force that had been helping him helped him again. Taxi carriages had already begun to hover at the new fairgrounds, and so hailing one was easy enough. For a few extra coins, the eager driver helped load the crate and the dolly right into his taxi. Then the cab took him all the way to Market Street and dropped him two blocks away from the Pacific Majestic Theatre—San Francisco's Finest.

After assisting him in unloading the crate, the satisfied taxi driver moved on to his next fare. He would quickly lose any detailed recollection of a nondescript man dropped off at no particular location.

The nondescript man had risked leaving the sealed crate outside the theatre's backstage door while he followed Duncan, so he hurriedly made his way back from the restaurant, moving along at a quick dog trot.

He was there within two minutes. His property had been respected. Then it was a simple slip into the deliveryman persona, and onward through the theatre's receiving entrance with the dolly and the crate. His research had already showed him that the theatre had no guards on duty in the backstage area before showtime.

Like the finest background player, he flowed onto the scene, blended in, and moved through it without drawing attention. His character projected the perfect attitude: casual, bored, impatient, a working man who radiated the potential for the kind of annoyed and annoying conversation that nobody wanted to hear. Others would avoid his company without even thinking about it. He knew that because the master had known it—in a distant past, he had observed James "J.D." Duncan pulling that particular slight on various marks, plenty of times.

Randall and Shane said goodbye to Duncan at the restaurant's front door ninety minutes after leaving The Sea Mist together. He proceeded on to the theatre to prepare for that evening's show while they went inside and ducked into a booth.

The manager spotted Shane and came over scowling, ready to ask why an off-duty employee was in the restaurant. Blackburn calmly gazed at him and said, "He's with me. We'd like a couple of beers." He dropped a dollar coin on the tabletop.

The manager recalculated his attitude, offered a brief, tight little smile, then snapped up the coin and shuffled off to fetch the drinks. Once he was out of earshot, Blackburn muttered, "I don't see how they can object, as long as you spend money here."

"He's on my back, anyway," Shane quietly replied. "Wants to move me out of here, make me cover the extension restaurant they're opening on the exposition grounds."

"Really? Why not just play along? It would probably be a much more amusing place to work."

Shane smiled and nodded. "First we'd better get through tonight's show with Mr. Duncan. And I have to tell you right now, I don't see anything with him."

"Nothing?"

"It's as if he's covered in a thick coat of paint. No light shines through him at all, that I can see. That's not a sign of something being wrong with him, necessarily. It's just that I can't tell if his story is true, half true, or some cooked-up fantasy."

The manager arrived and dropped off their beers, sneaking a quick look of disapproval at Shane before quickly following with an obsequious smile to Blackburn. Blackburn caught his gaze and silently held it, blank-faced. The manager moved away.

"I'm sorry that I can't do any better with this one, Randall," Shane added.

"No need to apologize," Randall replied, sipping at his beer. "I've never seen a man so close to outright hysteria for no particular reason."

"Maybe this is a tendency, you know, with people who go into public life. Entertainers."

"So someone is out to get him, but he either can't or won't tell us who it is. He's sure that he's being followed, but can't say why. He got the city brass to make me follow him around and look for unknown assassins who could strike from any direction."

"But he only needs security during performances."

Blackburn exhaled through his teeth in frustration. "Just tell me. As far as you can tell, is he in his right mind?"

Shane took a slow gulp to cover for some thinking time while his impression of Duncan came into focus. "I don't think he's insane. He doesn't seem delusional. With the exception of his conviction that someone wants to kill him, he speaks in a perfectly rational way. But something has him off balance."

"Want to guess what it is?"

"I will, but only after stressing the speculative aspect of my answer."

"Ah! Well, then." Blackburn raised his glass to him. "Consider it stressed."

"Whatever it is that troubles him, that's the real source of his fears, not some remote assassin."

"And of course," Blackburn spoke for both of them, "if his fears *are* real, then the time when he's the most vulnerable is right where I can't do him any good at all."

Shane completed the thought. "Any fool with a handgun can bring Mr. Duncan down when he's all lit up on the stage."

Blackburn drained his mug and dropped it with a thud. "All right, then. All I see here is an old-fashioned babysitting assignment. But I still need for you to come, at least for the big public appearances."

"You mean until you can dump the assignment."

"Amen."

They stood up to leave. Blackburn turned to where the manager was leaning against the bar and nodded to him. The manager gave his standard gracious imitation of affability, and since Shane was right next to Blackburn, did not even attempt to slide in a threatening look.

"Come on," Blackburn muttered while they walked out, "we've got just enough time to catch an early dinner before we report backstage."

"At home?"

"That would take too much time. We'll just stop in someplace where your manager doesn't work. Vignette knows to bring Miss Freshell along with her to the theatre if we don't get back on time."

Shane grinned. "I know Vignette will get there on her own. She isn't going to miss a good show just because we don't turn up. But aren't you worried that your sweetheart might take offense?"

Blackburn gave him a wry look. "Miss Freshell was not feeling herself that day, Shane. You know that as well as I do."

"No, I wasn't talking about—"

"What, you're referring to her ongoing clashes with Vignette? She just needs time to—"

"Not Vignette."

"Well what, then? She always seems to go out of her way to make a pleasing impression upon you."

"She does, Randall. I'm not—"

"Has she said something?"

"What, to me? Hardly."

"Well then, what are you trying to say to me? Why are we discussing this? They'll meet us at the theatre. Can we go get some supper or not?"

"We can. Let's go. I'm only admiring your fearlessness."

"Shane . . ."

"You haven't even specified to her whether you will meet her before the show?"

"She knows we're working! She doesn't expect me to sit with her."

"No, she doesn't expect you to sit with her."

"What, then? Damn it, Shane!"

"Can we agree that Miss Freshell is a published author of romantic novels, and that in some circles she is something of a celebrity?"

"Get to the point."

"Can we also agree that as your fiancée, she is likely to expect special treatment from you?"

"I arranged their tickets already!"

"Tickets. But such a woman, a woman who has read from her books in public, a woman who is engaged to marry—*she* won't notice if you don't show up to greet her before the show, though. Will she?"

They walked in silence while Blackburn absorbed the concept.

"The question of whether I meet her before the show or after the show—don't you think that's something of a technicality? Miss Freshell is a reasonable woman."

"Miss Freshell is a proud woman."

"Not proud in the wrong sense of the word."

They continued on down the sidewalk.

"All right, Randall. I'm sorry I asked."

"No need to apologize," Blackburn said, looking troubled. "I know you mean well."

"Thank you."

"Certain things, in a private conversation, a man can ask."

"That's fair."

"You think I should meet her and Vignette before the show begins, don't you?"

Shane adopted an exaggerated nonchalance, just for fun. "I think Vignette will be fine, either way."

Moments like this reminded Blackburn why he had remained a bachelor for so long. He walked along in a busy silence until they found an inexpensive café and turned to go inside.

J.D. always arrived at the theatre well ahead of showtime, taking advantage of the enforced privacy backstage to maximize his concentration, do his exercises, and make sure that his makeup was perfectly applied. Tonight's special preopening show was enough of an occasion to make it worth spending a good part of the late afternoon at the theatre.

All proceeded as normal, for quite a while. He sat at his makeup table applying darkener to his temples and warming up his voice. The silence backstage was the perfect backdrop for his imagination. He prepared himself by visualizing that night's two-hour extravaganza. Naturally, he would dither away the first half by calling up volunteers and having them do the usual tricks, while he covertly worked his suggestions into the audience.

That interaction with the individual audience members would serve its true purpose of ferreting out the ones that struck him as ready to play along. Out of those, he was usually right about half the time. And it was they who served as the capstone of his show, at the end—when he triggered them and watched their reactions convert a theatre filled with sophisticates into a gaggle of delighted children.

His mental rehearsal was in full swing when he decided to go ahead and get dressed, even though he still had an hour and a half until the house opened. The sensations of being made up and dressed in his stage clothes always helped to heighten his readiness and, these days, seemed to help clear his thinking. He stood up and stepped over to his dressing room closet.

His performance clothing had been delivered and placed there for him, early in the day. J.D. opened the door and looked at the suit rack to select the evening's jacket. It was not an unpleasant chore, something of a ritual. A few languorous moments drifted by. Style being a showman's first statement, the choice was not without meaning. Sometimes a pattern to aid in eye-dazzling the folks, sometimes a bold black for mystery. He was already in cake . . . cake up . . . caked makeup. His makeup was already on, that is, meaning that from now on, every little choice he made was a part of that evening's sow. Not *sow*, as a farmer sows a field, rather *show*. *Show*, was what his inner voice was trying to say: every little choice he made was part of that evening's *show*.

Something tickled at his lower peripheral vision. It was just a flicker, but enough to drop his gaze down to the floor and land it squarely onto the young woman's body.

She must have been beautiful once, but was now quite obviously deceased. She was wadded into a ball, with her arms wrapped around her bended legs, as if she had been packed into a box. There was no smell of decomposition, at least not enough to overpower the strong scent of greasepaint and the various stage makeup products.

It finally hit him. Time froze.

J.D. was a beached fish gasping for air. He stared at the sight before him and felt a rushing sound fill his hearing. It rose and fell in time with his pulse.

He found his knees shaking and felt them losing the strength to stand. Instinctively, he grabbed on to the doorjamb for support. His balance reeled away, and with a flood of alarm he realized that he was an inch away from passing out.

He dropped to his knees and lowered his head. He had been to this point often enough to know what to do: Suck air in and blow it out, fast and hard.

J.D. kept his eyes jammed shut and stabilized himself enough to remain conscious. But when he opened them again and found himself staring directly at one of the dead girl's feet, a second wave of shock swept through him.

The shock intensified while he forced himself to look upward, all the way to her face. She had powder around her mouth and nose. It looked just like his secret elixir.

The resulting tableaux was perfect. Its message was conveyed with clarity, bright and shiny as a well-lit marquee. And the message told him that this scene was precisely the same as it would be if this unfortunate woman had a noose tied around her neck—with the rest of the rope coiling its way directly back to him.

Panic hit him like a drop through the gallows. His body reacted before his mind could, and it threw itself into a frantic backward crab-walk, blindly repulsed, not thinking at all. He traveled away from the girl, straight across the floor and directly into the opposite wall with the back of his head. The awful impact was rock hard, through his skull, his teeth, his skeleton. This time, when the sensation of falling snatched him away from the world, he was powerless to stop it.

J.D. crumpled to the floor and slumped against the wall, unable to do anything more than make involuntary twitching movements while he tried to remain connected to himself. Inside, he danced on the deck of a violently rolling ship. One second . . . two . . . possibly three . . . but then his muscles went limp, all balance eluded him, and he fainted dead away.

CHAPTER TWELVE

AT TWENTY-ONE, SHANE Nightingale had never felt burdened by an overactive sex drive. Under the right circumstances, free from his usual self-haunting, he could view a woman's beauty and charm with the animal purity of a lustful desire. But he was fortunate among most men because sexual longing did not drive his days. What there was of it could be self-corrected effectively enough, on the occasional basis.

Thus while he steered Randall through the early arrivals to rendezvous with Vignette and Miss Freshell, he reminded himself that he had no real idea of what level of urge drove Randall's manhood. A fellow so obviously virile might require the presence of a woman at some point in his life. He might feel that it is something he simply has to have, in order to live. Shane could only assume that something like that was driving Randall now.

In that vein, he encouraged Randall's best behavior in matters regarding Miss Freshell, in spite of other choices that he might prefer to see Randall make. Even though she lived at her hotel and never stayed for the night, she was still at the house often enough to feel like a boarder. Randall had never become seriously involved with a woman in the years that Shane had known him, so there was nothing for comparison.

And so Shane never said a word to him about his reservations about her, because he owed his life to Randall Blackburn in ways that Blackburn himself would never know. Starting with the day nine years ago when Blackburn inadvertently drove away Shane's deadly tormentor.

Randall had never wanted anything except for Shane to thrive. Nearly everything that Shane knew about being a good and decent man, he had learned from him. Therefore, if Randall needed this powdered creature in his life, that was it. Shane could never do anything to spoil whatever happiness Miss Freshell might bring.

So he made sure that Randall intersected with Vignette and Miss Freshell, who arrived as scheduled in the theatre lobby. At Shane's prompting, Randall had already picked up their tickets. Miss Freshell was greeted by her fiancé before the show so that she did not have to go stand in the will-call line, and was personally escorted to her seat, along with Vignette, by both men together.

Miss Freshell beamed so brightly with pleasure at this treatment that Randall finally grasped the concept. His eyes widened and a smile crossed his face. He glanced at Shane and wiggled his eyebrows. Shane snorted back a repressed laugh.

When the two women reached their seats, Shane and Blackburn dropped them there to wait for the show to begin while the men began their duties for Duncan.

Shane resumed his place at the front of the house, discreetly looking back up the aisles and studying the audience members while they filed in. Randall was at the back wall, watching from behind.

Shane was so grateful for the chance to be of use to Randall, to work at his side, that he would gladly accompany him on any duty at all. Nevertheless, they were saddled with a completely unreasonable goal for this performance. He could understand the frustration that Randall had to be feeling, in spite of doing a good job of hiding it. Randall had been abandoned to this assignment by an angry boss, and now was under orders from this Mr. Duncan, a man whose judgment might be reasonable or might not. As for that moment, their job was nothing more difficult than to look out for anybody who might want to do harm to Duncan, by whatever means, at any point during the night. That was all.

Is that man over there raising a cigar, or does he have a derringer in his hand? What is under that lady's tall hat?

Shane's biggest challenge in this was that he could all too easily imagine such outbursts of personal violence, and the many reasons for them, coming from practically anybody. He had found that so far in his life, the passing of nine years since the Nightingale murders had done nothing to dim their impact upon him.

If we really had the power to see so deeply into a crowd of strangers, we would be the ones performing up on the stage.

On the other hand, Duncan claimed to be doing that very thing when he was "reading" an audience. Could he really do that, Shane wondered, without any sort of stage trickery? If so, was that why the man seemed to have no idea that his request to Randall was so unusual?

Or was it that Duncan was not willing to trust his own "abilities"—not with his own life on the line—and that Randall and Shane were there to compensate for skills that the great Master Mesmerist did not really have?

No answer was likely to appear before the evening's performance got started. The theatre was quickly filling up. Shane felt countless impressions beginning to overwhelm him. The sheer number of people presented a crushing burden on observational skills that he had never employed on a scale so large as this.

He soon he forgot about everything else, lost in the sensation of walking into a strong headwind formed by countless impressions.

"Ten minutes, Mr. Duncan!" came the cheerful voice of the stage manager through the locked dressing room door.

"Thank you!" J.D. called back, according to standard backstage protocol. With that, he was now duly warned of the impending curtain time, and management had heard his confirmation. That would satisfy them for the moment.

The dressing room had no window, so with the door shut and bolted, nobody could see him pacing before the open dressing room closet with the dead female occupant slumped at the bottom.

He had only been unconscious for a minute or less, and even though he woke up blissfully ignorant of what it was that had scared him in the first place, that moment of innocence vanished as soon as he opened his eyes. He found himself staring directly at the young woman's blue and gray body.

At that moment, J.D. saw all his self-imposed rules about avoiding the elixir before a show going out the dressing room's nonexistent window. He went for his makeup kit and saw with relief that it had not been violated.

There was no way to know why this girl was in here taking his powder. But she had obviously experimented with too much of it and died as a result. He seized the opportunity to jolt his own mind beyond the shock of the situation, using the magic of the elixir.

Dr. Alzheimer had been kind to J.D. after the diagnosis. He connected him with one of the chemical engineers who worked on developing the new substance, abbreviated MDMA, then got him his large supply. He showed him how to use it to hold off the disease's symptoms, to keep his memory working longer and to burn through the fog—but all of it was predicated upon the repeated warning that too much elixir could stop the heart. Stop it cold.

Since his own heart was not stopped by the renewed sight of the body—as it easily could have been—he figured that he was strong enough to justify prescribing a double dose for himself, show or no show. He needed a clear head. He needed to either run from this horror or think a whole series of very smart and clearheaded things to do in response to this. As it was, shock had fogged his brain so terribly that he could scarcely remain in the moment and form some sort of a plan, without an extra boost.

Still the clock, he knew too well, would not stop ticking. An audience was coming. Some were already there.

He spooned the elixir directly into his mouth while he resumed pacing. Clarity. He needed clarity. He needed to know what happened, but even more than that, he needed to know what in the hell to do with a dead body in the closet at ten minutes before curtain time.

The elixir's effects came on quickly because he was already scared, with his heart thumping away. Or was it the expectation? The old magic of expectation.

He could already feel his thoughts clearing a bit. His memory felt strong enough, and his brain did not seem to be locking up on him the way it sometimes could, stiffening like arthritic legs. He took a few deep breaths and asked himself, *Is there a way to deal with this? Is there?*

He made himself look at her. Beautiful once, now ash gray of skin and sunken in her features. How long had she been dead? He touched her flesh; no sign of rigor mortis. This was supposed to tell him something, but he could not recall what it was. That question fell into the what-happened category, anyway. He needed to focus on what to *do*.

"Five minutes, Mr. Duncan!" came the warning call through his closed and bolted door.

"Thank you!" He threw back the expected reply in a strong voice. Confident. Ready for a fine performance. Absolutely nothing that you would find troubling in here, folks.

That bought him five more minutes. Good, then. They were all still with him, so far. Management believed that he was just seeking out his solitude in the final minutes before the show. Why worry? He was in his dressing room, right where he was supposed to be, was he not? He had answered his time calls from the stage manager with energy that was appropriately cheerful and alert. Everything in good shape so far—eh, folks?

He realized that the elixir was already bringing him the magic of sustained optimism, in spite of the lack of any justification for it. Yes, there was a mysterious dead girl in his dressing room closet with his secret powder spread across her mouth and nose. But looking on the bright side, he had almost five minutes to go before showtime, and so far nobody knew a thing.

He breathed deeply, enjoying the feeling of getting too much oxygen to the brain, and breathed even deeper. This was more like it. This was getting to be very, very interesting, now. Dead girl. His powder. Why?

Just an accident on the part of someone who was too curious for her own good? Someone who found out about the elixir and just had to try it?

Who could say what she thought she was taking? He moved close to her and studied her face. She was dressed nicely enough, like a working girl in a store or an office. Her clothing was badly rumpled, missing buttons, torn in a couple of spots. What did that mean? Did it happen to her while she was still alive, or was it some-how done only after death?

She must have died here, hiding like this. Maybe she heard someone coming after she got into his supply. Then of course it hit him.

His supply traveled with him, and he had not arrived until late that afternoon. She did not make her way into the closet while J.D. was in the theatre, which meant that she was already in there when he arrived.

Meaning that if she had the elixir, she brought it in with her. Meaning also that she was the one who broke in, the last time!

Of course! J.D. was jubilant! Mystery solved! Somehow, she had found the elixir the last time. She took some away with her after robbing him, but she liked it and returned for more today. She took the last of her own while she waited for him to arrive, waited in the closet after sneaking into the theatre, and hadn't realized that she was taking too much.

Her heart gave out under the sheer power of her dose, just as the chemist had warned J.D. that it could do. "Anybody," the man had emphasized to him. "Anybody's heart will stop, with too much. It does not matter if you are young and healthy."

And as if to underscore the point, there was a cautionary tale played out, right there on the floor.

"Two minutes, Mr. Duncan!" came the stage manager's voice. "Overture starting up!"

"Yes indeed!" J.D. hollered back, but accidentally put far too much energy into it, like a man shouting across a mountain canyon. He clapped his hand over his mouth, but it was too late to bring it back. *Oh well, bigger fish to fry.*

Moving fast now, he pulled his empty costume trunk from the corner, flung it open, set it down, bent to the girl's body, picked it up, surprisingly soft, not stiff, wadded her into the trunk, folded her arms inside, closed the lid, clamped the lock shut, and pocketed the key.

"Dum, dah-dah-DUM-dah DUM!" He hummed at the top of his voice, along with the orchestra's rousing notes of the overture's conclusion.

"Mr. Duncan, sir, please! *Time!*" Now the voice sounded concerned.

But this time, J.D. flung open the door and offered his best smile to the waiting, fidgety stage manager.

"Yes indeed! Time to thrill and amaze!"

He hurried across the backstage area and into the offstage wings, leaving the mystery girl safely locked inside his costume trunk for the duration of his performance. Whatever her story might happen to be, she was not under any circumstances going to stow away in his life and bring him down in some terrible scandal.

Did he not have enough troubles? His afflicted brain was rotting out from underneath him. It was all happening just the way that the doctor had warned him. At first, the elixir gave him a slight advantage, made his performances godlike. Later, it only brought him up to his own standard.

The jumping shadows appeared, pulling at his peripheral vision, and he knew that the faces of the audience were again going to look as if they were painted onto balloons. But at least he had already worked under the influence of a heavy dose once before, and gotten away with it.

This time he only had to repeat that success and go home. Take the trunk somewhere and get rid of it, of course, but then go home. Because if he allowed himself to touch the horror of that girl's death for one second, his skin would stick to it like a tongue on a frozen pump handle.

His battleground was the stage. As long as his memory held up well enough for him to line up the right setups with the right triggers, he could coast through this one and take his bows—then go deal with the loaded costume trunk somewhere at the edge of town and hide until he figured out what to do.

It struck him that the elixir was really straightening out the old negative attitude. He felt a brief pang of guilt over his earlier lack of appreciation. Now as he reentered his familiar performance world and prepared to step out into the concentrated spotlight beam, he decided that everything was looking pretty good, all in all.

Suddenly, he felt as if he could not launch into the show quickly enough. He remembered that the folks out there were friends. All of them, friends, out there in the house and looking up at him. Each one of them had doubts about his powers, and yet was also ready to be amazed, hungry for the state of head-smacking disbelief.

Duncan knew why. If he confirmed their belief in unseen things, in powers that some people called magical, then by implication all their other intangible beliefs might also prove just as true.

When he demonstrated invisible mind control over perfect strangers, these poor sophisticates were lifted from the humdrum existence of a doubting Thomas and stepped, if only for a moment, onto the grassy turf of faith that was proved true, right there before their own eyes.

Out there on the stage once again, with the exquisite tingles of the concentrated spotlight beam ricocheting around inside of him, he could practically feel the thick leather reins draped through his fists. He had control. He clearly felt it. He was squarely in command of his faculties, and ready to drive this audience like a wagon team. They would find out where the open road took them all, together.

CHAPTER THIRTEEN

INTERMISSION
THE PACIFIC MAJESTIC THEATRE—
SAN FRANCISCO'S FINEST

NEITHER VIGNETTE NOR MISS FRESHELL felt like venturing into the lobby's pressing intermission crowd, so they kept to their seats. Vignette would have been content to spend the whole time watching the people making their way in and out of the theatre, but once their row of seats was otherwise empty, Miss Freshell leaned close to her. She spoke in a soft and very private voice.

Vignette could smell the powder on her skin.

"I don't know about you, but I think that I've seen a change in Randall since you agreed to work with us at the Ladies' Hospitality League. I think he's relieved."

Vignette's head whipped around toward her. "Relieved over what? That I'm getting stuck with a bunch of wax mannequins posing as nice married ladies? Or is he just relieved that you'll leave him alone about it now?"

"No need to bite my head off. I am simply convinced that this is the best thing for the family."

"The family?" Vignette glared at her for a moment, rejecting a whole list of responses, and finally settled for saying, "Why?"

"I told you, I like for Randall to be happy."

"Yes of course," Vignette replied, her voice rising a bit too high.

"Especially since Shane and I don't give a damn about him. We don't care whether he is happy or not, do we?"

"That is certainly not what I meant, dear."

"Vignette."

" . . . What?"

"It's 'Vignette.' Not 'dear.' "

"I see. You prefer blunt conversation."

"I prefer honest conversation. If you're such a big writer, why is honest conversation so difficult for you?"

"You are being too personal, Vignette. I cannot help but note that you have consistently been that way since Randall and I met."

"That was only a few weeks ago, Miss Freshell. A few weeks."

"And?"

"And now we need *you* to monitor whether or not we're doing our best to make Randall happy?" Vignette leaned in close and fixed Miss Freshell's eyes in her gaze.

"Lady, just tell me, one woman to another: Who the hell are you?"

She would not have been particularly surprised by a slap across the face, but she was still unprepared for the reaction she got. Miss Freshell's veneer of benign affability melted off her like a thin layer of wax under a flame. The visage that it revealed was hard and cold. The eyes were made of flint.

"I'm the one who will be taking Randall back to New York City once the exposition is over, as soon as we are married."

"He's never mentioned that."

"He doesn't know."

Vignette barked a sarcastic laugh. "Well, that was honest!"

"I thought honesty was your calling card, dear."

"All right, what if he refuses to leave San Francisco?"

"I don't believe he will."

"No, tell me. What if he won't go to New York? Do you still want him then?"

Vignette noticed that Miss Freshell stared at her as if she were a piece of three-day-old fish while she considered her reply. She finally spoke in measured tones.

"Here is what we're going to do, dear. We're going to tolerate each other for the next ten months while I am writing and promoting this book, and until the exposition is over. Then we will say a fond farewell when I take Randall and the new book back to civilization."

"If you're willing to be honest, or blunt, or whatever you want to call it, why don't you tell Randall that you have these plans all worked out for him?"

"I intend to, so don't bother threatening to tell him yourself." Miss Freshell shifted on her, again. This version was poisonously sweet. "Vignette Nightingale. Both names are made up, correct?"

"Vignette. Just Vignette."

"What, not Nightingale, as well?" Freshell smirked. "You two don't look like brother and sister to me. No resemblance at all."

"Don't pretend that you know anything about us!"

"I don't need to. The point is that we are women. We understand illusion as an essential tool of life. A touch of makeup, a good corset. Illusion lubricates our way."

"Please. You sound like one of the Ladies' Hospitality League."

"I am one of them. You know that."

"Do you have to sound like it?"

"And most of them already know what you are still waiting to find out—that in a world dominated by men and their brutality, we of the fairer sex must protect each other. Illusion is the main thing that protects all of us. Illusion is also something you understand, dear, in your own way. And just as well as the rest of us."

"You haven't said anything about your feelings for him."

"Romantic love? Like the plays they put on here?"

"You see something wrong with that?"

"Nothing that most of the women performing those plays don't already know."

"I am not following you at all."

Miss Freshell's face took on an expression that managed to be sour and sultry at the same time. "They understand the particular comfort that a woman frequently finds with another female. They enjoy the ironic fact that society allows us to walk, hand in hand, touch, laugh, flirt, even lie down together, and accepts it all as harmless."

"It's not?"

"It is," she laughed. "Of course it is! But not in the way that the men think. It's harmless because there's nothing wrong with getting comfort where you can. Especially under their noses."

"Under the men's noses . . ."

"That's it," she fairly sang. "It's been harmless for centuries, Vignette."

She laid her hand directly over Vignette's. "And it will be harmless for Randall, as well."

Vignette's stomach slowly dropped while she absorbed that, but before she could come up with any sort of reply, a large man and his wife came back to reclaim their seats and needed to step across them. That squashed the conversation.

Miss Janine Freshell, who had lost at that moment all chance of outliving the title "The Eastern Whore," gave Vignette's hand one final pat. She then pulled her legs in to allow the couple to pass. Vignette did likewise. The wife passed first, and Vignette watched the Eastern Whore flash an utterly charming smile at the husband when he sidled by. Some old married man.

He smiled back at the Eastern Whore, surprised by the intensity of her gaze, then managed to make himself look away. Of course he failed to stop himself from looking back. He was snagged by her illusion—as if that fat old man was a nineteen-year-old buck and Miss Janine Freshell was spread out naked before him—as if maybe the two of them would meet up out back and run off somewhere together. Vignette watched the flickers of fantasy cross his face, just as if the Eastern Whore had loaded the moving pictures into a nickelodeon.

A sense of the woman's power overwhelmed her. Without a doubt, Miss Janine Freshell could teach the Great Mesmerist a thing or two about making people see things that are not really there. That frightening command of illusion was the only aspect of the Eastern Whore that Vignette no longer called into question.

There was very little backstage activity during the intermission; J.D. worked alone in these close-up presentations. The stage manager was back there, but without a backup cast or supporting players to oversee, he tended to his check-board and pretended to work while a couple of black-clad stage hands quickly swept the stage.

J.D. had the hallway outside his dressing room all to himself, except for Detective Randall Blackburn and his assistant Shane something. Night-bird. Nightingale. The two men politely stood back near the offstage wings and gave J.D. plenty of room to pace, which he continued at a frantic rate.

He only traveled a few steps in each direction before turning around, so that he remained close to the door of his dressing room. People were less likely to get curious about the contents of that big trunk in there if they never saw it in the first place.

So for now, basic tasks: keep them away from the dressing room, finish the show, wait until everybody is out of the theatre, remove the trunk, take it far away, get rid of it, go back home, sleep for days.

A simple schedule, by God. One that made sense. With plenty of time to figure out everything later on. Deduce the why of it. A dead woman, complete stranger, hiding to steal his elixir.

Or perhaps he would drop it all into that same dark pit where so many other memories had been disappearing of late. How would that be? Let the cursed affliction serve some purpose, eh?

"Perhaps it'll even give old J.D. a whiff of luck and let him forget her altogether," he said out loud.

"Excuse me?" replied Detective Blackburn.

"What?"

"Who is it you want to forget, Mr. Duncan?"

"Oh that. Nothing! A line! I do lines before the show starts again! Warming up and all! You understand!"

"Sir, if you could hold still a minute and have a conversation with us—"

"Go right ahead, Detective!" Duncan cried, pacing like a man trying to make up for lost time. "I do this! Intermission! Keep the blood all fired up, eh? You understand!"

"Yes sir."

"I know you understand!"

"All right, then. Mr. Duncan, we've looked at every single audience member tonight. If anybody plans to cause trouble, so far they aren't doing anything to give themselves away. Nothing suspicious at all."

"Perhaps because of you, eh? Good, gentlemen! Good work!"

"The thing is, sir, there are a lot of the big rookie officers who would like nothing better than to do body guard duty for you."

Not even J.D.'s labored pacing kept him from noticing that Blackburn's assistant was staring. It felt like a spotlight beam. He could feel the heat of it.

"Detective, did we not have this conversation? You come highly recommended!" He clapped his hands twice in a row to relieve a little more of the energy overload, wiped the sweat from his hairline, poured water from a pitcher into a tumbler, replaced the pitcher, and drained the glass, all without breaking stride.

"Just ignore the jumping shadows," J.D. reminded himself.

"I don't see any jumping shadows, Mr. Duncan."

"What? No! *Lines,* remember? Reciting. So forth."

"Mr. Duncan, I wonder if you could tell me who recommended me for this? It's some sort of a mistake, that's all. Then we can match you up with some guy who is a real bulldog. Any one of them would jump in front of you before they would allow you to take a bullet."

J.D. clapped his hands together. He hit them extra hard without meaning to, but noticed that the concussion released a little explosion of energy. He clapped hard again, felt a bit more of a release, and immediately began to clap once with every other step. Stomp, stomp, clap. Stomp, stomp, clap.

He remembered that Blackburn had just asked him a question. So he raised his voice over his own background noise.

"Come now, Detective! There's got to be worse duty than guarding me—eh?" Stomp, stomp, clap.

"Of course. It's not that."

"Because I have to tell you, she expected you to see more of the potential in this assignment!" Stomp, stomp, clap.

"She?" asked the other one, Night-something.

This is why you don't talk to people when you're like this.

"She, he, whoever it was, I'm not saying, I can't recall, it doesn't matter." Stomp, stomp, clap. Stomp, stomp, clap. "Just please watch them as they leave the theatre, don't let anyone come back here after the show. No fans, no autographs."

"You said 'she,'" Blackburn interrupted, taking a step toward him. "There aren't any women in the command chain, Mr. Duncan."

J.D. stopped pacing. It felt good for the truth to be out. One less thing. A rush of affection for Detective Blackburn washed through him, filling him with empathy for the man's plight. A manly fellow such as this detective would surely take offense at having his fiancée meddle with his career. How sad, he thought with an inward sigh, that Detective Blackburn could not allow himself to appreciate the fruits of his woman's ambition. So many men suffered from that character flaw.

J.D. walked over to Detective Blackburn and embraced him. The detective stood still for a moment, then gently pulled his arms from around his neck and stepped back. J.D. could not repress a sad little laugh.

"It's a real shame, Detective. She meant well."

"Who did, Mr. Duncan?"

"See? You just said 'who,' but you didn't ask. It wasn't really a question! Oh my friend, we are brothers in the fools that they make of us, are we not?"

That Shane fellow spoke up again. "You are referring to Miss Janine Freshell?"

"Gentlemen! Gentlemen, please! She wanted it kept from you, but I have no doubt this is the best way. Trust in me! Go home and embrace her! Give her your thanks!"

Detective Blackburn cleared his throat and found his voice. "Mr. Duncan, why would my fiancée have any influence in this department?"

"I don't know that she has any at all, Detective. But she is a published author, here in San Francisco to write her next book. If anybody is listening to her, I'd guess that it's not the department officials, but the local politicians they work for, eh?"

He watched Blackburn turn to the Shane fellow. The two men had a heated conversation for another minute or so. Despite all the empathy that filled him for his fellow suffering humans, J.D. was careful to keep himself posted between them and his dressing room door. He busied himself with pretending to warm up his voice while he silently rehearsed stories to get these two to leave the backstage area.

"Just tell them you have to concentrate!" he shouted.

"What?" replied the detective.

"The *show*! The part where I have to *concentrate*! That's all! But in fact, I need to concentrate now. I mean, before curtain time. Just alone. Here. So thank you."

"Why would Miss Freshell want me to guard you?"

"Oh, I really think that this is a private conversation for the two of you. As for now, please just watch the crowd after the performance, then you can go. I'll ring you up on your new telephone tomorrow afternoon. Opening week, coming up! Big week!"

Blackburn again turned to the Shane fellow and exchanged

meaningful looks and a few murmurs. Then he turned back to J.D. and looked him straight in the eyes. "Mr. Duncan, my captain has ordered me to accommodate you, but I'm going to get to the bottom of this."

"Fine, fine! But for now, if you could—"

"It's all right." Shane stepped close to them. "We can discuss this with the captain or someone. Later. So, Mr. Duncan, we'll go ahead and keep them away after the show."

"Excellent!"

"And you don't need an escort home, or anything?"

"Nothing! Thank you! Good work! I'll be sending my compliments up the chain of command! People never hear enough praise of a job well done, eh?"

"Yes, sir," Shane replied, taking Blackburn by the shoulder and physically turning him away. "We'll go on out, now."

"Thank you, gentlemen! Good night!"

Nightingale. That was it. Shane's last name. He watched Shane Nightingale keep his arm on Blackburn's shoulder and walk him out of the backstage area and back into the main house.

With the backstage finally empty, J.D. sagged against the door of his dressing room and took a deep breath. Moments later, the opening music blared from the orchestra pit, leaving him with less than a minute until his cue.

Nothing else to worry about at this particular moment but the triggers for the setups that he had carefully planted in the audience during the first half of the show.

The triggers, he thought. *The godforsaken triggers . . .*

The nondescript man had been very careful not to leave any revealing marks when he cut his doorway into the dead space behind the fake cliff in the caveman display. It remained carefully concealed. His own work during the unmanned late shift had allowed him to insulate the place for sound. And tapping into the alternating current lines running through the display for the background lighting was no challenge at all for a determined man with nothing else to do. Electricity afforded a mercifully quick death..

There was the unexpected problem of heavy dampness inside that closed space. During those few days when he thoroughly enjoyed his random captive, the place had become positively steamy. He kept her alive until the last minute, on the day of Duncan's show, but that was all the time he could spare her. It had gotten so close inside of there that he needed to get out for a while, anyway.

In the meantime, he made use of his acquired skills, starting with a couple of interesting things that he picked up the first time desperation drove him to get relief. After his escape, when James "J.D." Duncan turned on him and sent him away, he began life on the run as one of the lucky pukes who got to spend ten hours a day on the working floor of a Chicago slaughterhouse. It was the last stop before falling into the belly of Hell.

Still, to the determined man, the man motivated by the scorching need for vengeance, there are lessons to be taken even in humiliation. His time on that killing floor taught him a handy bag of tricks for killing, tricks for handling a carcass, tricks for quickly stripping a large dead creature to the bone.

Like the trick of using the tapped electrical line that he had run down into the dead space to administer repeated shocks to both ends of her spinal cord after she was dead. This handy slaughterhouse trick effectively delayed or even prevented rigor mortis from setting in—offering him the opportunity to transport her body and deliver it in any position that he needed to place her in, without having her stiffen up on him.

The floor in the dead space had taken on so much of the air's moisture that he had to use great care in working with the electrical lines. The second time that he got a small shock through his thick leather gloves, he realized that the floor had become dangerously wet.

Now, back in the dead space after making the delivery to the theatre, he noticed that the floor had not dried out at all. This was despite the fact that nobody had been in the space for hours. He had left the hidden entrance door slightly ajar without giving away its position, enough to allow a draft to move through.

Instead of drying, the floor was more damp now. Maybe a pipe joint somewhere. The entire fairground was built on artificial land, chunks of the old city that came down in the Great Earthquake nine years earlier. The artificial land was shot through with water pipes of every size and description, to service the countless needs of the exposition's fountains, displays, and fixtures.

At least there was no foul smell, so he wasn't looking at a sewage leak. Slow leaks could be ignored, but a bad one could draw attention. So he would have to watch the floor: one more thing.

He sat up on the work table and was finally able to enjoy that special feeling of being alone in a darkened place, the site of his recent exhilarating forays. He felt the rare sensation of being at ease in that glorious foyer of Hell where right and wrong meant nothing, and no one else had any power but him.

He savored the thought of the fiasco that the girl's body would cause at the theatre, once it was discovered. He enjoyed trying to decide whether Duncan would find it, or if one of the crew would get there first.

And the touch of putting the powder that he stole from Duncan last time all over this girl's mouth and nose—would they connect it to Duncan? They would, he decided, or an anonymous note would be delivered to City Hall Station the next day. That was the beauty of it. He didn't have to sweat the details of Duncan's downfall, he only had to stand back at a distance and give him the push.

He had set a disaster in motion, but trusted in circumstance to add the finishing details. With the body deposited inside Duncan's dressing room, there was no way for the famous man to walk free. The only question was what specific form of disaster would come crashing down on him.

He was tired from his many exertions. But he had earned the

right to sleep. He could finally allow himself to let go and give in to it, all the while chewing on the expectation of the story that would be coming out about Duncan in the next day's newspapers.

He had a list for Duncan:

(a) Public humiliation;
(b) professional destruction;
(c) personal failure;
(d) lack of any opportunity to recover;
(e) all hope of leaving a respected legacy destroyed.

Oh, yes. He had a list. And in the case of James "J.D." Duncan, a checkmark was going to be required next to every single item—then and only then could the nondescript man say that his mission had been accomplished.

At long last.

CHAPTER FOURTEEN

TONIGHT, HABITS INGRAINED AFTER forty years of experience combined to steel his resolve. He considered it a masterful stroke of self-hypnosis on his part, to insist upon being the Amazing Duncan. His real product was not hypnosis, anyway. It was the persona of James "J.D." Duncan. On a night like tonight, that might be all he needed, if he pulled it off just right. The key to the technique was that everything he did had to imply a secret meaning.

The first rule that he would teach to aspirants, if his knowledge were the sort of thing that one shared, was this: "The folks will buy it if you sell it like you mean it." And for him, the message had always been the same: "Ladies and gentlemen, I am James 'J.D.' Duncan—*And Now You Are Hypnotized!*"

Shane stood at his position in the side aisle near the front of the stage, fascinated and baffled at the same time. Something very strange was going on with Duncan, stranger still because Shane could not tell if this was a planned part of the performance or not.

He glanced at the audience again and confirmed that they all seemed to be wondering the same thing. *Where is he going with this?*

They were hardly ten minutes into the second half of the show, with no threats to Duncan visible in the audience. However, as for whatever it was that was happening up on the stage . . .

Duncan screamed with laughter. He pointed straight at the crowd like an amused parent catching a child in some lovably foolish endeavor.

Shane felt his insides begin to knot at the recognition of something from the Nightingale murders, which after nine years still seemed to have happened yesterday. The only other time in his life that he had witnessed such a high state of stimulation in a grown man was in the ranting of Tommie Kimbrough while he destroyed the Nightingale family. The common element of *overexcitement* in these men was what struck him. Tommie in the act of murder and Duncan in the act of giving a performance, both displaying states of excitement far higher than the occasion called for.

Even though Tommie had been in the process of committing multiple murders, he knew that he was safe from discovery or intervention. And yet Shane had listened to him kill with the frantic energy of someone who was fighting for his life. Tonight, Duncan's state was clearly far more intense than anything he might need to put on a stage show. Shane could see perspiration pouring off Duncan's face. Strands of his hair were splayed across his forehead. His hands visibly shook when he gestured to the crowd.

He crouched forward, as if to guffaw at the audience again, but abruptly stopped cold. He did not move for several long seconds.

Then gradually, his face relaxed, he stood up straight, dropped his arms to his sides. He looked over the entire audience, opened his arms and spoke as if he were delivering the Sermon on the Mount.

"My Dear Ladies and Gentle Men, this has never happened to me before! Perhaps it serves to underscore this miraculous exposition being hosted here this year, or perhaps it is—and really, I personally believe this to be the case—perhaps it is the aggregate effect of the mental powers represented by this august body, right here in this theatre today!

"Because I must confess that you have overwhelmed me, tonight. Over one thousand of the city's greatest minds and strongest personalities, people of high education, people of great skill, even one or two who actually have both—ha!—Joking! Laugh along with us! Ha-ha!

"And yet if you will permit me to be quite serious for a moment, my friends, you must allow me to humbly inform you that the strength of the mental waves created by the sheer power of your collective thoughts has overwhelmed my ability to employ the mesmeric skills."

Shane shook his head in wonder. A bargain was being struck with the audience and everyone could feel it. J.D. offered them the flattery of assuring them that they would not see such a thing happen again. The experience was exclusive to them alone. Why, the retelling, the bragging rights, the envy of friends and relatives!

He gave them an elaborate version of a bow that Shane recognized as something from the Far East. It was just unusual enough to give the crowd the impression that he was ending the performance for them in a unique way. He gave the clear sense that it was fitting that such an overwhelming audience should share this secretive gesture with him.

Shane immediately whipped around and peered into the darkness, taking in the faces of the audience. He saw a smooth sea of rapt witnesses to tonight's oh-so-special event. His stomach twisted again. This man was on the verge of passing out up there, but everybody seemed thoroughly charmed by him. It was a dark art, knowing how to tread the thin territory between what people look at and what they actually see. Shane thought again of the late Tommie Kimbrough, who had so boldly walked among San Franciscans as a female, and been ignored by many of the people he would later victimize because they never really saw him when they looked in his direction.

• • •

It was late. Traffic was minimal. No one bothers with a solitary man pushing a heavy load, and despite the constantly changing condition of the sidewalks and street surfaces, he sweated his way along the endurance route without interruption. In just under an hour, he was far enough into the twisted Chinatown streets that he was able to pull into a deep shadow in a narrow alleyway. He used the darkness for cover while he unstrapped the crate from the dolly, then opened the crate and pulled the body out.

Strangely, there was still no rigor mortis. She was a deadweight rag doll, still flexible but presenting considerable challenge to a man who had just pushed a heavy load across the city. He had to bend over and breathe for a few seconds, just to get some strength back.

That was it, then. This would have to be the spot. He pulled her over his shoulder and staggered a few feet to a large trash pile that stood awaiting disposal. He quietly dropped her forward and onto the pile, then pushed enough of the trash over her to cover her from sight.

A garbage pile in Chinatown. It was harsh. J.D. was not without compassion. But anyplace where he could leave her without being seen was fine for the job. Show her the same level of respect that she had showed to him, breaking in the first time, stealing some of the elixir, liking it enough to want more, then coming back today and lying in wait to ambush him. She might have accomplished all of it if her own greed had not caused her to consume the last of her stolen powder while she waited to rob him of the rest.

Who in Hell *was* that young woman, and why would she do these things to him? Expose him to accusations about her death, about the elixir? Could the Devil himself come up with anything worse?

He did a slow turn, checking all directions. The night was velvet black. No one was stirring anywhere in the neighborhood. Time for all good folks to be sleeping. Industrious people, the Chinese. Up in the morning with the first rooster.

Good enough, then. He strapped the empty trunk back onto the dolly and silently pushed the rig away, leaving the mystery girl to her fate. He found his way back out of Chinatown and onto the main city streets with only a couple of wrong turns in the Chinatown maze.

He did not mind. His load was now feather light, with only the empty crate strapped to the dolly. At this point he was only a few more checkmarks away from completely dodging tonight's terrible bullet.

He returned to Market Street, but crossed over and into the warehouse district. He made his way over to the loading dock for the nearest warehouse, and dropped off the empty trunk, trusting that they would assume it was left there in the course of doing business. They could either put it to use or throw it out.

Two more blocks down the alley parallel to Market Street, there was a smaller warehouse. He placed the dolly neatly next to the rear shipping door. It was a good dolly, strong wheels, stolen from the theatre but without any identifying marks. They would find some rationale for keeping it.

And that was it. Hail a taxi back to the hotel, head straight on up to his suite of rooms and stay there for the next two days.

Chances appeared high that he would never know the dead woman's motives for such odd behavior. His only clue was the backstage door slipping shut just as he turned around during that first night's show. It was surely caused by her, sneaking out after robbing him. She must have taken along a sample of the powder; perhaps she had been curious as to what a tiny little bit of it might do.

End you up in a garbage pile like this girl here, is what it might do. Unless you use it right, he reminded himself.

It was an enormous relief to flag down a decorative hansom cab and feel its low center of gravity whisk him around corners with the smooth glide of a carnival ride. The draft horse's rhythmic clicking of iron-clad hooves against the granite paving stones was a reassuring sound. Slowly, while the icy fog caressed his burning forehead, he embraced the fact that he had actually circumnavigated his way around certain disaster on this night. The sort of disaster that starts gossip and speculations, which are then fed by idle minds and active mouths until they form a litany of complaint. The sort of disaster that ends a career.

But now luck, Fate, or Divine Intervention had seen to it that he found himself safely on his way back home, undiscovered, even on this sudden heart attack of a night. He could explain later to his City Hall employers about his behavior onstage. Dismiss his "crowd sensitivity" as a reaction to food poisoning or something, instead of a surprise dead girl and an unwise shot of elixir.

They would never fire him over something like food poisoning. It would risk provoking an outcry in the newspapers. And what with the world's fair just now opening, and all those hungry tourists, he could count on City Hall to remain silent about his little faux pas, just as he could always count on his audience members to feel the need to play along. They offered up conspiratorial silence while barely even realizing that they were doing it.

But sleep, now. Sleep was what he needed. Exhaustion tugged at him, even from beneath the cloak of chemical stimulation. When the cursed elixir wore off, he would finally sleep. But who could tell when that might actually occur?

Sleep, he optimistically pleaded to the same God who was allowing his brain to slowly turn to mush. He believed in the power of sleep at that moment more than he believed in Heaven and Hell. In spite of what his racing heartbeat tried to tell him, sleep was what he needed most of all.

CHAPTER FIFTEEN

BY THE TIME THAT next morning rolled toward noon, the dead space behind the fake cliff was becoming too creepy even for the nondescript man. Once the girl was gone and he was alone there again, the place lost its meaning to him. And now the emptiness was a constant reminder that every hour spent alone in there was an hour wasted by not accomplishing his mission.

By this point, the nondescript man had whittled his life down to a picture of simplicity. Work, eat, sleep, hide. Lay low, avoid people, stalk Duncan just as a big game hunter stalks a man-eating lion. He was unstoppable in this mission, because he did not care if he died in carrying it out. He had a hard time trying to picture life after the mission anyway.

The broken pipe or whatever it was under the floor of the Hall of Science was doing nothing to improve things; there was now a decidedly wet feeling to the mortar flooring. It seeped in from below, rising so evenly that he could not tell anything about its source.

Mold was beginning to show on the underside of the rock outcropping. Like everything else, the "rock outcropping" was made out of a gluelike mortar that was smeared and shaped over wooden forms and support beams. The mold seemed to find the substance to be an inviting home.

He knew, along with most of the workers and none of the public, that this mortar over wooden supports formed every cubic yard of the exposition's brand-new architecture. There were only a few rare exceptions, such as the Oregon State Pavilion, a copy of the ancient Greek Parthenon built entirely out of Oregon logs. Otherwise, pavilion after pavilion was wood and glue, stretched and painted to look like anything you want it to be. It was the same with nearly all the architecture built upon this brand-new land.

The brand-new land was also brand-new landfill, composed of the city's rubble from the Great Earthquake and fires, just nine years earlier. That disaster had struck a city that was brand-new itself, at the time that it crumbled under the earthquake's powers. Thus even though the pulverized newness beneath every visitor at the exposition was beautifully masked, the essence of failed newness was everywhere.

Instinct alone had compelled him to hole up in that dank, dark place while the same events that he wanted to read about in the newspaper today played themselves out. It did not matter that he could not explain his reasoning about why he did not check into a rooming house or maybe even splurge on a decent hotel room for a night or two, to make himself comfortable while certain events unfolded. He only knew that the idea of handling things in that luxuriant way would have given him a superstitious feeling, a feeling that he would tempt Fate if he dared to make himself so comfortable while he was on his mission.

Suffering alone in the darkness was a time-honored way of petitioning the Lord to grant your wishes. Perhaps he had overdone it by hiding in the dead space? Buyer's remorse flashed through him; he would have loved to get those hours back. Especially since he had already established that the Lord was known to be an unreliable partner, prone to absenteeism.

When he could stand it no more in the dead space, he told himself that enough time had passed for the day's newspapers to have the story. Perhaps he could venture out?

Why not? he had to ask. He sneaked out the concealed door and quickly stepped away from the fake cliff and fake vegetation. None of the people milling around looked in his direction, and he was out of the display area in no time.

Even a man on a mission could excuse a short break for some coffee, maybe eggs and toast, and of course, most of all, a good morning paper to read. He only wound up at The Sea Mist restaurant because he had followed Duncan there, that last time. Otherwise he would not have been aware of the place. He had done very little exploring around the city, even though he arrived in San Francisco nearly two months before Duncan himself.

He had made his way to the port city as soon as Duncan's booking for the exposition was set. Once he arrived, he assumed the life of an ordinary workingman. That existence consisted mostly of labor.

But he was a patient warrior. Waiting was simply part of his mission. Waiting and blending in and establishing a genuine presence. It worked in unpredictable ways. He had no idea that his desire to give orders instead of take them would get him promoted to crew chief, back when he signed on to the vast construction team. And he could not have known that the promotion would ultimately present him with the opportunity of this hidden place.

All he knew was that it felt right to be forever pressing forward with things, with everything, as long they somehow pushed him toward Duncan. Meanwhile, the communal shower and the workers' laundry allowed him to remain clean enough to pass in polite company. He understood the value of a generally presentable personage when traveling incognito.

And so while he walked out of the fairgrounds and into the city, the Sea Mist restaurant seemed as good a place as any to break his long fast. He would do so in the disguise of a simple workingman, while reading all about the delectable details of Duncan's surprise encounter with the well-planted body of Revenge girl.

He bought a paper at a newsstand when he neared the restaurant, but forced himself to proceed on into the establishment without reading any of it, not even the headlines. When the waiter came to take his order, he recognized the dark-haired young man— the same fellow who had walked away from the restaurant the other day with J.D. and that big police type. He clearly recalled the three of them leaving the place together.

He could still see their image, walking down the sidewalk: the dark-haired young waiter, reed thin; the police type, dangerous looking; and the great Master Mesmerist himself. Three friends, out on the town. A last walk.

So for now, he carefully kept his attitude neutral while he dealt with the young waiter. There was no point in drawing attention, and for him, hiding in plain sight was effortless. Most of the time it was a far greater challenge to make himself remembered.

Still, the nondescript man slipped into his most opaque bubble and willed the waiter to serve him without remembering his face. Like a snake that sees in the dark, he sensed the lack of energy in the waiter's eyes. He could feel that he was passing beneath the young man's attention.

He felt the tantalizing pull of the news article in every fiber of himself. Still, his discipline was such that it was only after he was comfortable in the cozy restaurant and safe inside his protective bubble of anonymity that he opened the paper and greeted the day's news about Duncan's big pre–Opening Night show, less than twenty-four hours earlier.

Shane hardly noticed his first customer for that day's lunch shift: single fellow, big man. In his thoughts, Shane was absorbed in the question of why Vignette was so compelled to take risks. The most she had ever been able to tell him about it was that she did it when she felt suffocated to the point that she was going to tear her own skin off unless she did something outrageous. Something that would break through and let her breathe.

He was still daydreaming and putting on a fresh pot of coffee when his sole customer jumped up from the table, moving so sharply that he might have been choking on his complimentary bread.

The motion caught Shane's attention. The man did not utter a word, but his eyes suddenly bugged out while he stared at the newspaper that he was holding. He slowly stood up. It was only after a moment that he seemed to wake up. He abruptly looked around, then sat back down again, making a little show out of re-folding the paper in an imitation of calmness.

Shane could see that the man's breath was heaving while he held the edge of the table with both hands. His eyes rapidly darted around without pausing, seeking something that they did not seem to find.

It all registered in Shane's attention, but did not seem to mean much. The man might have been reacting to some outrageous political article. Or maybe he had just found out that he lost a big bet on a horse race.

Then, when Mr. Duncan came in and called Shane over to one of the back booths, the customer's astonished gaze moved from the newspaper article to Duncan's face. Shane hardly noticed; Duncan was already a local celebrity. He could tell that the customer was fighting the urge to stare. Most civilized people would do the same thing. He gave it no more notice than that, and forgot about the man.

"Sit down," Duncan instructed him from his seat in the booth.

"We're not supposed to sit down on the job, Mr. Duncan."

Duncan took a deep breath while he rubbed his hand all over his face. He looked up at Shane with a brief smile, then grabbed Shane's upper arm and pulled him into the booth.

"I persuaded the police to rig your home with a telephone so that I could communicate with Detective Blackburn, but no one answers today. They answer, I think, but they don't speak."

"I was out this morning."

"Someone else, then. They pick up the line, then nothing."

"I can ask."

"Good. That's not why I'm here. This is too dangerous to put over an open telephone line, anyway. You know that the telephone operators can listen right in on those calls, don't you? Any time that they want to! Think about that!"

"I've only used a telephone a few times, so far. There's nothing for me to—"

"All right, listen." Duncan dropped his voice level and fixed his eyes on him. "I'm telling you this in person because no one else is supposed to know. For tonight's opening, I am going to hire two of the stagehands. They're going to do their regular jobs, but also watch everything the whole time. Backstage. I'll tell them they can earn a big bonus if they find something. You know. Whoever's doing this."

"Doing what, Mr. Duncan?"

Duncan appeared to consider whether he might answer, but then his face clouded. "Nothing. I mean, whoever it is who might want to take some sort of deadly action."

Shane leaned across the table and nearly whispered, "Sir, it's very plain that you've got something on your mind that you are not telling us."

"Mr. Nightingale, please don't bother to—"

"I respect a man's right to privacy, Mr. Duncan, but I've got to tell you that you give me the distinct impression of a man who knows something that could help us to do the *very thing* that you want us to do. But for some strange reason, you choose not to tell us."

Duncan's face formed a heavy smile.

"I am sorry if it appears that way, Mr. Nightingale."

Shane just looked at him.

"At any rate, nobody else is to know this: You and the detective will cover the audience, and my men will cover the backstage area, for each show."

"All right, Mr. Duncan," Shane said, rising. "I'll tell him."

"I'll be performing tonight at the Palace of Fine Arts, four fifteen-minute shows in a row, with ten minutes between each one. You'll need to watch all four audiences, going in and coming out."

"With only ten minutes to clear the area and bring in more people?"

"It's a small venue, seats a hundred and fifty. They set up the chairs, build the whole set out of curtains and rods and poles. You could clear everything out in ten minutes, people included. My men will keep everyone away, backstage."

"Good enough. I'll make sure we're both there by eight-thirty, if that's all right."

"Yes, but tell him in person!" Duncan insisted. "Not on the telephone!"

"From me to him." Shane gave him a wave, just to move the older man along, then headed off to the kitchen in hopes that Duncan would leave. The thought of hiding out for a while by helping out the dish jockeys with the rinsing and washing seemed pretty good.

Duncan looked different today. He had lost the electrical glow in his eyes. He seemed about four inches smaller and twenty pounds lighter. There was a deep fatigue about him that Shane had not seen in him before. He got the impression of the man as a half-filled balloon, and wondered how he planned to give four opening-night performances that evening, even if the shows were short.

In the showman's depleted state, he painfully reminded Shane of himself, back in the Nightingale house. Shane had reached that same beaten-down point when he finally crawled out from his hiding place in the kitchen pantry and struggled to his feet among the bodies, in a house that would soon go up in flames.

Everything inside him would resist any hint of moving in that direction again. If necessary, his legs would stand and run in the other direction, even while he was sleeping.

CHAPTER SIXTEEN

HOURS LATER
BACK AT THE FAIRGROUNDS

THE NONDESCRIPT MAN USED UP the last of the fading afternoon light in a fast hike around the exposition grounds while anger and disbelief rotated through his brain. The Divine conspiracy against him was obviously increasing its reach, because the newspaper had said nothing—*nothing!*—about a missing person report for a young woman her age.

That much might have been tolerable, if it were only that much. It had not been long since she had disappeared, and who knew what kind of family she came from? (Maybe they were concerned people, but then, maybe not. Fair enough.) But the real stab in the heart was that the paper also said *nothing* about Duncan, other than to provide a pleasant little review of his performance.

To judge from the cursed news article, all that happened at the theatre was a nice little family show. Absolutely nothing suspicious in old J.D.'s dressing room, no sirree. According to the review, nothing whatsoever threw the Great Mesmerist off his game. A lovely time was had by all.

Except for a certain nondescript man who knew for a fact that there was a dead body in Duncan's closet all through the show. It was simply not believable that one, the stagehands; two, the star himself; and three, the cleaning crew, *all* somehow missed that tiny detail backstage.

He wanted to scream. He needed to scream, just the way that Revenge girl had: into a nice tight gag that would hold in all the sound. With no such release possible, he pressed on with his walk-and-mutter all around the exposition grounds.

He even hiked all the way up and down the Zone, twice. The sixteen-block strip of amusements and rides greeted visitors at the front gate and led them into the main fairgrounds. He could move around the Zone unchallenged, since his work pass hung on a string around his neck, right out where anybody could see it. A workingman. People left him alone. Once, a confused delivery boy tried to stop him to ask directions, but he pretended not to hear and kept on walking.

Visitors brushed by him in a thin but steady flow. Their eyes were completely out of focus when it came to recognizing potential danger from someone like him. The feel of their excitement was nearly contagious. These early visitors were additionally eager for the coming opening ceremony, beginning as soon as darkness fell. The president of the United States himself would be turning on the electric power to the fairgrounds, *all the way from Washington, D.C.!*

Rumors of fakery abounded throughout the city. It was obvious that no such thing was possible. People who knew of no other form of municipal power except natural gas speculated that the light switch must be located somewhere on the fairgrounds, and that the president was simply in on the joke by agreeing to keep up the illusion for the national prestige.

Otherwise think of the waste! Think of the waste!

The rumormongers pictured the entire flow of electrical energy being directed around the country from the generators, to Washington, and then back to San Francisco, the way that a flow of gas would be—instead of being activated by one remotely powered switch.

Others found both possibilities intriguing. Either the feat was impossible and represented an international hoax, or it was real, against apparent logic. If so, it would only prove itself to be another of the miracles of science that marked these soaring times.

The public's anticipation and excitement made them beautiful. They sometimes displayed happiness to the extent that he physically hungered for the chance to crush it in his bare hands.

If he could spot one who was beautiful enough to be worth the risk of capturing, then the very act of snatching her and getting her back to the dead space would be nearly as good as anything that came afterward. He could easily vent enough of his rage through the victim's fear and pain that he would be able to survive another day to continue his actual mission. Duncan's uncanny luck or whatever it was could not last, and thus it could not prevent the inevitable. The mission remained.

He had just reached the top end of the Zone for the third time and was about to turn around again when he noticed a single-story pavilion, the "Ladies' Hospitality League Center."

No one noticed that the nondescript man paused to observe the people who were wandering in and out of the place. Some of them emerged carrying little souvenir mugs filled with steaming cider. He smelled the hot cinnamon when one young couple strolled by, happily sipping away.

Disgust overwhelmed him. Unmannered pigs, stuffing themselves. He took a good look around. As quickly as that, the visitors were not beautiful anymore. Some of them needed a good mud hole to roll in. He felt such a compelling need to crush the complacency out of one of them, just the right one of them, that it became a sharp pain under his ribs.

He turned again toward the Ladies' Hospitality League. An interesting place. There ladies were charged with the job of showing hospitality, meaning that they were likely to be less standoffish than regular women. In a place like that, his lack of an appearance would not count against him; it was their job to notice him.

One would be enough, as long as she was the right one.

He moved toward the door in an utterly nondescript fashion. There was no sense in dropping the cloak until it was time to get one of the hospitality ladies to see him. Not that the cloak always came off when he wanted it to, but that was something else.

Blackburn stopped at the door to Vignette's room. She was seated atop the bed with her shoes off, reading her new hardback copy of *Huckleberry Finn*. He tapped lightly on the doorsill.

"Is that the one that came in the mail last week?"

"Yep. They send a different one every month unless I write and tell them to stop."

"I've read that one. The character of Huck reminds me of you."

"He what?"

"Well, in spirit, I mean. Some people have to bust out from the way that things are in their lives."

She searched for a response, but every suggestion her brain provided was sticky and complex and did nothing to move the awkward moment along. The best she could come up with was "Well, you're about to go?"

He laughed. "Yeah. I'm meeting Shane at the restaurant, maybe take him somewhere for dinner before we have to show up at the fairgrounds."

"She said that there's going to be all sorts of food there. They give it away."

"That's it, then. We're just doing an hour or two with Duncan at the Palace of Fine Arts, then I guess we'll come on home. Want me to stop by the Hospitality League on the way out?"

"No, we might be gone already. They close up at ten o'clock. I'll just . . . ." she sighed. "I'll see you guys back here."

Blackburn grinned. "You *might* enjoy meeting those women, you know."

She offered a wan smile. He chuckled and walked over to her, pecked her on the cheek, then headed for the door.

"One thing, though," he added. "Don't say anything to Miss Freshell, but I can't stop feeling interested in exactly how the department found out about you. Curiosity, I guess. I just called the Fairmont Hotel on the telephone, how about that? I left a message with the bell captain to post on her door after she leaves. I want her to meet me in the restaurant there after the park closes tonight. So I'll be home late."

"Why keep it a secret from her until she gets back?"

"Old habits, I guess."

"What habits?"

"Well, not that it means . . . in this case . . . You don't want to give people too much time to think things over before you talk to them. If you can avoid it."

"Mmm. But that really applies more to your detective work than your personal life. Yes?"

"Old habits."

"It's about me, isn't it?"

"No. It's about her and me, and you."

"All right. Good. But it's still pretty late for a social visit."

"This one's overdue. Anyway, Mr. Duncan tells me that he tried to place a call to this number here, today. He thought someone answered but wouldn't say anything."

"I don't like the things. A bell tells you what to do. Just because a bell rings, you have to stop and pick up the telephone receiver and talk to whoever wants to call you and interrupt what you're doing."

"You answered it, then?"

"I picked it up. What are you supposed to say when you pick it up? Nobody told me. I've seen people use them and yell things like 'Ahoy!' and 'Yoo-hoo!' They sound like idiots."

"Just say 'hello.' Or say your name, that's good enough."

"Anytime the damn thing rings? I have to stop and take messages from just anybody who happens to—"

"No, Vignette! You can ignore it. Just don't pick up the receiver and say nothing and then hang up again. All right?"

"I was hoping they could take a hint."

"Vignette."

"All right."

"And be cooperative with Miss Freshell. Treat her with respect."

"Randall, I promise you, I realize that she is your fiancée. I never allow myself to forget it."

"My God, do this for me, Vignette! It matters. It matters, or I wouldn't ask."

She paused, then sighed. "All right, Daddy," she replied with an impish grin. "But just because you asked me so nice."

"Good, then," he smiled and turned to go. "Last thing . . ."

"Don't call you 'Daddy'?"

"Thank you."

CHAPTER SEVENTEEN

OPENING NIGHT
FEBRUARY 20TH, 1915
THE PANAMA-PACIFIC
INTERNATIONAL EXPOSITION

THE GRAND OPENING OF the Panama-Pacific International Exposition went splendidly well for the city of San Francisco, whether the American president helped to fake the impossible chore of turning on the lights from Washington, D.C., or not. Either way, it was safe to assume that not one person who wandered the six hundred and twenty-five acres of newly made land and manufactured wonders had ever seen anything like it.

The Remington Rand company had a giant typewriter, twenty-five feet high, that actually typed the day's headlines. The Tower of Jewels glittered with hundreds of thousands of individually hung glass gems that vibrated in their mountings with the wind. Hidden controls operated automatic fountains in beautiful patterns of water sculpture. And everywhere, brand-new electric lights, an unknown phenomenon to many visitors, illuminated everything better than daylight, just as soon as the sun went down.

The visitors were confronted with and overwhelmed by the world's first modern theme park. The entire fairground glowed like some sort of enchanted fairyland filled with themed architecture. While the beguiled families strolled along in a state of awe, it tended to be only the breadwinners who noticed that the entire exhibition was a complex machine that efficiently caused all of a person's cash to disappear.

Over in the northwestern corner of the grounds, the elaborately designed Palace of Fine Arts and its reflecting lagoon were set up for James "J.D." Duncan's series of brief, intimate shows. These performances consisted entirely of personal hypnotic treatments, "plumbing work" as he called it, on the essential energy flow of the individual audience members.

Since he did not remember to hire anyone to watch his backstage area as he had told Blackburn that he intended to do, he now paced amid the temporary curtained "backstage" without any protection at all. Only the fact that he had forgotten the matter altogether kept him from being alarmed over it.

Shane and Blackburn kept watch on the crowds, coming and going. Occasionally, their eyes met and they shook their heads, acknowledging that neither one knew what they were supposed to be looking for.

Vignette quickly discovered that the work of the Ladies' Hospitality League in their pavilion at the top of the Zone was the hardest "easy" work she had ever attempted. After Miss Freshell arrived with Vignette in tow, there was a flurry of chirpy introductions among the members, pleasant ladies who ranged in age from a couple who were younger than she was, right up through old great-grandmothers who were there with two or three generations of family women, all working together.

The names and faces came at her so fast that she went into a smile-and-nod mode, to get herself past the moment without offending anyone. After that, the job seemed to mostly consist of wandering around the pavilion and passing out cider or snacks to anyone who wandered in. Each lady was to engage them in pleasant conversation, as if it were somehow any of their business how these people got there, why they came, and how many relatives they brought along to the exposition with them.

To Vignette, these women all appeared to have taken on some sort of military commitment to bombard every hapless wanderer who stumbled into the place with more food and affection than they had ever experienced.

According to Miss Freshell, the lesson had been learned at the Chicago World's Fair, years before—people, it seemed, were even more inclined than they might naturally be to send plenty of glowing reports home about a visit to a place, when the people at that place gave them tons of free cider and muffins, reliable directions, and an overabundance of cheerful attitude. So said one of the ladies, anyway.

And so for nearly four hours, she was in character as an enthusiastic volunteer, entirely because Randall asked it of her. The look in his eyes and the tone of his voice when he made the request were like nothing she had ever seen in him before. It nearly stopped her on the spot and forced her to blurt out a question about it. She managed to keep quiet, but the effect remained. She was going to do this thing. She was going to find some way to make it work, even though some dark part of her heart throbbed with the fear that, with her crammed into this place, things could not turn out well.

In the meantime, the Ladies' Hospitality League position was the same as a regular job, in most ways. The grim fact was that it was the same as a regular job in all the ways that mattered. Every attempt at a job that she had ever put herself through, back when she still attempted such things, turned out badly in the end, and the end never took long in coming.

She knew that the part Randall found most troubling was that she was never fired for incompetence or carelessness. She was fired because people simply did not like having her around. She got the message. She even understood their point of view on that, since she was usually the one who felt repelled first. The problem was that she had never been able to put the reasons for the thing into words for him or for anyone else.

It was never the job, it was the role. Always the damned role. To her experience, any one of the few jobs that a woman was allowed to do was either something that was stupidly simple and repetitious, or was a position of direct servitude under some male boss. Meaning that she could either choose to be slowly strangled by the dreadful boredom of a repetitious job in some factory, or she could be the unofficial concubine/secretary of some executive, which would require a daily mantle of subservience to all things male.

There was also retail sales work, of course, which required the ability to suffer fools gladly in the constant flow of presumptuous, demanding, cigar-smoke-blowing men who found it baffling that you do not live to serve their whims.

She tried twice, in her late teens, and only got into a fistfight with the merchant marine that first time. The second time she had the wisdom to turn around and walk out of the store and never go back when the manager passed behind her so closely that he deliberately rubbed his stiffened member across her buttocks.

If she had been holding a sharp object, Vignette knew without a doubt that she would have shoved it into his groin. She knew that a prison cell would kill her, so she was grateful to have been empty-handed in that moment.

It had always struck her as odd that factory work and clerical work both caused the same reaction in her. In both environments, she quickly developed a suffocated feeling, one so strong that she could not ignore it. When things reached that state she was a goner, as far as the job was concerned. All somebody had to do was shout at her, or grab at her, or, worst of all, sneer at her in some condescending way, and that was it. She had given up punching people for a long time now, and usually managed to get out without spewing much verbal anger. Sometimes, though, some sorry bastard thought that he was going to put one over on her for no other reason than that she was there alone. Then she had to let it out.

She restrained her urges to fly into him and tear at his throat by allowing herself the wonderful luxury of hurling such a forceful, venomous tirade into his face that he was certain to have *never* heard any other woman talk to him in such a way, except perhaps his unmannered whore of a mother.

Oh, the looks on their faces. Sometimes the cigar smokers actually had the thing dangling freely off of the lower lip, stuck there by a little spit and tobacco juice, just because their mouths were open so wide. Few of them ever gathered their wits enough to match her verbal onslaught.

Vignette's favorite moment of every job was when she was quitting because some man pushed her so far that her anger was perfectly justified. She realized that she was taking a physical risk by allowing herself to explode on some snarling male animal, but the act itself reminded her that she was still alive. She was still Vignette, a living soul, not just a collection of forced behavior and the brunt of endless disrespect from others. And if a man felt the need to use her for some kind of verbal punching bag, then the opportunity to throw sheer wildness into his face was one she would not ignore.

So far, it appeared to her that she had succeeded in getting herself hated for it just about everywhere she went. On those jobs, even other female workers avoided her or openly opposed her. They did not care for the way she shook things up. She may have been looking at them as if they were sleepwalkers shuffling through a giant maze, but they were comfortable in their ruts and did not want her interference.

That evening, while Vignette walked around the pavilion, she could not help but notice that these ladies also seemed to be very comfortable in the smile-and-serve role. If they were not actually having a swell time pretending that their visitors' jokes were funny, she could not tell.

She wondered if it were possible that they really enjoyed this so much. And if not, how did they hide their feelings so well? It baffled her. Her face had always seemed to be a signboard for whatever she was feeling at the time. Poker would never be her sport.

Tonight, in this situation where she could not allow herself to fail, she felt the old constrictions like belts tightening across her chest. There was nothing to do but ignore it, so she put extra effort into rushing up and greeting many of the visitors before the other ladies had the chance to get close to them. She hoped that it came across as perky and enthusiastic, since it helped to move the hours along. But she could not tell if she was fooling the ladies or not.

"Vignette?" It was the Eastern Whore.

"Closing time already?" Vignette asked, as if surprised that it could be so late.

"It certainly is! You have been wonderful tonight! I am proud of you, and I plan to tell Randall that, too!"

"Why are you so happy? I'm suspicious."

"I am not happy, I'm cheerful. It helps people to receive difficult news if you are cheerful when you present it to them."

"So why are you being cheerful with me?"

Miss Freshell playfully hesitated.

"Oh, all right. What's the news, then?"

"Vignette! I'm just playing with you! But the fact is, we'll be using a team of two ladies every evening, to stay behind and finish up here after closing time. Each team will be taking turns at the shifts for a week at a time."

"We don't get to go home yet?"

"All we have to do is put the supplies away and get the place ready for the cleaning crews to come through later. Probably half an hour, maybe less."

"Aren't you hungry? I'm starved."

"Well then," said Miss Freshell with a perfectly serviceable smile, "let's shoo everybody out, lock the doors, and get started!"

She sashayed away, swinging her low-hemmed woolen skirt. Something was out of kilter about the woman's behavior; Vignette had never seen her willingly extend herself to anybody, and her relationship with Randall seemed to consist mostly of getting him to do things for her. What sort of delight could she be finding in this little performance here?

Vignette had a bad feeling in her stomach. It told her that her very discomfort was the source of the Eastern Whore's delight. Then she hurried after her, realizing that it must be later than she thought. Even though the cleaning crew was not due for another half an hour, one of their janitors was already pushing a broom, over near the back wall.

The nondescript man had walked directly to the pavilion's storage closet. It was unlocked, as he predicted, so he reached in and took out a push broom. He had used push brooms many times in the past, doing reconnaissance work. He found it to be a perfect way to move around a room anywhere you want to go, while blending into the background. Most people tried not to notice janitors anyway. He smiled. It was as if people were afraid that if they made eye contact, you might ask them for help with the chores.

When he combined his naturally nondescript qualities with the invisibility of a janitor's work, he moved around as unnoticed as a very light breeze. He kept his eyes on the broom head; peripheral vision told him plenty.

While the rest of the ladies filed on out of the building, two appeared to be staying behind. The younger one, boyish looking, had nothing to recommend her to him. But the elder of the pair was something to see. Oh, she was too good. She even fit the pattern, that same image that always sank its hook deep inside him and pulled him along as helpless prey: sophisticated looking, with honey-colored hair that made her seem more pure to him than a darker woman. Sweeter to destroy.

If he was to survive to complete the mission, he had to find another stopgap female victim. And this one, this one could be her ten times over. She appeared so polished, she was nearly waxed and buffed.

With that, the idea struck him fully formed. If he could get her back to the dead space, he could probably expel enough rage to get him through several more days.

He decided to spend a couple of evenings doing his reconnaissance work in this end of the Zone, get the story on these hospitality ladies or whatever they were supposed to be, and start looking for opportunities to separate her from the tomboy long enough to spirit her away.

If the tomboy had to be eliminated, that was that.

CHAPTER EIGHTEEN

BLACKBURN FELT COMPLETELY ADRIFT in the fabulous hotel restaurant. He knew that the unfamiliar environment was filled with observers, carefully eyeing one another. He was as comfortable as a man in a tub of spiders.

His state of tension at the unfamiliar environment was minimal compared to his dread of the task facing him. He was left vulnerable by his lack of skill at coping with a situation like this. His shoulders were already so tense that the muscles had tightened all the way up his neck and under his scalp.

Still, he had to laugh when he imagined the reaction down at the station, if they ever found out that he had finally used the new telephone at home for the first time—to call the Fairmont Hotel and have a messenger take a note up to her room. In that single moment, he grasped the appeal of having one of the telephone devices at home, and why Duncan had wanted him to have it. The showman could reach Blackburn as easily as Blackburn contacted the hotel. He made a mental note to check and see if this new telephone company was publicly traded.

His message to Miss Freshell was that he had to see her right away, and to please meet him in the hotel's Laurel Court restaurant. All she had to do was dress and come down from her suite. He knew that the place was reputed to be a top-tier establishment, but he had never actually been there. When he arrived, it was a shock to discover how gilded and ornate the place was—and how obscenely expensive.

Still, it felt morally right to do it there, or as close to morally right as he knew how to make it. All he wanted to do was talk to her, but in his gut he felt as if he planned to beat her up, and was simply showing her the courtesy of doing it near home so that she wouldn't have to travel far afterward.

He was certain of nothing else. Even if she could magically produce some reason for why her wishes had anything to do with his current working assignment, there would still be the bigger issue, the thing about turning in Vignette to Blackburn's commanding officer. The dread in his stomach had blossomed into the realization that the police must have learned about Vignette from her. He had been wrestling in the back of his mind with this, but no matter how much he tried to rationalize it, it was simply not something that he could swallow.

And for reasons that he had not even taken the time to think through yet, the issue turned out to be the capstone of a whole stack of things that were bothering him about his whirlwind relationship with Miss Freshell. It felt so fine, for a while, to be pursued by a woman—a woman who was not unattractive, an author of romance books.

She originally sought him out to interview him for her new book, but he quickly realized that her company was an addictive pleasure, and asked to see her again. His personal stiffness relaxed and dissolved in the presence of her laughter and her animated conversation. She compensated for his social awkwardness so well that they could even have a social life. Nearly every part of it was new to him.

Tonight, while he sat at the table and waited for her to come down, his skin felt overly warm under his itchy wool suit, as if his garments were woven from strands of pure heat and nervous tension. He checked his old pocket watch and saw that she was not late yet, but he craned his neck around, just to make sure that she was not just out of sight behind one of the gilded marble columns that supported the triple-domed ceiling.

"Randall?"

Caught him from behind.

He stood up, smiling while he turned around to face her. He kissed her cheek and seated her, watching for any hints about her mood. Throughout the greeting, however, her face remained a pleasant mask. She said nothing more.

He sat down, placed his napkin over his lap, smiled at her, and scooted his chair in. He arranged the napkin again and took a sip of water. He had expected her to jump into the pause, the way she always did.

She did not.

That one tripped him up, right off. She always had before, every time he had seen her since the first day they met. Now she merely gazed at him through a glassy façade. Her half smile did not invite comment.

In the past, he had only seen her use quietude as a tool when she was angry. She certainly had nothing to be angry about at the moment. She always preferred a nice restaurant to eating at his house with Shane and Vignette. This place was one of the most posh that the city had to offer. Ordinarily that would be enough to delight her. Moreover, Blackburn's unique means of arranging the date with her via telephone should have been more than enough to put her in the mood to launch into a conversation right away.

He took another sip, stalling while the waiter filled a glass for her. After the man moved away, Blackburn looked at her again. Her face remained a pleasant blank.

And still she said nothing.

Outside the hotel, Vignette was dressed up and girlish enough to sashay right past the two gallantly costumed doormen and into the hotel. She knew that her conscience would bother her if she got caught, so she arrived full of determination to do no such thing.

Eavesdropping on Randall's telephone conversation was hardly a proper way to find out when Miss Freshell would be leaving her room. If Vignette got caught there and was also proved wrong, she would look like an utter fool and everyone would hate her.

She could not believe that she was wrong. Not about this. So she faded back into the shadows of the hallways on Miss Freshell's floor, waiting for her to leave her room. It never occurred to her to wonder what she would do if the room were clean of evidence. That could not happen. If it did, then the sugar-cookie version of life that Miss Freshell claimed to represent was real, and Vignette would have no way to stop her from actually dragging Randall away to New York City.

Two couples passed Vignette on their way out for a late night. She covered by rummaging around in the complimentary ice box as if she were stocking up for a party. The guests ignored her, chattering away.

Moments later, Miss Freshell's door opened. She came out smoothing her hair with one hand while she pulled the door shut with the other. She never even glanced at Vignette, whose head and shoulders were in the ice box while she made scraping noises. When Vignette raised her head, she was just in time to see Miss Freshell walk away with the air of a salesman on the way to close a deal.

She stood up, brushed the ice chips from her hands and closed the ice box lid, then walked directly to the door of Miss Freshell's empty room. Using a nail file pulled from her pocket, she jimmied the door latch almost as quickly as it would have opened with a key. Vignette had not done the lock on a hotel room door in a long time and was surprised that such simple mechanisms were still being used. But she filed that fact away, just in case.

Inside the room, with electric lamps still burning, she made a quick visual scan and identified her target: a large traveler's trunk that had been converted into a filing cabinet.

Thirty seconds at the filing cabinet was enough time to locate the correspondence. There, the fancy stationery of Miss Freshell's publishing house stood out among all the other typing paper and carbon copies.

The most recent letter to Miss Freshell explained it all. Vignette's hands trembled like those of an archaeologist who has just made a vital discovery.

Randall sat in the conspicuously opulent dining room and felt solid, visceral fear despite the surroundings. It was the kind of thing that he only expected in dark alleys with armed criminals. He knew that his relationship with Miss Freshell was at a crossroads and he was prepared to confront the crisis. But to do that required verbal skills and negotiating abilities he had never possessed. Years of self-imposed solitude had left him dangerously low on skills for dealing with any woman in a nonprofessional capacity, whether she was verbally skilled or not.

A sunken feeling came over him. He realized more with each passing moment that she was far superior to him in this arena. Janine Freshell was not going to be forced into confronting anything. Even her way of holding a silence without being mean about it— women could do too many of those things, he thought.

Most of the time, Miss Freshell made it easy to be with her. More than easy, it was effortless. Still he remained aware, deep down, that he was not the one who made each encounter so seamlessly smooth, even though she did so much to convince him that it was his humor, his character, and his strength that was making it delightful for her to be in his company.

The wave that carried them was primarily generated by her. For a while, he had been glad to be borne along by it, since in the rest of his life and career he was always the strength and the enforcer. The sheer novelty of having a female be attentive to him, concerned for him, interested in everything about him—he found it overwhelming. And he went for every bit of it.

Randall believed that a gentleman must formalize such an intimate state with an engagement ring. He did. She accepted with delight. With their engagement official, the sexual romps that she discreetly provided made it wonderful to be owned by her.

However, whenever he veered too far from whatever path she may have chosen for the moment, he felt that luscious wave flatten out and die. Motion resumed only when the course was corrected to her liking. Then the wave picked right up, her personality sparkled, and she danced through any social occasion with equal measures of charm and ease.

At the moment, the wave was flat, the air perfectly still. Her smile remained, though, while she silently demanded he tell her what it was that he wanted to see her about, and demanded it by simply refusing to speak first.

In the eye of a hurricane now, Blackburn could actually feel his hands shaking under the table. He started to pick up his water glass again, nearly knocked it over, and decided to refold his napkin instead. He felt driven to handle this delicate thing just right, and at the same time he thought of kicking down a door, doing it with words.

"Did you send the note telling the captain about Vignette?"

" . . . I beg your pardon?"

A self-conscious flush went through him over his clumsiness. He realized, in that sinking moment, that he had forgotten to say anything at all to greet her after she arrived. It felt as if he had already spoken to her, greeted her. He would have guessed that he had done so. But the busy feeling in his skull came only from the furious pace of his thoughts. He had not actually said a word—until he opened things up with an accusation and essentially began the conversation by pulling out his revolver and blowing his toes off.

He cleared his throat. "That was not well spoken. I'm sorry. I have to admit, I'm feeling a little nervous."

"You ought to become accustomed to dining in places like this. You deserve it."

"No, not because of—I meant—"

"You only feel uncomfortable here because you aren't used to it, Randall. If you realized how you dominate a room like this with your presence—"

"Janine . . . please. I know that the question is awkward. I apologize again. It's awkward for both of us. But out of respect for you, I am coming straight out with this . . ."

She waited, doll-like, telling him nothing.

"Janine, I can't figure out the time line for when you found out about Vignette from the cops who came in to install the phone, as opposed to when the captain—"

"Of course the men didn't tell me, Randall."

" . . . They didn't tell you anything?"

"They told me how to use the telephone."

"I mean—"

"You mean, did I find out from them? No, Randall. I did not. The captain found out from me. I wrote a confidential note to him and had the officers carry it back to the station when they left."

"And you were there at the house when they arrived, because—"

"Because I knew they were coming to install the telephone and that nobody would be there but Vignette, meaning that she might or might not get out of bed to let them in. I knew you needed help with making sure that the telephone got installed while you were away."

"Janine," Blackburn quietly began, "I have to tell you that Vignette thinks you only came over so that you could give the officers the note. I'm sorry, but she's really got it in her head."

"Well. I'm sorry, too, Randall. Why would I need to use the officers as messengers? Why would I not simply post a letter? I could do that, anonymously, and still sleep late."

She smiled that smile again. It was gracious, even though she done, now. But by the time that the exposition closes down, she will have had almost a year of association with women who will set a sterling example for her in terms of personal decorum. They can also help her."

"Yes, but—"

"*Help her,* Randall. Help her as she goes along in life. Have you thought about that? You seem to want to see her as still being just a girl, but she can hardly stay at home forever."

That one stopped him cold. Blackburn sighed, angry with himself and with the situation, furious at his inability to land a blow on the truth. He hated what Miss Freshell had done, but he also understood her reasons. He hated the way that she did it, but he also had to admit that it would not have worked if she had told either of them first.

It was demoralizing to still feel so angry with her without understanding why. But Miss Freshell seemed to sense everything that was going through him. She reached across the table to take both his hands in hers.

"A single woman's social contacts are priceless to her, Randall. I doubt that a man as independent as you are can begin to grasp what that means for her. They can make all the difference in the quality of her future. Now, I understand that this inheritance of theirs won't do much more than keep body and soul together, correct? Didn't you tell me that?"

He felt himself blush. It was incredible. She had been dishonest, manipulative, and conspiratorial with both him and Vignette, and nevertheless she had just convinced him of the perfect sense in all of it.

The question that challenged him was simple. How important were his personal opinions about the way that things ought to be done? How important were they, compared to a plan of action that wound up helping Vignette to learn things that she needed to know and he could never hope to teach her?

In his judgment, he still owed her for her adolescence. He had skated past her change from a girl into a woman. She just never

was clearly annoyed. Just gracious enough to remind him that she had the potential to get the wave moving again, if things went right.

"All right, but the problem I am having is, how did you know? If everybody else was fooled, who told you about it?"

"Vignette did," Miss Freshell smiled, cool as a watercress sandwich.

"I think not."

"She did. Not with words, and not deliberately, of course. She thought that her wig fooled me, just because I didn't mention it to her."

"All right, you knew that she cut her hair. That was enough to tell you what?"

"Nothing. It was the fact that she was hiding it from everyone that was the mystery for me. Randall, we both know that she is completely closed off to me, but we also both know that she is floundering around without any real direction. You've been so good to her, and I know she probably wouldn't be alive without you. But you haven't been able to guide her in being a woman. Who could expect you to?"

She had nailed him. Like mounting a bug on a straight pin. Part of his sensitivity over the topic of his adopted children was his fear that he had not done enough for them. He could not deny that Vignette had lacked a woman's guidance throughout her life. There must have been things that he could have done to help her develop social skills, if he had possessed them himself.

"So I paid one of the boys who works for the concierge at the Fairmont to carry along a description of Vignette and wait outside your house early in the morning, and stay there until she came out."

"You *paid* someone to—"

"Well, I wasn't going to do it, was I?"

"It doesn't seem—"

"*And* he followed her to the police training ground, watched her duck into an alley and come out wearing a man's clothing! Ha! She must have had someplace to hide a bag, back there."

"You knew." Blackburn could hardly react.

"Women sense things, Randall. Surely you realize that."

"Not just women."

She sighed. "Yes, I know about Shane. The point is that I found out about Vignette's reckless and immature little game. I give her points for initiative, and all. But please, Randall, she could hardly have considered the possible impact on you."

"Well, office politics is not something she . . ."

She flashed him a coquettish smile. "So, then, don't you want to have someone in your life like me, who is there to consider what it could do to your career if a certain person pushed her little joke, or little experiment, or whatever she wants to call it?"

"But Janine. Why not just come to me? Or even, even just go to Vignette herself, if you didn't want to bring me in on it? Why not just go and appeal to her?"

"Oh, my goodness, do you hear yourself, Randall? You want me to go and make an appeal to her? She is nineteen years old, an adult in most ways, and insists on behaving the way she does. What appeal can I make to her? Tell me!"

"She deserved to be treated with more kindness than to betray her like that."

"Excuse me! I would only 'betray' her if I failed to address her predicament. It is so clear that what she needs is to be thoroughly exposed to an atmosphere where she can absorb important social skills. She would've never listened to a suggestion from me, especially about such a thing as working in the Ladies' Hospitality League. But I was positive that she would be more receptive after her careless little game was exposed. It was her sense of being chastised that made her agree to go along. You can see that, can't you?"

It hit him like a brick. He did see it. She was right. Not only that, but he had been pleasantly surprised when Vignette agreed to work with her. So why did he feel that he was being robbed, somehow, at that moment? Each little point that Miss Freshell brought up made sense to him. Still, it all felt wrong.

The problem was that he had gone to the Fairmont Hotel th evening already filled with suspicion that she had been decepti and manipulative with him. He arrived determined that if it wa true, he would break off his engagement with her. The simple trut was that he could not abide the thought of her lying to him in suc a way—especially involving Vignette.

But now his momentum had dissipated. He was stuck in his po sition, while Miss Freshell, it seemed, was not done with hers.

"Randall, look me in the eye and tell me that you would have been able to convince her to even *try* this arrangement, if I had merely come to you, and then we 'simply asked' her? What would be her motivation to cooperate? But now, after being discreetly but very definitely exposed, she is temporarily embarrassed enough to *try* this."

"Did you think nothing at all about the risks of doing it this way?"

"I did. And I thought about the risks to her of continuing on her unworkable path until something really dreadful came of it."

"You've really got that much concern for someone who treats you the way she does?"

Miss Freshell smiled one of her good smiles.

"No, Detective. My concern is for *you*. I know that you will be happy if she pulls herself together and makes a place for herself in the world. I also know that she has you so tightly wrapped around her finger that you'd have never stood up to her, without this."

He had one last objection before he would be out of ammunition.

" . . . You tricked her, Janine."

She deflected that one with a gesture that actually reminded him of swatting away a pesky fly. "What I did was to 'trick' her into a whole new chance at life. You're welcome."

Randall dropped his head, beaten.

She reached for him and lightly drew her fingers across his cheek. "So tell me, do I know my fiancé, or do I not? This is the kind of thing that a good woman wants to do for her man, Randall. Make his life better. Naturally, Vignette can't appreciate what I've was clearly annoyed. Just gracious enough to remind him that she had the potential to get the wave moving again, if things went right.

"All right, but the problem I am having is, how did you know? If everybody else was fooled, who told you about it?"

"Vignette did," Miss Freshell smiled, cool as a watercress sandwich.

"I think not."

"She did. Not with words, and not deliberately, of course. She thought that her wig fooled me, just because I didn't mention it to her."

"All right, you knew that she cut her hair. That was enough to tell you what?"

"Nothing. It was the fact that she was hiding it from everyone that was the mystery for me. Randall, we both know that she is completely closed off to me, but we also both know that she is floundering around without any real direction. You've been so good to her, and I know she probably wouldn't be alive without you. But you haven't been able to guide her in being a woman. Who could expect you to?"

She had nailed him. Like mounting a bug on a straight pin. Part of his sensitivity over the topic of his adopted children was his fear that he had not done enough for them. He could not deny that Vignette had lacked a woman's guidance throughout her life. There must have been things that he could have done to help her develop social skills, if he had possessed them himself.

"So I paid one of the boys who works for the concierge at the Fairmont to carry along a description of Vignette and wait outside your house early in the morning, and stay there until she came out."

"You *paid* someone to—"

"Well, I wasn't going to do it, was I?"

"It doesn't seem—"

"*And* he followed her to the police training ground, watched her duck into an alley and come out wearing a man's clothing! Ha! She must have had someplace to hide a bag, back there."

"You knew." Blackburn could hardly react.

"Women sense things, Randall. Surely you realize that."

"Not just women."

She sighed. "Yes, I know about Shane. The point is that I found out about Vignette's reckless and immature little game. I give her points for initiative, and all. But please, Randall, she could hardly have considered the possible impact on you."

"Well, office politics is not something she . . ."

She flashed him a coquettish smile. "So, then, don't you want to have someone in your life like me, who is there to consider what it could do to your career if a certain person pushed her little joke, or little experiment, or whatever she wants to call it?"

"But Janine. Why not just come to me? Or even, even just go to Vignette herself, if you didn't want to bring me in on it? Why not just go and appeal to her?"

"Oh, my goodness, do you hear yourself, Randall? You want me to go and make an appeal to her? She is nineteen years old, an adult in most ways, and insists on behaving the way she does. What appeal can I make to her? Tell me!"

"She deserved to be treated with more kindness than to betray her like that."

"Excuse me! I would only 'betray' her if I failed to address her predicament. It is so clear that what she needs is to be thoroughly exposed to an atmosphere where she can absorb important social skills. She would've never listened to a suggestion from me, especially about such a thing as working in the Ladies' Hospitality League. But I was positive that she would be more receptive after her careless little game was exposed. It was her sense of being chastised that made her agree to go along. You can see that, can't you?"

It hit him like a brick. He did see it. She was right. Not only that, but he had been pleasantly surprised when Vignette agreed to work with her. So why did he feel that he was being robbed, somehow, at that moment? Each little point that Miss Freshell brought up made sense to him. Still, it all felt wrong.

The problem was that he had gone to the Fairmont Hotel that evening already filled with suspicion that she had been deceptive and manipulative with him. He arrived determined that if it was true, he would break off his engagement with her. The simple truth was that he could not abide the thought of her lying to him in such a way—especially involving Vignette.

But now his momentum had dissipated. He was stuck in his position, while Miss Freshell, it seemed, was not done with hers.

"Randall, look me in the eye and tell me that you would have been able to convince her to even *try* this arrangement, if I had merely come to you, and then we 'simply asked' her? What would be her motivation to cooperate? But now, after being discreetly but very definitely exposed, she is temporarily embarrassed enough to *try* this."

"Did you think nothing at all about the risks of doing it this way?"

"I did. And I thought about the risks to her of continuing on her unworkable path until something really dreadful came of it."

"You've really got that much concern for someone who treats you the way she does?"

Miss Freshell smiled one of her good smiles.

"No, Detective. My concern is for *you*. I know that you will be happy if she pulls herself together and makes a place for herself in the world. I also know that she has you so tightly wrapped around her finger that you'd have never stood up to her, without this."

He had one last objection before he would be out of ammunition.

" . . . You tricked her, Janine."

She deflected that one with a gesture that actually reminded him of swatting away a pesky fly. "What I did was to 'trick' her into a whole new chance at life. You're welcome."

Randall dropped his head, beaten.

She reached for him and lightly drew her fingers across his cheek. "So tell me, do I know my fiancé, or do I not? This is the kind of thing that a good woman wants to do for her man, Randall. Make his life better. Naturally, Vignette can't appreciate what I've done, now. But by the time that the exposition closes down, she will have had almost a year of association with women who will set a sterling example for her in terms of personal decorum. They can also help her."

"Yes, but—"

"*Help her,* Randall. Help her as she goes along in life. Have you thought about that? You seem to want to see her as still being just a girl, but she can hardly stay at home forever."

That one stopped him cold. Blackburn sighed, angry with himself and with the situation, furious at his inability to land a blow on the truth. He hated what Miss Freshell had done, but he also understood her reasons. He hated the way that she did it, but he also had to admit that it would not have worked if she had told either of them first.

It was demoralizing to still feel so angry with her without understanding why. But Miss Freshell seemed to sense everything that was going through him. She reached across the table to take both his hands in hers.

"A single woman's social contacts are priceless to her, Randall. I doubt that a man as independent as you are can begin to grasp what that means for her. They can make all the difference in the quality of her future. Now, I understand that this inheritance of theirs won't do much more than keep body and soul together, correct? Didn't you tell me that?"

He felt himself blush. It was incredible. She had been dishonest, manipulative, and conspiratorial with both him and Vignette, and nevertheless she had just convinced him of the perfect sense in all of it.

The question that challenged him was simple. How important were his personal opinions about the way that things ought to be done? How important were they, compared to a plan of action that wound up helping Vignette to learn things that she needed to know and he could never hope to teach her?

In his judgment, he still owed her for her adolescence. He had skated past her change from a girl into a woman. She just never seemed to have any questions about it. He knew that she was not taught about that sort of thing in their private school classes, beyond general biology. At the time he had been grateful to have an excuse to dodge the thorny issue. Now it shamed him to realize that.

He never asked himself why a young girl expressed no curiosity about her body or about sex, when she felt so completely free to talk about any other thought that breezed into her head. Why had he not wondered a bit more about that?

Since Miss Freshell had caught him red-handed at being a fool, then was he also a fool for thinking of breaking it off with her? Perhaps the sense of strangeness that caused him such concern was just his own reaction to the way that life was like, with a woman. After all, was there anything that he knew less about?

For years he had been listening to the married officers complaining about their wives, trying to figure out how to deal with the women in their families, trying to figure out what they wanted. Was that this?

The answer was clear. As long as Miss Freshell's motives were pure and her aims were achieved, who was he to say that she had to do things in the same way that he did?

He had been a colossal idiot.

Blackburn's sense of honor left him so embarrassed by his mistake that he dared not proceed to the second issue, about what she could possibly have to do with him being assigned to guard James "J.D." Duncan. With a trace of dread, he suspected that there would turn out to be another obvious explanation, one he failed to see until it was pointed out to him.

He could not stop himself from raising his eyes to meet hers. On its own, his face formed into a rueful smile. He had no thought of doing it; it seemed to happen by itself.

Immediately, Miss Freshell's eyes revealed that she saw and understood. In acknowledgment, she knitted her brow in a sympathetic pull to the middle and offered him a sexy pout.

And now that he had indicated that he was coming around to her way of thinking, Blackburn immediately felt the momentum begin to build. The tide soon lifted them off that momentary sandbar and the evening's energy wave began to pick up speed.

The rest of the meeting, which he soon realized was now a full late-night dinner, went by as smoothly as spun silk. He noticed that she ordered more than she was likely to eat, and that all of it was from among the most costly selections on the overpriced menu. Still, his conscience bothered him so much over his unfounded anger and suspicion of her that it never occurred to him to object.

Neither Blackburn nor Miss Freshell was looking across the dining room in the direction of the stairway coming up from the grand lobby, so neither saw Duncan stroll up the stairs and into the restaurant. He intended to have a quick late dinner alone, mostly ignoring the food and using the drinks to counteract the remains of the elixir, then retire up to his suite. He walked along with his habitual tunnel vision firmly in place. J.D. had long since found that if he looked straight ahead while he walked and did not meet anyone's eye—and perhaps pretended to be just a touch hard of hearing—he seldom had to endure gushing conversation from civilians. He was in no shape for it.

A busy waiter passed by him just as a fork fell from the waiter's tray. It landed near Duncan's foot, and was just enough to cause Duncan to glance in the waiter's direction, next to the table where Detective Blackburn and Miss Freshell sat profile to him.

He recognized her immediately, felt a quick impulse to start in her direction, but stopped in his tracks as he realized who was with her. Detective Blackburn was there, even though she had assured Duncan that Blackburn was revolted by extreme luxury and would never step inside such a place. Hadn't she said that?

Duncan could not deny that his memory for immediate things was eroding, such as being able to recall where he had just come from. But his memory for things that stretched out over time was still fairly good, and his relationship with Janine Freshell had gone on long enough for him to remember it well.

He had also not forgotten her engagement to the detective. The practiced showman kept his face entirely neutral while he flicked his gaze away from their table and smoothly turned around, back toward the stairs. He tapped his head as if he had just forgotten something, in case anybody watching was curious about his change of direction. Then he walked out of the restaurant.

There were other places to pretend to eat and actually drink: smaller places, within a couple of blocks from the hotel. The wise choice was to go someplace where there was no risk of Detective Blackburn spotting him and somehow connecting Duncan with the woman that the bigger and much younger man was supposed to marry.

Policemen, he reminded himself, were famously vindictive about such things.

Vignette stepped out of Miss Freshell's suite and quietly closed the door. Then she fixed her face with an expression of benign affability and focused her eyes straight ahead with such intensity that nobody would think of speaking to her. She remained protectively masked all the way back to the lobby, out the door, passing the glorious doormen with a playful wave and striding off into the night.

Vignette could have grabbed a cable car right there, but instead she started off down the hill, moving at a steady little dogtrot that she called her "city stroll." She could do it for long blocks, even up most hills. And if she could have done it unencumbered by the long skirt, she would have happily darted in and out among the other pedestrians. Weaving circles and figure eights in the air all around them, she would be like a thieving swallow who has just picked up something very bright and shiny indeed.

‖ CHAPTER NINETEEN ‖

"WHO KNOWS WHY the forgetting occurs?" Dr. Alzheimer had rhetorically asked. He continued, with a sly grin that kept you from knowing if he was making a joke or not, "Perhaps the victim of this malady will first begin forgetting those things that he or she considers beneficial to forget. Who can say? Underneath all manner of social expectation, cultural taboo, religious conviction, and even the individual ego itself: hard truth. Bitter, like the inside of a rotting nut. The husband who no longer remembers his wife. The wife who cannot recall her children. The businessman who forgets his partner. The doting grandfather or grandmother who remembers none of the family at all. Hard and bitter truth. But then," he added with a mischievous grin, "who can be certain? Perhaps only random memories, dying."

J.D. sat in a chair on his ornately tiled balcony, nude underneath the bedspread that was wrapped around him. He fought the urge to turn around to make sure that nobody was sneaking up on him. He had already checked several times. Some ghastly thing made of fear and dread had him in its grip. Somebody was coming after him. He felt it. He could not get any clarity about it, but the feel of it was strong despite the gray stuff. The mist . . . not clouds . . . fog.

The dread of it came from his inexplicable conviction that he deserved to be hunted down. Why? He pressed his memory hard. Why would he deserve it? Even his worst audience humiliation gags were tame, compared to anything that would set somebody off on a path of vengeance. He was gentler with them than he had been with his own ferry . . . funny . . . *family*. His own family.

What then? No answer. Nothing. He looked out to sea. From the top floor of this hilltop hotel, the ocean was a broad expanse that filled the western horizon. The view was spectacular, even for one in his state. His suite's main balcony was so well enclosed on both sides, and so protected from above by its overhanging roof, that he felt like an isolated dweller in a floating cave. As always, the site of an open ocean filled him with a sense of hope, a feeling of new departures on fresh journeys. The sensation was a welcome relief from the turmoil churning inside him.

But it was gone in seconds, and the grim truth was left facing him. *The elixir is not working anymore.* He counted it up: six words. Six words put him on a short road to a permanent end. He still felt the physical stimulation of the powder, but the clarity that had always come along with it was now frequently missing. The fog stood in its place.

Worse: In recent weeks he had been finding that the clarity borne by the elixir seemed to arrive only to tease him. The clarity would descend, and in a flash he would see complete answers to problems that had seemed insurmountable, only moments before—but then the clarity would simply vanish.

With every passing day, it came less often. Even when it did, it was a flimsy clarity that tended to snuff out like a candle flame, all on its own.

As soon as that happened, there was the fog again. And each time, the fog was thicker by another degree and it took him longer to battle his way through. Now, whether he was growing a tolerance for the elixir or whether his malady was simply advancing, the loss of clarity was hard upon him. He stared again at the blue strip of Pacific, but this time took no comfort. The loss of his clarity was the same for him as the loss of a violinist's hands. He might plug along and survive, but James "J.D." Duncan would be gone forever, fodder for the dustbin.

How bad was he? He tried to think back to the way that he was during his European tour, when he first went to see a doctor in Munich for slight memory problems. He was referred by another physician who had read of this doctor's work in the field of memory and thought.

On the day that he first went to Dr. Alzheimer, he had not yet suffered any visits from the fog. His problem was just a growing tendency to forget things from a few moments before. His lifelong absentmindedness had expanded to interfere with the substantial memory work that was required for his performances. Back then, he thought that losing a trigger phrase once every week or two was a big problem. Now he longed for such a mild condition.

There was no real way to measure the change, but he could no longer doubt that he had reached substantial mental impairment. How long could he keep up the charade?

He had two days until his next round of performances. All he wanted to do during that time was to hide in his floating cave, and for those two days at least, to be safe from making a fool of himself and protected from exposing this terrible and growing weakness.

The last of the late afternoon sunlight was creeping up the wall while Shane slept sitting up in a chair, still holding a screwdriver in his hand. The disassembled parts of a brand-new seventy-eight-RPM record player were scattered on the floor around him. He had just brought it home from the exposition the day before, and wanted to figure out how it produced sound, but soon discovered that the question was more interesting than the many components of the answer.

He was still sleeping when a repeater bell began to ring. Just as he awoke and began trying to figure out what the ringing bell meant, he heard Randall's muffled voice.

"This is Detective Blackburn."

The telephone. Even half awake, Shane realized that he had never heard Randall answer a telephone before. So that was how he did it. Which meant that Shane could answer with "This is Shane Nightingale" if the thing rang while he was there alone. He filed it in his memory with a small sense of relief. Answering the telephone: one less thing.

He drifted in and out of sleep for another half hour or so, surfacing just long enough to track Randall's progress: water running, the thumping of closet doors, Randall's footsteps down the hallway and at the front door, the door closing, the lock being turned from outside.

He would get up in another minute or two, he told himself. It was so pleasant to float between waking and sleeping. The range and speed of his thoughts in that half-waking state were joyous for him. Anything he thought about seemed to spring up all around him, as if he had been magically transported. He often thought that if he could somehow play a game of chess in this particular state of mind, he would be hard to beat. He could see so many steps ahead, like the best champion players. It was almost like looking into the future.

In that fluid state, he could visualize points of connection between almost any two people, places, or things, just by thinking about it. He could perceive patterns that would completely escape him, otherwise.

He saw, as if for miles ahead, the broad layout of his own life. Things that happened months ago or years ago displayed points of connection with his current position, so that he not only saw all the forces that had propelled him to this specific point of his life, but also many of the opportunities that he missed the first time. Tiny signs or clues that had moved in front of him unnoticed now came back to him with a vengeance.

And with that, the realization seized him in a strangler's grip: right there in the restaurant. He had missed one. Just the other day. He was all glossed over, as usual, and his brain was thus slow enough that his memory recorded what his attention itself did not register.

The man alone at the table—he was the sole customer at The Sea Mist when James Duncan dropped in at the end of Shane's shift. Duncan was so full of fear and suspicion that Shane had allowed it to distract him. Now, a quick reread of his own neglected memory confirmed that the lone customer had been doing a good job of pretending not to pay attention, while watching everything Duncan did.

The clues had all been there. Shane missed them by being too lost in his own thoughts. He shook his head in frustration. There had been too much anger hiding behind the lone customer's expression. His eyes were flint hard. Unlike some audience admirer who just wanted to eavesdrop on the showman, this man had been sitting on a steam pipe of emotion. The customer had a tall and broad-shouldered physique—a remarkable-looking man. His icy stare was as penetrating as the one on Duncan's posters, but the intensity of this one was sour. There was filthy energy behind it.

Every homicide case that Shane had helped Randall to crack over the past nine years had a perpetrator with eyes that looked like that. Even back in the Nightingale house all those years ago, as a terrified boy paralyzed by mortal dread, he had peeked out from his hiding place to catch a glimpse of the killer's eyes. They were the same. Eyes so hard that they looked like stones. That kind of perpetrator might have a smooth face and project an innocent attitude, but the eyes were like flat rocks.

Shane had never asked anyone else if the similarity was obvious to them. It was the same with any of the heightened perceptions that he had inherited from his terrible day and a half in the Nightingale house. There, he was force-fed an education in human evil by the nonstop diatribe of the family's slow killer, and he had learned far too much about the darkness of human nature.

He sensed that to talk about such things at all was to invite questions. The trouble was that all the answers pointed to the same shattering event. After nine years, not a soul alive knew what happened in the Nightingale house but him, and he hoped to die that way. If he should live to a hundred and ten, he yearned to die with the intact secret of his frozen cowardice in that place.

His soul had been so thoroughly tarred by shame while he hid in that little pantry, pissing himself and listening to the sameness of the infantile babbling to which Mrs. Nightingale and both of Shane's adoptive sisters were reduced, one by one. There was no way to get the tar off.

The legacy of knowing, however, was also his remnant of those crimes. It aided him as often as the grimness hit. Now, because of it, he was certain that the man in the restaurant posed an active danger to Duncan.

In the next instant he wondered what he was supposed to do with a piece of information like that. What did he really have, anyway? One, somebody was angry with James Duncan, and two, this somebody had been in The Sea Mist, glaring at him.

So what? If the man had been casing the place, then he now knew how to smoothly move through that environment, just as Tommie Kimbrough had done in the days before he struck at the Nightingales. With that, Shane realized that of course the man was there doing reconnaissance. It had only been a watchful exercise at the time, which was why Shane got no sense of immediate danger. There had not been enough to puncture his daydreaming state.

Now with Duncan already as jumpy as he was, Shane decided to keep the realization to himself. He could just keep an eye out for the man. If he ever showed up around any of Duncan's performances, then Randall could pull him aside and check out his story.

He left it at that.

CHAPTER TWENTY

THE STREETS WERE quickly darkening with an incoming fog. Late vendors trundled home from their markets in horse-drawn wagons while isolated cars and trucks weaved in and out among them. Blackburn drove his trusty used Model T with care; traffic was especially dangerous because of the random mix of animals and loud machines.

He pulled the Model T to the curb just a few yards from the front door, with its giant marquee that permanently announced "The Pacific Majestic Theatre—San Francisco's Finest." The theatre's lights were off for the night, and the grandiose swirls of the building's façade were laid over with shadows. Huge classic faces of comedy and tragedy hung above the theatre doors, peering through the foggy darkness.

All through his short drive to the theatre, he tried to think of why Captain Merced would call him at home on his telephone and order him to come to this remote place at this late hour, on a day off. What was there that could not be taken care of at the station?

If he and the captain had been on better terms, it might seem as if he were being called in to consult on a crime scene. Considering the ridiculous punitive assignment that Merced had inflicted upon him, nothing like that was likely.

His imagination could supply plenty of possible scenarios, none good. He had to give the captain credit for his flair for the melodramatic in having Blackburn meet him up on the second floor—the same place where they spoke on the night of Duncan's first show. He supposed that the little man saw some symbolic value in that, something to increase his stature in his own eyes.

He felt certain that he would have to stand for another sneering lecture from the little bulldog. He reminded himself that this time he could not fall for being provoked into stupid action again, no matter what the man decided to shoot out of his mouth.

He tried the theatre's front door and found it open, so he went on inside. There was just enough ambient light from the newfangled exit signs that were always on. So he moved across the lobby and up the stairs for the second-floor balcony, expecting to wait around for a while before the captain showed up. It took him by surprise when he topped the stairs to see him already standing up there, with two other men in plain suits on either side.

The three stood shoulder to shoulder, across the width of the balcony's hallway. Each man held a cigar, three red dots floating in the balcony's grim shadows. Blackburn observed that despite the fact that each of the cigars was freshly lit, the air was already blued by swirling smoke. These boys had been pulling on their stogies pretty hard. Nerves?

Absolutely nothing good could come of this meeting.

"Watch your step, Detective," Merced called out.

"Thank you, sir. I can see well enough."

"No, I mean *stop*!" Merced called out.

Blackburn froze, confused and growing alarmed.

"You don't seem to understand, Detective. You could do real damage in a fall, here. Hard clay tile over concrete like that stuff is."

Blackburn had not moved. "Why did you want me to stop, sir?"

"Isn't it obvious, Detective? Look down! At the floor! Just a few feet in front of you!"

He looked. There was nothing but a long crack running the

width of the hallway. In that moment, he recalled stumbling over that same crack the last time he was there. "What, this? This crack?"

"The one you so expertly spotted and reported to the City Hall Station. My station. My precinct. You damn well should recognize it."

"Yeah, I noticed it the night of Duncan's first show here."

"Detective, the gentleman on my right is Wilford Cron. He represents Golden Bay Insurance Company. They cover this building."

"Hello, Mr. Cron. Captain, am I supposed to keep standing here?"

"Indulge me a moment, Detective. The gentleman on my left is Nathaniel Simmons. He's the head of Chief White's personal security force."

"I've heard about you, Mr. Simmons. Hello."

Like Mr. Cron, Mr. Simmons said nothing in response.

"Detective." Merced took a thoughtful pull at his cigar, lighting his face with a brief orange glow. "It may interest you to know that the crack that I just saved you from tripping and falling over, possibly even breaking bones on that hard tile floor, is a very long crack indeed. In fact, it runs through the entire second floor. One end to the other."

"Yes, sir," Randall replied, at a loss as to where this was going. "Crack runs one end to the other." He remembered telling the desk sergeant to make a report on it, but after that he had forgotten all about the thing.

"You do not understand, Detective, but you soon will. That's why we're all here." He took another pull at the cigar and continued without looking at him. "It may also interest you to know that this crack also runs down both walls on either side of the building, vertically, and then across the floor of the entire backstage area. From one wall to the next."

"That sounds as if you mean—"

"I mean," Merced interrupted, "that it runs all the way around. The Pacific Majestic Theatre—San Francisco's Finest, is completely broken into two separate pieces."

Blackburn felt mildly surprised, but still had no sense of why this bizarre meeting was taking place. He did not have to wait long.

"Detective, these men are here to personally assure you that they are acting with the full support of Chief White and the Golden Bay Insurance Company."

"Acting as what?"

"Official representatives. To assure you that this will all be done with quiet support in the background."

Blackburn let out a dry laugh. "All right, gentlemen, I'm getting lost."

"Detective," Mr. Cron said, "this building is built upon the ruins of the theatre that collapsed in this location during the Great Earthquake. It is barely eight years old. Furthermore, it brags of being one of the most modern post-earthquake buildings in the entire city. Do you understand?"

"No sir, not yet."

"The city adopted strict earthquake-proofing requirements for everything constructed after the Great Earthquake. Showing that we learned from it, you know."

"It didn't last long," Mr. Simmons from the chief's office butted in. "City Hall realized that the codes were too strict. Everything was taking too long, buildings were costing too much money. But still, this was right after the Great Earthquake, and the city was desperate for investors. You see, Detective? We had to make sure that buildings got constructed, one way or the other. We had to get our people working and our city rebuilt."

"Gentlemen," said Blackburn, "the entire city knows that this theatre is built on one of those new steel frames. Why should a crack matter? Something like this, you get some mortar, some new tile, you patch it up. Right?"

Mr. Cron blew a thin stream of smoke and replied, "In the best of worlds, yes. However, certain compromises were deemed necessary in constructing this place . . ."

"What. There's no steel frame?"

"Oh, it's built on a steel frame, all right," Mr. Simmons said.

Mr. Cron completed the thought. "They could have used more steel . . ."

"So these construction codes . . ." began Blackburn.

"They are well-intended rules, and were actually followed in some cases," Mr. Cron the insurance man replied.

"And eventually dropped, in practically every instance," added Mr. Simmons from the chief's office. "Time, effort, cost."

"And we have to consider the foul timing of this," Mr. Simmons added. "It's like the Devil planned it! We've just now got the god-damned exposition off to a successful start, just now looking like maybe the big gamble paid off and we'll get a whole mountain of this city's debt taken care of. So you think about everything that this implies to the rest of the world, think of what it would mean to the city's entire reconstruction effort, if word got out."

"Detective," Merced went on, "the city is many, many millions of dollars in debt after building those exposition grounds up there. There is no way that the exposition can pay for itself, even though we're running it for ten months."

"Then why do you—"

"The exposition exists for the purpose of pulling investment back to San Francisco on an international level, for the first time since 1906."

"All right, gentlemen, but this is not clearing things up for me at all. The theatre is broken in two, and what, you don't want people to find out?"

"The maintenance man here was questioned. He knew about it but wisely kept his mouth shut until you reported it. He has been paid off and already left town. He was given enough to retire on, and he's a young man. Do you understand?"

"All right. It's vital to keep the flaws in this building secret, because they're not supposed to exist. Now you can't let anybody find out. Is that right?"

"That's it," Merced replied, "as far as the problem. But then that brings us to the matter of the solution."

"Let's go downstairs, Detective," said Mr. Cron, the insurance man. "Let's all go on down, shall we?"

They moved in silence down the stairs, through the theatre house, and back behind the proscenium arch, until Mr. Cron stopped them in a deep backstage area. They were near a stack of canvas flats that had been leaned against a wall for storage.

"Fire hazard," Mr. Cron the insurance man muttered, pointedly glancing over at the flats. "Canvas on a wooden frame. The main stage curtain is fireproof, not all these drapes back here. All flammable."

The three men stopped together, shoulder to shoulder, facing Blackburn. This time he wondered if they were doing it deliberately. There was a pregnant pause, awkward in the extreme, while the men studied their cigar tips and Blackburn waited for the second phase of whatever was going on.

He rubbed fatigue from his eyes for a moment, then decided to push things along again. "All right, we can all see that the crack is in the floor down here, too."

"Yeah, we already know that. It's the flats that worry me, Detective," said Mr. Cron. "Some of them even look like they might have been done in oil paint. Who could be that foolish, using such a flammable type of paint? Why? Just to achieve some particular effect? It's not worth it."

Blackburn felt it hit him over the head like a falling spotlight. There was a heavy pause. His stomach seemed to spin in a full circle.

When he spoke, he kept his voice soft and low, as if there were a sleeping monster in the room that they ought not awaken. "Mr. Simmons, when you speak for the chief, I assume that he in turn is speaking for City Hall?"

"That is correct, Detective. Every responsible member of our city government realizes that this most unfortunate idealism we all felt in the aftermath of the earthquake did not meet with acceptance in practice. It's not that we were wrong in abandoning the codes; it's that they were ridiculously high in the first place."

"Except that here," Blackburn began, "it does seem as if they ought to have been just a tad higher, though. Yes?"

"Don't get smart! Goddamn you, Detective, your report on this place is out there now. There's no way we can get back every copy, or get to everyone who might have seen it. If you'd kept it quiet, we might've found some excuse to close the place. Discreetly. Now we have to make sure that nothing that may have been 'rumored' about this place matters, anymore."

"Captain," Mr. Simmons jumped in. "You have to admit that the detective has a point. Who can deny that the place could have been built better?"

"Those cans of kerosene shouldn't be stacked back there. You know. Too close to the flats," said Mr. Cron the insurance man.

"Oh, son of a bitch, Mr. Cron, you can stop all that right now. I understand, all right? You plan to burn down the theatre to hide the fact that it's in two giant pieces. You're here, Mr. Cron, to demonstrate that the insurance company is accepting of this plan, for some reason."

"For a very *simple* reason, Detective," Cron replied. "Paying to rebuild this theatre will be a fraction of the damage that we would take on if there was a major structural failure while this place was full. I don't even want to think about it."

"And you're here," Blackburn continued to Mr. Simmons, "because everybody from Chief White, right on up the command chain, plans to look the other way while this place burns down tonight instead of falling down tomorrow."

"Fair enough," said Merced, taking another thoughtful pull on his cigar.

All three men looked away from Blackburn and studied their cigars again. He wanted to shove the things down their throats.

In the back of his mind, he already knew where this was going, but it was so terrible that the thought had not made it into his awareness yet. Instead, he felt a sharp pain of anxiety twist itself through him.

"Detective Blackburn likes it blunt. He likes plain talk. He's not one for dancing around the beast—eh, Detective?"

"I suppose not. Why don't you just tell me?"

"I am telling you, if you are listening, Detective!"

Mr. Cron finished it off. "I know it's hard to believe, Detective, but my company strongly prefers that this building should come down due to fire. And soon."

"Very soon," added Captain Merced.

"So why are you . . ."

Denial would not protect him any longer. The shock was like a stomach punch. He took a deep breath and turned to Merced. "Captain?"

"Sticks in your craw to play lifeguard for this Duncan character, doesn't it? Don't answer; of course it does. It's outrageous, Detective, the unfair punishment that your 'daughter' is causing you to absorb. She must have an ironclad conscience."

"She doesn't know."

"*Yet*, Detective. You've held out for a few weeks, a handful of performances. But you miss the real work. Of course you do. You're a detective, for crying out loud, not a nursemaid!"

"My sentiments exactly. And all that time that you make me waste on him is time that I can't be helping out with the things that are really wrong with this city, Captain. So what the hell are we talking about here?"

"What we're talking about is that we have a meeting of the minds, after all! Congratulations!"

Blackburn lowered his voice to a whisper and directed it privately to Captain Merced. "Sir, please . . . what's going on? I've spent my life fighting crime. You're trying to hand me the job of burning this place? Sir, whatever personal beef you've got with me, is—"

"Stop!" yelled the captain. His voice filled the backstage area, rang off of the walls. He let the following silence hang while he walked away for several steps, then stood with his back to him, taking another deep pull at the cigar. Finally, he turned back around and silently stared at him.

It was Blackburn who spoke up. "Why would it even occur to you—gentlemen—to come to me with this?"

"What," said Mr. Simmons. "You think that a job this vital is going to be handed to the local firebug? Maybe you think we should offer a reduced prison sentence for some hardened criminal to come and take care of this?"

"It's a fair question," Blackburn replied.

"Ha! You expect me to go back to my company and tell them that there is a professional criminal somewhere out there who did the job for us, and who now knows what really happened here? I'm supposed to tell them that someone like that has our lives in his hands? Is that what you suggest?" asked Mr. Cron.

Captain Merced's voice was cold and flat. "Detective Blackburn, you're gonna wait here all evening, until midnight, when everybody in the district is at home. You don't leave and come back, because you would increase the chance of being spotted. Once things are quiet, you're gonna set this place on fire and let it burn until the whole ground floor is involved. Then you go sound the alarm. That way, the fire crew gets here in time to contain it to this building."

"You'll be a hero, actually," added Mr. Simmons from the chief's office. "We've sent a message to Duncan to meet you here, telling him that you have news regarding your work. You just say that you arrived early, luckily for all, because you will discover it in time to keep the damage limited to this building!"

"What are you afraid of?" asked Captain Merced. "That you'll get *arrested*?" He broke into a loud laugh, joined by the other two.

"And you can be sure that the insurance company isn't going to come after you!" chimed in Mr. Cron, which set off another gale of laughter from the three men. They all seemed to feel much more relaxed, now that the truth was out. It was time to limber up their senses of humor at his expense.

"All right, all right," Merced called out. "So I guess by now you understand that this is actually your lucky day. You do this little job—an easy job at that—while everybody looks the other way. In return, you get a nice little article in the paper and, get this, now: freedom from James Duncan."

"We understand that you want that," smiled Mr. Simmons.

"Nothing wrong with wanting that," Mr. Cron agreed.

"Except for that pesky little thing about it being a major felony, gentlemen."

"Which I am standing here telling you is not any sort of a problem for you, Detective. This is my precinct. There's nobody else to come after you."

The scene had become so surreal that Blackburn felt as if he could lose his balance and fall. He could not believe that he was actually having this conversation.

"Listen to me, gentlemen," he began, with his constricted temper boiling toward explosion while he forced himself to remain calm. "This thing. This plan. I guess it sounds nice and neat to you, and I see how it could hide the architecture problem from outsiders. But my whole career in police work has shown me that it's the unexpected things that get you, every time. You can plan all day long, but there will always be something."

"Like what?" Merced demanded.

"What if the fire got out, somehow, and started to spread?"

"I don't see how that could—"

"I don't either, Captain. That's my point! It will always be that one thing you didn't see. And when that one thing happens here and this fire spreads, it won't necessarily be restricted to property damage. There could be lives lost because of this thing! Think about what I'm saying to you."

When Blackburn finished he was nearly panting with exertion and a sense of near panic. Merced's response did not help.

"No. You think about what I am saying to you, Detective Black-burn. You will do this. You'll be a local hero and finally go back to your real job. You'll get rid of that fleabag you've been ushering around. I understand that your duties consist of watching audience members."

All three of them had a good laugh over that one. They knew that this was a situation where they could safely push this big man, pretend to stare him down while his hands were tied.

"You two fellows don't know me, but Captain Merced, I can't be-lieve you ever thought that I would do something like this."

Blackburn knew that this was the time to walk out. There was nothing more to be said to these fools. But the nausea of dread in his stomach seemed to express his predicament. His legs did not move.

Mr. Simmons of the chief's office spoke up. His voice sounded kind and understanding.

"Detective Black—Ah . . ."

"Blackburn."

"Yes, sorry: Blackburn. As soon as you came inside, your vehicle was moved to the City Hall Station. After you do this job, you can retrieve it. Otherwise, I will burn this place myself and we will frame you for it and use your car as evidence that you were here but that you ran off." His voice remained kind and quite gentle while he continued. "We'll talk to the newspapers about how we picked the car up after our men spotted you here. We'll say that the fire was already lit. We had to find you and take you in."

"You can't make a story like that stick."

"We have an entire city administration who thinks that they can, Detective," Mr. Simmons assured him in the voice of an old and dear friend. "Which is why an absurd story like that will 'stick' just as well as all the other absurd stories that are out there."

"You know," Merced addressed the other two, "Detective Black-burn's adopted kids are young adults now. Old enough to get by on their own. If he was in prison, say. But after you've met them both—I hate to say it—but they do strike you as being a bit lost. I intend that not as an insult, simply an observation." His grin reminded Blackburn of a tomcat's fangs.

"The detective might not get a prison sentence, though," countered Mr. Cron. "Because of his clean record, and all."

"No, maybe not," agreed Merced. "In that case, he'd only have a busted career and a public disgrace and no future in this city whatsoever. But then, that's not so bad."

"Not bad? That would be getting off easy," added Mr. Simmons of the chief's office with a scholarly nod.

"After all," concluded Merced, staring into Blackburn's eyes, offering an entire future to him, "it's not like this is going to be an actual crime on the record books."

"Damn it, Captain, I'm the last man you ever should have thought of for this job!"

"Exactly! That's why you're perfect! Your loyalty to this department is well known, Detective. You are above suspicion, unless we decide that we have to make you look bad. Plus you can keep a secret. That's why you." He imitated a big, warm smile. "You might not like this assignment, but you gotta love this department! Hell, everybody knows you're a fanatic!"

All three of the men laughed at that one. A fanatic, yes. Laugh, nod. Smoke, nod.

Blackburn was astonished. Most of his energy was being lost to the struggle to refrain from leaping at these men and making them all regret that they ever came to him with this. He felt his world turning upside down.

"Chrissakes, Detective," commented Mr. Simmons, who sounded as if he was tired of reasoning with an idiot. "Why don't you try thinking about how lucky you are, for just one minute?"

CHAPTER TWENTY-ONE

WHO'S THE BIG IDIOT WITH THE BROOM? Vignette wondered. The janitor outside the pavilion's main entrance had already gotten on her nerves. Tall man, pale Anglo features, age thirty-five or so. She toyed, for a moment, with the idea of crossing over to him while moving her ankle-length crepe-de-chine skirt with that inviting sway that tells the world, "I am succulent under all this, but far too refined to let you see." She could arch her back just a little extra, subtly moving against the fabric so that the cream-colored silk jersey of her fitted, high-necked shirt would catch the light to the advantage of her breasts.

She could embody the league's ideal Hospitable Lady by bearing him a tray of watercress sandwiches and honey tea, clicking the low heels of her pointed shows along the hard floor until they nearly touched his own, then shoving the hospitable tray of tea and sandwiches straight into his face, knocking him off balance and sticking her foot behind his to trip him so that he fell backward and struck his head on the steps. *Oops! Excuse me . . . but welcome to San Francisco!*

Vignette's days at St. Adrian's Home for Delinquents and Orphans had given her a wide and sharp awareness of the lustful gaze from males. By the time she was six or seven, she had learned to think of the male lust-gaze as a big, invisible tongue. She could almost feel the warm slobber that it left on her. The trick was to be able to tell the difference between the stupid and sloppy feeling of the ordinary ones, and the sour, metallic sting of the dangerous ones. If you can get to where you are able to identify them in an instant, you will have information that you can use to stay out of their way.

Since her world was filled with monsters posing as decent people, such as that idiot janitor outside, it would be the trademark of a moron to reveal indiscriminately her depth of awareness about the things she had seen. With an effort, she turned her back on the big man. She shook her head. The slobber dogs would always be out there; she had problems far more pressing.

Meanwhile, the effort of keeping herself compacted down into the vanilla mode was again causing her to feel crammed into clothing that shrank by the hour. Her head throbbed in the back, and it was painful to breathe. She tried to imagine doing this "volunteer work" for the entire duration of the exposition and felt her chest constrict at the very notion of it.

"Miss Nightingale!" came the chirpy voice from across the room. She looked up to see Janine Freshell headed her way, absently flicking a bit of clotted cream off the silk georgette bow at her neckline.

Vignette constricted the muscles in her toes and then tightened every muscle all the way up to her neck. It helped to displace the strain of keeping her face relaxed and pleasant.

A moment later, Miss Freshell took her aside for an intimate conversation. "All right, then! Closing time! My, you have been *so* enthusiastic. Bravo! I tell you, Vignette, the sense of poise that one can develop from—"

"I saw that letter from your publisher, Janine. I know what you're doing."

Of course Miss Freshell did not grasp it, at first. "Excuse me? I believe the proper form of address for me in this situation—"

"Janine. Stop. We both have to stop. I can't do this, here. You can't do what you think you're doing, either. We both have to just stop it."

"I think that you had better explain—"

"I'll go any damn place that I need to go, if there's something I have to find out. It's nothing to get into your hotel room over there at the Fairmont. I could do things like that when I was eight."

"What are you saying? My room? You're saying that you've been in my room?"

"Are you always this slow? I smelled you from a long way off. So I went past your hotel door lock like nothing and sorted through that work file of papers you keep in that big converted trunk. And I found your letters from your publisher." She fixed the Eastern Whore with a crafty grin. "That one good one. It tells the whole thing, doesn't it?"

Miss Freshell's face hardened back into her real self. Her eyes went cold.

"You would never do such a thing. And young lady, I have half a mind to tell Randall what you just said!"

"You came here already connected to James Duncan. You agreed to come here, put him together with the detective you've snared, and persuade your publisher to take one more book from you. All because Duncan is so convinced that someone's trying to kill him, so that you're hoping they will try and he's hoping they will fail."

Vignette watched it hit home, then. Miss Freshell's face drained to a bluish white. She snapped at her in a sharp whisper, "Vignette! What you are talking about is a crime! You *cannot* break into a person's room and go through their private things!"

"Yeah I don't care about any of that. You went after Randall like a hunter goes after quail. I'm not going to let you get away with it. Do you even hold any love for him at all?"

There was a long pause. Vignette could almost hear large gears shifting, vast pieces of heavy machinery stopping and reversing direction.

Miss Freshell smiled. "Hardly a little thing like quail. Think of it as bringing down a big, friendly bear."

"You're using Randall for your own ends."

"Oh, God almighty, Vignette! You are a grown woman now. What world is it that you intend to inhabit?"

"What's that supposed to mean?"

"It means that everything I am trying to impart to you by way of exposing you to the women you work with, here—women who are able to behave at this level of sophistication whether they are in re-fined company or not—it's all aimed toward helping you get a grasp of how to move through the world. Your little inheritance isn't going to carry you."

"Oh, so you know about that, too, then?"

"I know what I need to know, Vignette. Like you."

"None of that makes it all right for you to crash into our lives. You can't just sweep Randall up like a toy, because he's a lonely bachelor and vulnerable to a collection of feminine wiles—all just to suit some little plan."

"Yes, I'm a grown woman, all right." Miss Freshell snorted out a badly repressed laugh.

Vignette nodded. "I'll say this much for you: You know how to laugh your way through life. You've got this spiderweb set up to catch whoever's after Duncan, just so you can write the story. I wonder how you got to Mr. Duncan?"

"Same answer, Vignette. I'm a single woman in a world ruined by its men. We have a war breaking out in Europe that is going to bring us to the edge of mankind's destruction, again at the hands of the men."

"Meaning what, then?"

"Meaning it's time for you to grow up. You're one of us. Randall was there to be taken. If it wasn't me, it was going to be another woman. He was ripe. I thank you and Shane for it."

"Me and Shane?"

"I think—no, I *know*—that living with you and having this family that you have, it made him want the next step in life. Hell, he's already raised the children. Would you deny him a wife?"

"You're not a wife! You're a hunter and he's your big, friendly bear. You're using him and Mr. Duncan and Lord knows what else to get your next book published! You hope somebody will go after J.D. so you can write about it and just happen to be married to the detective on the case. You're doing this to save yourself!"

"Uh-oh! Now a woman can't even save herself through a man, in your view of life? Interesting. Isn't that a lot like walking around hungry in an orchard full of fruit, but refusing to reach right out and pick it?"

Over Miss Freshell's right shoulder, Vignette happened to catch sight of the front entrance, where the big janitor had been standing, pretending to sweep. There was nothing there. She supposed that he was off pretending to work somewhere else.

By now, the visitors had all trickled away and the last of the other hospitality ladies were calling out goodbyes and heading off into the night, making their way across the closed fairgrounds toward the main exit. In moments it would be just the two of them left to make sure everything was ready for the cleaning crew.

Even though there was nobody close by, Vignette spoke softly enough to compel Miss Freshell to listen. "I'll tell Randall what you're doing unless you go away and leave us alone."

"Tell him."

"What?"

"Tell him. Maybe the best way for you to learn about your own power is by watching mine, since you clearly know nothing."

"Are you out of your mind?"

"No, and I am not exaggerating when I say that it's probably best if you tell him. When you see that he will not believe you—and that he will refuse to believe you, no matter what kind of evidence you show him—then you will start to get the message. It's about power. You need to learn about yours."

Vignette hated the way Freshell's remark made her feel, all the more because she hated her own suspicions that there was truth in it.

"I'm going to the ladies' room, Miss Freshell. Why don't you do the finish work for both of us? Then we can go catch a cab and discuss whatever you plan to do, just in case Randall surprises you and listens to me."

"You are being very unwise."

"I don't want to hear anything else!" She turned and started for the ladies' room. It caused her to miss the expression on Miss Freshell's face, but it was a welcome relief to get away without having to deal with another protest from her.

The pavilion was empty except for the two of them now, and the sounds of her own footsteps echoed around the large space while she made her way to the ladies' room. The awkward confrontation made her feel all the more aware of the noise. The trip seemed to take forever.

She heard a flutter of fabric behind her, and wondered whether Miss Freshell had dramatically spun around to walk off in the other direction.

She never heard any footsteps, though, so she decided not to press her luck by turning around and inviting another comment.

Inside the ladies' room, she made it a point to take her time in using the facilities, carefully washing her hands, patting cold water on her face, fixing her ridiculous wig, all so that Miss Freshell could finish the closing work without her.

She abandoned the attempt to use her fingertips to brush the false hair, horse hair, whatever it was. The stuff felt like dried grass. Everything she did to it made it look worse. The activity used up time, but otherwise served only to remind her that the absurd wig was the very embodiment of everything that was happening to her. It was another sign of falsehood that society expected her to wear, if she wanted to achieve any sort of acceptance from the world around her.

She had made things so much worse when she cut off her hair and took the irresponsible risk with Randall's career. Not only was it idiotic, but as a further mark of shame, she still could not think back on it without a thrill of satisfaction.

She thought of people watching a horse race, seeing their horse pulling ahead. She was her own damned horse. To hell with all of them.

Except that she had not stopped and considered the possible effect of it upon Randall. She had a sick feeling in her middle that plainly told her that she should have done so. This was the man who had made it possible for her to take such an outrageous risk in the first place, by raising her with love and respect in a safe home. After it was over, he even avoided coming home and screaming at her, or striking out at her the way that she knew most men would.

He only pleaded with her to understand that he had to be able to trust her. By the time she came down from the anxiety that first went along with being discovered, it broke her heart into pieces to realize that she had put him in a position to have to beg her to be trustworthy. She hated the memory of his words.

Worst of all was the endlessly repeating reminder that she had always been able to trust *him*. She could not think of a single time that he lied to her, and never once had he threatened her or done her the slightest harm.

What were his crimes? Why, he had made her use her little inheritance from the Nightingale family to get a private education, all the way through high school. He pestered her to study. He made sure she earned her diploma when so many girls rich and poor did not. He never pressured her to become anything that she did not want to become; he only encouraged her to find a place for herself that involved working and striving in the world instead of hanging back from it.

It had been over a year since her graduation and she had done nothing to build a life. But he somehow managed to pester her gently, without throwing any sort of defiant challenge at her.

Randall had never even questioned her claim to be Shane's sister. Even as the pair grew older and revealed no hint of family resemblance, Randall stayed blind to it just as well as Shane did. It always overwhelmed her to think of it—so she tried not to do it often—but all she ever had to do to join this family was to give both of them a made-up story about seeing Shane's records back at St. Adrian's. For that, Shane handed over his last name and half his modest inheritance from the Nightingales without the slightest hesitation. Then Randall took them both into his life and not only adopted them, but did his stumbling best to keep them healthy and well.

On the rare occasion that she could restrict her thoughts about men to just those two examples, then in that limited frame she perceived so much more of the beauty of maleness that ordinarily escaped her. When the usual presences were removed—lust-licking stares or grotesque words whispered or shouted, the potential for violence and the violence itself—then a vacuum of silence remained that allowed subtler male energies to take their place and quietly speak to her.

These two men—her fake brother who became a real one by doing nothing more than living that way, and the adoptive father whose little family she joined with a lie—they lived out the truth of the male capacity to latch on and hold fast to the role of protector, day after day, season after season, year after year. They lived out the truth of calmly but strongly standing up for anything that you know to be true and right. They lived out the truth of always seeking and preferring a civilized response to the world, but of also being willing and able to protect one's own safety, even if violence is required. And although that capacity for violence is real, in such men it is never employed against the innocent, and it freely takes on lethal risk to protect another.

It was only because of those two examples that she had any hope of finding a life that would not require her to be a liar simply to survive. If there were two, there had to be more somewhere. She had so many little memories, over the last nine years, of both Shane and Randall refusing to have anything to do with a situation that would involve being deceitful in some way. Neither of them preached about it; they both just seemed to have an instinctive aversion to falsehood: Randall, because he saw the worst of it every day, and Shane for whatever reasons he carried.

Even if Shane could do nothing more than work in a restaurant, with his condition, she had to acknowledge that he was still out there in the world, living his life. And Randall had fought off attackers so many times in his work that she was certain nobody could ever make him do something wrong, just by threatening him.

It was because of Randall that she knew it was all right to believe in heroes, even in a world that is in large part a giant ash pit. But in spite of all that, she had gone ahead with her mad inspiration to get around the manly police structure's assumption that women could not do the damned job. The sheer challenge of it had pulled at her the same way that she imagined the sky will pull at a grounded bird.

Her ultimate betrayal of Randall left her unforgiven in her own eyes because she still could not, absolutely *could not* look back on any of it without feeling that burst of pride. The fact that she actually put the plan into motion instead of simply fantasizing about it, as she had a million others, why, that alone was remarkable. Not only did she do it even though it was utterly insane, the sheer audacity of it all somehow became her greatest asset in pulling it off.

She knew that the more she stepped outside the boundaries of social convention, the easier it was for her to move things around. Miss Freshell had prattled on to her about a woman's power of illusion with corsets and a makeup brush, but she did so without having the slightest grasp of the power to be had in successfully shattering a false taboo, proving it wrong. It made Vignette want to crow like a sunrise rooster . . . when, she reminded herself, she deserved to feel nothing but shame, of course.

CHAPTER TWENTY-TWO

INSTEAD OF SUGAR, J.D. stirred a fraction of a teaspoon of the elixir powder into his piping hot room service coffee. This was his favorite way to consume it, when he was free to give in to its power. A long Monday night off in the isolation of this lovely suite was an ideal time and place to amplify his dosage further than usual, safe from prying eyes. He had, after all, recently been forced to learn that he could indeed maintain his self-control under the effect of much larger amounts.

He sensed a freedom of some kind that was to be found by hovering near the loss of control. Perhaps it was that place of mental release that his audience marks always went to, but that he had never been able to enter himself.

There was no doctor in the United States to monitor his condition. American doctors. Bonesetters. And he would check into an American hospital for an examination on the same day that he swam in an open sewer for exercise.

He knew what to look for, anyway. All a doctor could do was help him to face it. Dr. Alzheimer had taken care of that by introducing him to just the right chemist. He had a bagful of self-diagnosis open on the table in front of him.

The ornately colored tiles lining J.D.'s main balcony framed his view of the ocean far below. The balcony carried a familiar feel in the handiwork of the mosaic. If he looked closely at the single tiles, they seemed to be randomly placed. But if he pulled away a few steps, an entire panorama came into focus. By the same token, he was certain that if he pulled back from his jumbled thoughts and viewed them from a distance, the whole picture would finally reveal itself.

The question was simple enough, after all: *How bad is it?*

How bad is it compared to when it started? Say three years ago. Be more honest, say five. Five years, then. Five years of what he had never allowed himself to define as a slow disintegration, but what he had always recognized as precisely that. Relentless disintegration, a sandy beach eaten away by the tides.

How bad is it? He didn't even know what "it" was until he had the evil curse or the good fortune, depending on the time of day that he thought about it, to meet Dr. Alzheimer and receive his diagnosis. His condition was an example of the doctor's discovery: a new distance—not distance, *disease*—a new disease that slowly empties your brain of its contents and turns you into a godforsaken child.

How gentle the doctor was. "Every man has another inside of himself that he must keep hidden, if he wants the world's respect. This illness strips away one's ability to conceal the hidden man." The doctor did not mention females, in the fashion of his Germanic culture, but J.D. supposed that he referred to them as well. He was about to ask about that when Dr. Alzheimer smiled and added one last thing.

"Mother Nature is kind. As this illness steals your abilities, it also steals your ability to notice the process. Eventually, the problem is not yours at all. The problem, really, is for the ones who must take care of you."

It was enough to end the conversation. The doctor had smiled again, although his words could not have been more damning if they were uttered by Satan. Their cruel message was clear: *Whatever you have left to do, do it now. Get it done. Then, as soon as you possibly can, scuff away a little indentation in the dirt and line it with pine needles, so you'll have someplace soft to land when you fall over.*

The great James "J.D." Duncan had never been successful enough to earn real wealth. He was an aging man, married twice, abandoned both times by his wives because of his devotion to his work. Of course, he reminded himself, the love of card games had not been helpful. Various other women picked him clean, time and again, seemingly without effort.

Now this. This erosion.

His fingers began to shake a bit while the first of the elixir took hold of him. He used the remaining seconds while he still had enough fine motor control to peel scrapes of warm wax off the fat candle burning in front of him. He salted a bit of the elixir onto each scrape of wax and rolled it up into itself, burying the elixir inside.

It was a little trick that he came up with during his first year with the elixir, strictly for use on days off. The little wax balls were easy to swallow, and they could keep the elixir from getting into his system for as much as an hour.

Ever since the forced overdose at his introductory show, the idea of pushing his tolerance for the elixir gripped him. He felt compelled to experience every scrap of memory that he had left. He planned to swallow one or two of the wax balls and save the others for later, then go for a long walk and let the effects surprise him.

But at that moment an abrupt knock on his suite's double doors gave him a jolt. He bolted up from his chair and felt his heart jump.

Room service again? He had not ordered anything else. Besides, room service people always immediately announced themselves. No one had spoken.

He took a deep breath and turned toward the door. "Yes?"

"Mr. Duncan," came a muffled male voice. "It's Shane Nightingale. I'm here by myself, sir, and I'm sorry about the late hour, but can you come to the door? The hotel has been trying to get a message to you, and I was asked to bring it over in person."

Shane Nightingale?

Shane . . . Nightingale . . . A bolt of fear shot through him. It was obvious that he was supposed to know that name. Instead there was a blank spot precisely where the information about someone called Shane Nightingale ought to be.

"The hotel refused to come and knock, because you left word not to be disturbed, but they've been tucking notes under your door all evening."

J.D. saw several slips of paper on the floor within a few inches of the doorsill. He sighed. *This is the worst part,* he thought, *losing a whole person.*

It was not the loss of words, or the struggle to keep the trance triggers in his mind, or even the challenge of bluffing his way out of failed bits. The absolute worst part was finding out that somebody he was supposed to know had popped like a soap bubble and vanished in his brain.

His greatest threat was a situation just like this: one-on-one, where he had no escape. And it might just be more than he could do, to lie his way out of it. It required a dexterous level of fakery far beyond his means, to handle such an encounter without giving away his deficit.

But with his next deep breath, a fresh wave of clarity sparkled through him. Riding its effect, he reminded himself that he was James "J.D." Duncan, renowned mesmerist. If anyone could bluff his way through such an encounter in spite of the distance, not distance, *dizziness.* But no, it wasn't dizziness, it was disease. Disease. He lost the train of thought.

Forty years of almost continuous work in the public arena had earned him enough to take him through his marriages, even if they failed. He accumulated nothing. And what about children? Any children?

Any children? Any children?

The echo of the phrase was loud, swirling inside him with such force that he felt a rush of seasickness from the motion. He reached out a hand to steady himself against the wall.

What was he thinking about?

At that moment, he realized that the chemically fueled memory had completely reversed his mood, placing an entirely new and different lens over his eyes. He now saw that there was a lot to be said for the "die trying" attitude. So why not answer the door? Throw down the challenge.

Plus, J.D. could rely on maintaining as much clarity as possible for several more hours, since he had himself a bellyful of methylenedioxymethamphetamine—the next best thing to fairy powder sprinkled over the brain by elves. He felt it: rapidly dissolving, boosted by caffeine. It would light a bonfire inside his skull. *Good thing the folks aren't out there tonight.*

He decided that maybe he could entertain this Nightingale fellow for a minute or two, after all. Convince the man that he remembered him, then send him on his way and get right back to more amusing things. Surely he had mastered this elixir well enough to maintain the control necessary to accomplish that much.

He forgot for a moment that impulsiveness was a much bigger problem for him when he was under the effects of the elixir, and willingly acted upon the impulse to swallow all six of the little wax balls at once. He took a quick swig from the water pitcher, swallowing the wad with effort and dabbing at the sides of his mouth while he hurried over to the suite's double doors. That would keep him motivated to get Mr. Nightingale going on his way before the little wax balls melted, released their treasure, and the real trouble started.

At the doorway, he placed his hands on both doorknobs and took a deep breath. Then he pulled on both doors and opened them wide, adding a bit of dramatic flair, a matter of individual style. He was the Renowned Mesmerist, after all.

Out of all of her readers, Janine Freshell would have been the biggest fan of the way she died. She might have even stolen the death for her next book, the one that she did not get to finish, despite her resourcefulness in finding a way to revive her publisher's interest in her and insert herself into Duncan's need for a professional boost. The renowned mesmerist was a perfect antagonist for her next book: not the killer, but the cause.

As a woman who had never found any enjoyable use for her femininity except for the effect it created in men, she had adopted the persona of a ravenous whore by night and perfect lady by day. As such, she could hardly fail to secure the romantic interest of a certain bachelor who just happened to be the police detective whose name came up in newspaper articles more than any other over the past few years.

Her inspiration had come from a single piece of information that started it all, for her—received on the day that a distraught woman sought her out in hopes that the author of women's romance stories would be a sympathetic ear. The woman was older, never married, but had a fatherless son. The son was now a grown man, and his crazy and sometimes shameful behavior was steadily escalating toward violence.

The woman sought Freshell's help in appealing to the father of her crazy bastard child, whom she could no longer protect or control. But the father was a famous showman. He ignored the letters from the mother of his child, and refused to see her after his shows.

And so the woman begged Freshell to use her celebrity to make contact with the great mesmerist, James "J.D." Duncan. The older woman did not want anything from him, did not even care to see him, for herself. She only appealed for him to find a way of keeping their mutual creation from causing some sort of terrible harm to himself or someone else.

"Please," she had begged, "make sure Mr. Duncan understands. It's gone beyond anything that one woman can handle. Something terrible is wrong with our boy. God forgive me, but sometimes I look at him and I see the Devil."

In the brief time that it took Miss Freshell to die, there was a moment when a thought flashed through her, not in words, but as a series of mental images and fleeting physical sensations. Their sum total was simple: She was the one who set off the long and complex chain of events that eventually led to the fatal pressure that was now constricting her windpipe.

It began at the moment, months before, when she decided to accept the woman's appeal. She then lied to her and claimed that Duncan had refused to see her. In truth, she never contacted him at all. Instead, she arranged to meet him for her own purposes, using the opportunity to allow the woman to sit in a café across the street from her meeting place with Duncan, so that she could see for herself that Freshell was actually visiting with him, as promised. For that privilege, the woman paid Miss Freshell a wad of cash that she claimed represented every dollar she had, and which Janine Freshell gladly accepted.

With that, she only needed to convince Duncan that she could save his career, without mentioning her own. She persuaded him to press the San Francisco authorities to assign Detective Randall Blackburn as his personal body guard. It had taken her three anonymous threatening letters, left for Duncan at his stage door, to convince him that he needed a body guard at all. When she sweet-ened the pot by explaining that she had just gotten the fabulous idea to tail Duncan for the duration of the ten-month exposition, writing a book with him as a main character, his commitment was sealed.

And if none of those things guaranteed her doom, Miss Freshell instantly understood that the cause of her own demise had been launched the moment she contacted Duncan's criminal bastard with another note. This one was her masterpiece, written as if Duncan himself was the author, and delivered to the mental insti-tution where the son was incarcerated.

The note's contents berated the son to the point of never even using his name. It scorned him for frightening his mother and it mocked him for thinking that Duncan would ever have anything to do with a god-cursed wastrel like him. It did everything short of openly daring him to escape and come after his father. By the time she finished writing it, she could not think of anybody who would receive such a letter without wanting to kill the author.

God, how her publishers loved the whole plan! Perfectly set up, all she had to do was hang back in her Hospitality League position and allow the natural course of things to generate a story that she would access from the inside—perhaps even become a part of, herself. (She had not decided whether to use her own name for her character, too much fame being destructive for an author, after all.)

Everyone in New York understood that with such brilliantly structured conflict, her inside position would certainly yield a whopping good story. When the crimes that she anonymously helped to manifest finally took place, all of the breathless newspaper articles would only serve to whet public appetite for her book's in-depth details. After this one hit the bookstands, nobody would ever trap her in the "Women's Romance Writer" category, ever again.

Everything caught up with her too soon, that was all. Before she had the chance to complete her mission, the chain of events somehow boomeranged back down all the days and weeks since then, ending with the constricting pressure on both sides of her neck, forcefully applied just beneath her chin.

She had almost escaped it, at first. She even managed to keep herself beautifully alive throughout the initial attack, which came upon her without warning inside the pavilion. It was stunningly powerful, a large hand whipping around from behind her, clamping vicelike over her mouth. One moment she was trying to think of the most hurtful remark that she could to hurl at Vignette's departing form—the next, she was speechless, barely able to breathe, pinned by the powerful man's second arm, then lifted just high enough that her feet would not touch the ground.

As quickly as that, all power was taken from her. Her wiles did their best for her; she immediately relaxed, sensing that resistance would only aggravate her attacker. She went limp and allowed him to carry her out of the pavilion and across the Zone, which was deserted at this late hour. Her attacker bore her into an isolated group of low bushes that had a small clearing hidden in the middle, and plopped her down onto the ground. She wisely ignored squealing in pain and shock, knowing that this might aggravate him also. Instead, she tried to turn and meet his eyes. If she could somehow connect with him, she would be able to do something. Janine Freshell could always do something when she locked eyes with a man.

There was no way to turn her head. The pressure of his grip did not ease.

In response, she kept her body perfectly limp and offered no resistance of any kind. She slowly reached her right arm across to her opposite shoulder, then lightly caressed the top of his hand with her fingertips.

The effect was immediate and gave her a moment's hope. Whoever he was, he obviously had not predicted a seductive reaction. His grip dropped to half its strength.

Miss Freshell knew by now that this was no robbery. Her attacker showed no interest in her purse or her pockets. Could it only be sex? She wondered. Could *that* be all? Some stinking, penis-bearing shit sack was willing to risk kidnapping her and then raping her in this public place? Whoever this man was, he had to know that he would be shot on the spot if someone saw him, or that if he went to prison for rape, he would die there.

But she also knew that half of the world's population were morons and that you could always identify one by checking for a penis. So she continued the caressing motion and writhed her hips under him. The message was easy to convey. *Here I am, I'm your little victim. Feel me? Feel what you have trapped underneath you?*

That was the moment when his hand dropped from her mouth to her throat, squeezing with such awful force that all her thoughts left her, replaced by a fireball of panic. It filled her awareness to the point that she had no knowledge of when she began dying, or even when she finished. Her last coherent thought was that it felt as if she were strangling herself and could not stop.

She lost consciousness from the cutoff of blood to the brain before she had the chance to pass out for lack of air, meaning that her death was relatively painless. Janine Freshell would have also approved of that, given the circumstances. And since her new opus was never going to be completed now, she might have been willing to stoop to remaining within her romantic fiction territory if she could only be granted the opportunity to write a passage about her own demise.

The realities of spasmodic death would never appear on such pages: the panicked voiding of her bladder first, then a massive evacuation of her bowels when her instincts did their last bit of misguided service by lightening up her body, preparing her to flee. But the only flight left to Miss Freshell was, perhaps, the spirit from the body. The body itself would never travel again.

Panic occupied her while the hand crushed her larynx, shutting down the arteries. The panic only faded as her life faded, and still the grip on her neck was strong and determined. Before long, there was nothing left of Miss Janine Freshell whatsoever, except for an empty carcass, a stomach-wrenching odor, and all the lethal chaos that she had set into motion during her truncated life.

CHAPTER TWENTY-THREE

VIGNETTE STOOD FROZEN BEHIND the door to the women's rest-room for a full minute, listening. It felt like half an hour, but still there were no sounds from the other side. She had just finished deliberately rebraiding her hair and was considering coming back out again, when her very bone marrow seemed to grasp the fact that she had heard nothing out there for all this time. She figured that the running tap water might have drowned out a little of it, but some trace of noise ought to have filtered through.

Her blood ran cold. She had gotten careless. She became so busy with her little game that she forgot to listen and keep track of the cleanup noises outside.

The time spent behind the door straining her hearing was terrifying, even though she did not consciously know why. When she finally opened it, she eased it forward by millimeters, peering out through the vertical crack.

Nothing. She smoothly widened the crack—still nothing. At last she slowly and steadily pushed the door back, just far enough to slip her head out for a peek . . .

Not only was there nothing there, but nothing at all had been done to finish up. No wonder it was so quiet. Her first reaction was annoyance, since the Eastern Whore had obviously gotten her bloomers bunched up and trumped Vignette's exit to the restroom by walking out on the job.

Vignette stomped out into the center of the pavilion and slowly turned in a full circle. Unbelievable. Unless she was prepared to raise the ante by going home now herself, leaving the job undone, she was stuck. It was tempting to do exactly that, except that the aftereffects could go more to Randall than to Miss Freshell.

It was interesting, she thought, that this childish display revealed how much the Eastern Whore truly thought of the Ladies' Hospitality League, in failing to leave the place ready for the cleaning crew and risking embarrassment to them all. Freshell was the one who always complained to Vignette about how the male park managers were always waiting for the all-women's group to mess things up. They could howl about such mistakes for days because it made them feel smarter.

Nobody had to warn her about that. Such awareness came right out of her own experience. Women were never supposed to look too good in any business environment. If they did, people started to talk about how it was that this woman may have accomplished so much, what she might have done to get there, that sort of thing. Gossipmongers ruined lives.

It took her over half an hour to get things put away and push back all the little brochure tables so that the sweepers had clear room. She found herself putting extra energy into it for no other reason than that it made her feel angry to picture anyone saying that the women could not even manage their own working space at the fairgrounds.

By the time it was all done and she closed the main door behind her, leaving it unlocked for the cleaners as instructed, she was feeling glad that Miss Freshell had abandoned her in such a crude way. Maybe when Randall heard about it he would shake off whatever spell she had him under and give the woman a second look.

She walked out into the deserted Zone and headed toward the main gates. It was a brisk ten-minute walk for average people, and

Vignette could take it at an easy trot in a third of that time. It felt good to break out of the Gibson Girl mode, and she smoothly trotted along on the balls of her feet, so that the shoe heels stayed out of her way. There was nobody around to stare, except for a few straggling workers closing up. She stretched her stride and deepened her breathing.

The long skirt was of a thin wool, but still cumbersome enough to be a drag on her efforts. She grabbed up the front with both hands and let the rest drape off to the sides. She had only covered the first couple of blocks when she came to a small alley cutting across the sidewalk. Surprise stopped her cold at the sight of a full-sized female mannequin that somebody had left sprawled on the bricks just inside the alleyway.

The top half of the female form was concealed by the building's moon shadow, but Vignette could see the rest of it clearly enough: standard black leather high-buttoned, low-heeled shoes, the long ankle skirt of the same dark blue or black that all the women wore. This one had a simple slip, pulled up to reveal the dark stocking on one leg.

Such an elaborate mannequin. Somebody had to have been pretty damned careless to have lost it.

Vignette ignored a flash of dread. Instead, she managed to spend another few seconds in the relative comfort of ignorance by asking herself what the poor person who lost this mannequin was going to do. Vignette wondered if she should tell someone about it. Hell, she was only a volunteer, and had not volunteered to be on mannequin-chasing duty. Somebody who was on the clock ought to figure out—

Comfortable ignorance ended. She arrived at the sprawled "mannequin" with a part of her already recognizing the outfit. For a fraction of a second, she tried to remark to herself upon the similarity of the mannequin's clothing to that of Miss Freshell.

But by then she was close enough to see into the dark slash of the building's shadow. Miss Freshell's dying horror was perfectly captured, frozen upon her face in a nasty shade of bluish gray. The eyes were wide open and fixed straight ahead, so that they happened to be staring directly up at Vignette. The impact of the image hit her like a tree branch across the face. She froze to the spot, bending her knees and gasping for air.

She knew better than to assume the killer was gone; this crime had to have just taken place. She scanned the shadows for threats, for any movement. Her anxiety caused the ground to begin swimming beneath her. She pushed her breathing into its deepest and most forceful mode while she checked in all directions for a possible attacker.

Once she was satisfied that no one was about to pounce, she turned her focus outward, for someone to call for help. There was no need to check for a pulse. Death had laid its brand upon Janine Freshell and burned it in deep.

She's in God's hands, Vignette thought, *if you follow that sort of thing.*

She had to find a beat cop or at least see about a public telephone to ring up the police. Although she knew that the first thing Randall would want her to do was get away from there, she pulled off her medium-weight waistcoat and stepped close enough to the body to waft it down over the face and head. There was no other way to show the dead woman any respect or to protect the scene.

Her linen long-sleeved blouse offered scant protection against the brisk snap to the air, so she gathered her skirt in her hands again and started directly for the main gate, where there would always be a guard. She kept her speed lower than an open sprint, but her stride was still deep and fast enough to cover ground in a hurry. She poured her shock into the exertion.

Somewhere close by was the person who did this. She tried to imagine if the attacker was male or female, but saw that it could be either. Some male sex maniac might have struck out at her because he thought she was all alone in the pavilion. But with a woman like Janine Freshell, it could just as easily have been a jealous female—

perhaps the wife or girlfriend of one of Miss Freshell's necessary conquests, lying in wait to find her alone?

She was running so easily that the main gate loomed close in a quick minute, but the closer she got to being able to call for help, the more the awful dread filled her.

What about Randall?

What would this do to him? The more she thought about it, the more the terrible alarm filled her. Randall was going to be hurt by this, and she was beginning to realize what a blow it would be to him. She had to let him know. She had to be the one to tell him, not some unfeeling son of a bitch on the force.

The nondescript man walked as fast as a man can go without breaking into a run. Legs outstretched, back stiff, shoulders back, he covered ground quickly enough to be there and gone before anybody noticed him. He was careful to avoid giving the impression of a man running away from anything. He ground his teeth to the rhythm of his footsteps and timed his thoughts along to the beat: Left, right. Left, right. *Get it done, get it done. Get it done, get it done.*

All down the Zone until he reached the main exit. Through the exit and out to the taxis.

First bump in the trail—the taxis were all gone, at this hour. He admonished himself for not knowing that. No telling how long the wait might be.

So, still walking fast—not like an escaping murderer at all—he gave his best imitation of a man finished with his overtime and anxious to get home to his family. The nondescript man glided through the giant lighted gates, passing late-night employees here and there.

Before the second hand of the big clock above the main gate could make a single sweep around the face, he had disappeared down Van Ness Avenue, heading for Nob Hill and the opulent Fairmont Hotel. That was where Duncan was to be found. He saw clearly now that wherever Duncan was, he himself needed to be. No more of this stalling and cautious maneuvering. After tonight's debacle with the useless Revenge girl, it was obvious that he belonged near Duncan and no place else. *No place else.*

Duncan was the place to vent his rage, the only place, the proper place, the fitting place. Everywhere else he tried, the fires grew faster than he could beat them back. Revenge girls were either a very temporary waste of time, like the first one, or a panicky mess, like the one he had just left behind.

He could no longer tell whether he was being deliberately tormented by God or by the Devil, but it was clear that the big fix was in. Obstacles were popping up in every direction.

Just this very evening, the dead space under the false cliff in the Hall of Science had taken on enough water that it was only a couple of inches below the point where it would begin to flow into the exhibit. As soon as that happened, there would be frantic overnight repairs, water pumps, drainage lines, so that the spongy land would remain cleverly disguised from the visitors walking on top of it. His crew would probably get the work order.

So the dead space was no longer safe. It was useless to him now. Whatever the hell they had built the exposition's new land out of was making itself a bit more comfortable by settling down into the ocean bed.

He knew enough about ocean currents to realize that the sea had to have penetrated the millions of tiny airways and pockets among the chunks of crumbled streets and buildings that formed the foundation of the new land. By now, the sea had used its relentless pressures to push the water in through all the millions of microscopic pathways, pulling the water back out again with every changing of the tide. He pictured the land underneath the exposition as a porous reef. Every inhale and exhale of the tide forced the ocean water in or out.

He could practically feel the undermined land vibrating under his shoe leather. He could not get away from the exposition grounds fast enough.

At this point, he wondered, what else was he to think, except that this botched business with the new Revenge girl was a clear sign. It was a sign written in giant, bold letters, and it was telling him that things would continue to go badly for him unless and until he confronted the *real* cause of it all. Otherwise, he was surely doomed to be repeatedly derailed by the flimsiest of chance events. Unfairness of every sort would spontaneously manifest, always at precisely the worst moment, to keep right on ruining every single damned thing.

Like tonight.

This Revenge girl should have been perfect. Not really a girl, to be sure. As soon as he grabbed her, he felt the skin on her face. It was an adult woman's skin, not that of the very young woman she seemed from a distance. He registered the difference but felt no particular reaction. Within reason, age did not have to matter; besides, there were always unexpected breaks in the path with any publicly committed crime. Things happen, you take care of them, you move on.

But then came the proof that certain Forces were toying with him. Proof that unnecessary obstacles were being created by a cruel, outside hand.

She did not fight him. She was supposed to fight him. She did not fight him at all.

What, did the pathetic creature *want* to die?

He had pictured every detail of it. She was supposed to struggle with all of her body. She was to attempt to scream from beneath the iron fingers of his clamped hand.

Her resistance was the final ingredient. It was the key to sending him into that frenzy of exploding emotion that he craved so deeply, while every cell in his body throbbed in the act of annihilating her. The very point was to destroy, to desecrate, to reduce her to nothingness for opposing him. For tormenting him with her beauty, which, if he allowed it, would paralyze him into a state of worshipful awe. And since giving up power was, to him, the same as giving up life, his survival instinct would shred her out of existence at the moment she struck out against him. He was a spring-loaded trap, set for the first sign of a fight.

He needed to steal it from her; she was *not* supposed to offer it up. She was not supposed to go limp while he carried her, and then turn into a writhing whore the moment he fell on top of her. It was her hips, the feeling of her hips, moving against him, inviting him, urging him to come to her, grinding against his crotch, not recoiling at the feel of his quick erection but immediately moving in sympathetic and harmonious circular motions against him.

She pressed her face against the side of his while she moved her body, undulating in small movements that set off explosive effects in him, and it was as if she did not realize that the side of her mouth that pressed against him placed her slack lips in contact with the sensitive skin of his neck, with the tip of her tongue just naturally resting there between both lips so that when her slow and silent body movements caused her face to slide down his wide open shirt collar, toward where his neck and shoulders met, her tongue dragged slightly, just so slightly along his skin.

He felt his entire existence focused upon the tip of her tongue and hated himself for his weakness at the same instant that he yearned to give in to it. He was outraged at her audacity and grateful down to his bones when she opened her mouth and laid the entire flat of her tongue against the skin of his neck and pressed wet and soft flesh against him, pushing into his skin with her lips and her teeth.

His body stiffened into a plank. She kept it up, while he remained helpless within the fleeting ecstasy that she yielded up to him. In that single instant, he fully understood the old-time use of the word *witch*. This woman had used invisible power to reduce him to a stumbling schoolboy. She did it in moments, did it without effort. The unforgivable whore was not even breathing hard.

Then it hit him; from that moment on, he could not prevent her from knowing that she had done him in and that her wiles had overpowered him without effort. She had denied him her intended function while he sadistically dominated her, and she had denied it by first dominating him. Nothing had gone the way it was supposed to. Now—even as he felt himself coming down from the cloud of sexual release—he could sense her smug contempt.

She knew, and of course he could sense that she knew—her big, bad, abductor could be reduced to absurdity by something so insubstantial as a female's urgent invitations. It was backward. One of the reasons he had picked her was that he could tell she was a refined woman. She should have crumbled under his attack.

And so what did that mean for him, after this unexpected twist? Oh, that much was plain. All too plain.

She was most assuredly the type who would scream with laughter while she told her friends all about how she had exerted feminine mastery over a failed kidnapper. Her stories of a grown man who spontaneously ejaculated over a few wiggles and hip thrusts would set whole rooms into gales of laughter. She would light up parties with her tales.

Nobody would ever stop to consider *his* position. He was certain of that much. Not one of the bastards who laughed and applauded for her masterful, sluttish sexual skills would ever give a thought to how he had been left completely unfulfilled by this.

She was nothing like she was supposed to have been. From where else but the Devil could a woman get the power to plug into the very core of a man's being and trigger it as if it's nothing? How can any female do this in a matter of a few heartbeats, to a total stranger? She was too good for a simple thing of nature, in the way that she dominated him. The most awful thing about the act was its mercy. The relief, the relief, left him younger and lighter and faster and smarter.

It ought to have been sweet, revengingly sweet. But it was only sexual release. It did nothing whatsoever for the rage. Even with such otherworldly power, masterful power, nasty and delightful and shameful power, the rage remained unaffected. After he went slack on top of her, spent and foolish, she lay quiet beneath him. All she did was breathe. No crying, no attempts to talk. The Goddamned woman was far too smart.

Her breathing was just enough to remind him that she was still alive and delicious underneath him. Not only did she deny him her terror, she was making it plain that she was there to be taken again, if he had it in him. Her soft breathing and her utter, yielding stillness had already combined to restart the fire in him. Another minute or two of that from her, and he would find himself sexually paralyzed all over again.

How much of that humiliation was he expected to endure? He went against his own better judgment by moving her torso around so that he could look into her eyes. Her gaze shot into him and he nearly exploded.

There was so much of her in it. There was a smart woman of refinement and education, far beyond his, no doubt, and also a woman of taste. She was one who could hold her own in the company of strong and powerful men. This was a woman who surely had a number of those same strong men who would gladly shoot him full of holes if they could see him on top of her now.

All of those people seemed to look out through her eyes, straight at him. The glare was blinding. He noticed that his hands were around her throat and squeezing as hard as his muscles could contract. He squeezed as if he could cut through her neck with his thumbs and pull her head right off her shoulders.

All the while, he stared directly into the blaze of life coming from her eyes, the brilliant glow from her superiority over him.

He was the sole witness to the fact that she died in a very matter-of-fact and forthright manner, nothing abnormally disgusting, probably better than anything he could muster himself, under such circumstances. He held her gaze while her life faded away, sucking the last of the gravy from it.

It was over too soon. All of the love and friendship that a wonderful and polished woman like that was certain to possess in her life died away into nothingness, into darkness, while he sucked on her eyes with his stare and squeezed on her neck for all that he was worth.

Right there at the end, when she appeared to realize finally that her wiles had not succeeded in getting her out of this and that she would never leave that place, he saw the fear and anger flare in her. It was so beautiful, such a life force. First the fear, a garden-variety response and to be expected, but then, tastiest of all, her moment of indignation. That flash in her eyes when she realized that everything she ever knew, all that she hoped for, was all being taken away from her. Her knowledge of what it means to be a conscious living thing was being stolen from her, by this man above her. Yes, the man whom she had just so successfully humiliated. And how much good had it done her, to toy with him that way?

His murderous rage flared and strengthened the grip in his hands until he could have twisted off the head of a wooden cigar-store Indian. He barely restrained himself from screaming into her face while he destroyed her. Instead he whispered, counting on the fact that the hearing is the last thing to go. He told her to be sure and laugh with her friends about what she did to him, when they all got together in the Afterworld.

It was a crowning moment, limited only by the dismal fact that she faded in seconds. How he would have loved to sustain that bubble of time wherein she knew that her life was going and that he was the one taking it from her. Like a crystal snifter of rare cognac, he would swirl and sniff and quaff of her mortal terror, perhaps quietly reminding her of life's tiny moments of goodness and delight. Babies laughing, a spring rain, a lover's touch. He would make sure she was alert enough within her fear to fully appreciate that he was stealing all of it from her. Him. Shitty, old, piece of nothing him.

The distance from the exposition gate to the Fairmont Hotel was about three miles, but he was so filled with fire and chaos that he walked like an alpine hiker. In no time he found himself closing in on the opulent six-story stone building without straining himself at all. Electric floodlights had been installed around the outside of the hotel, illuminating the place like one of the exposition's displays.

He found a rare grotto of shadows within sight of the main entrance and hunkered down there. Fog was light and there was no rain. Experience gave him all due appreciation for that.

The nondescript man settled in to wait and observe. He knew that you learn things when you hang back and watch, sometimes things that you do not even realize you are seeking. For his lifelong curse of invisibility: to be unseen by women, unseen by potential male friends, unseen by the general public, unseen by a cursed, towel-dispensing attendant in a public toilet who seemed to intuitively understand that he would not be good for a tip—the tides were turned again. It would help him now to be such a painfully nondescript man as he knew himself to be, as he had been fated to be by cruel chance or by Divine Curse or by Satan's personally designed torment.

And so it was good to withdraw into his small patch of shadow. He felt lucky to have it. Nonilluminated places were disappearing in that city. He was already tired of the harsh glare of electrically lighted signs and powerful outdoor spotlights that had taken over within the last couple of years.

It would be just fine, he thought, when the exposition was finally over and San Francisco could peel off her wig and makeup, strip away her restrictive girdles, and go back to being a comfortable seaside lady with soft yellow gaslights that faded to nothing in the predawn fog.

There would be no need for the city to prove anything, then. People could finally stop using so much of that harsh electric light everyplace. It would be a long sigh of relief.

The only spotlight he wanted to see was the one fixed on his father's face while he answered for himself, while he explained his abandonment, while he bleated out a broken man's apology, while he realized that an apology was not enough, while he saw that his life was over, while he grasped that it was the nondescript son, the invisible one, back to settle his terrible score with the flashy father's inglorious end.

All he needed before leaving this painful life was the knowledge that his worthlessness did not mean that he had been powerless, too. He was not something that can be thrown away like table scraps.

The sense of power flashed through him. This was a big story for the newspapers. Even though most of it would die with the two of them, what remained would still be enough to cause a sensation.

He understood the publicity aspect of it clearly enough. How could he do otherwise? He had spent his invisible boyhood breathing in such talk along with his father's cigar smoke. Today, the newspaper stories to come out of this were so vivid in his mind that he could read them like actual newsprint.

He would speak to history, after all. John Wilkes Booth was just as famous as Abraham Lincoln, or close enough. And so when it came to the great James "J.D." Duncan, it was by the flashy father's absence that the nondescript son would be known.

CHAPTER TWENTY-FOUR

THE EXPOSITION HAD DRAWN a healthy crowd of visitors who appeared to have few concerns about the late hour, and Shane had no desire to get pulled aside for any friendly conversation. He kept his gaze on the floor while he moved across the hotel's grand lobby. But he kept his distance behind Duncan at no more than twenty feet or so, to avoid losing him among the milling guests.

He had wanted to walk out together, but in the showman's hugely fearful condition, he seemed convinced that someone could be trying to follow him. Shane was already realizing that he had made a mistake in telling J.D. about the strange customer in the restaurant who had stared so hard at him.

For his part, Shane felt equal mixtures of irritation and foolishness while they crossed the lobby. No one there showed any trace of potential for hostility, and despite Duncan's fame, nobody paid the slightest attention when he passed among them. A sense of celebration was sweeping the entire city, and these late-night guests were in the mood to stay out into the wee hours. Long-skirted ladies tittered while their derby-topped escorts swirled the air with fat cigars.

He finally made his way past most of them and trailed Duncan between the towering set of double columns that prevailed over both sides of the main door. Then they were out into the night. The

voices of the guests faded as soon as they were on the walkway leading out to the street. Duncan turned to the right and immediately
headed away from the hilltop. Shane casually followed, deliberately
looking off in another direction. As far as he could tell, nobody had
recognized the master mesmerist or shown any interest in him.

As soon as they passed the reach of the hotel's exterior lighting,
the rest of the area was dark enough, given the late hour and a typ-
ical fog bank. Shane was tired of the game already, but he dutifully
craned his neck in all directions. Not only was there nobody tag-
ging behind Duncan, there was nobody else visible out there at all.
The night revelers were all back up at the posh hotel; the dark
streets knew how late it was.

They were not completely out of sight of the hotel, though, so he
let Duncan pull even farther ahead, just to be certain that he
avoided making the frenzied man feel "crowded." He had no desire
for a repeat of the scene back in Duncan's fancy suite. They barely
got past the small talk while Shane waited for J.D. to get ready to
leave for the theatre to meet Randall.

It was clear that the moment was not going to get any more comfortable, so Shane went right ahead and related his memory of the
lone male customer, the one who had watched Duncan so closely
back at the restaurant. He only presented Duncan with the facts,
and had not gotten around to his conclusion. But with just that
much, Duncan's anxiety seemed to completely overtake him.

Shane felt a quick rush of guilt when he realized that he was
studying the man instead of helping him. The guilt was just strong
enough to cloud his judgment—he cooperated when Duncan suddenly demanded that they talk on the way to the theatre. The showman specified that they should get all the way outside the hotel,
away from any potential eavesdroppers, and that they must appear
to leave separately.

Shane only cooperated to remain on the showman's good side
long enough to check out his theory. But if the theory turned out to
be correct—even though he had to admit that it was based on noth-

ing more than Shane's cursed vision—it proved that Duncan had been covering up an important secret all along, one that explained his fears.

And he might not tell the truth about any of it.

Shane pretended to brush dust from his boots while he walked along, barely breaking stride, and managed to get a clear look behind and to both sides. There was not a soul in sight but Duncan himself, who suddenly spun around to face him. His eyes were wild, gazing out in all directions, as if he were searching for an avenue of escape.

Shane hurried down the hill toward him, but stopped a few yards away when Duncan whipped his arm out straight, holding up the flat of his palm.

"Halt! Shhh!" Duncan's face became a mask of concentration. "Did you hear that?"

"What?"

"Shhh!"

Shane stepped close and whispered. "What?"

"Out there. It's the buildings—sounds echo off the buildings. You hear it? Try to tell where a bouncing sound first starts, I don't know, it's more than I can do. The echoes are what keep tripping me up; otherwise I could point right at it."

"Good. Point at what?"

At that, Duncan turned to him, heavy-lidded with disdain. He spoke slowly.

"Point. At. The. Source. Of. The. Footsteps."

Shane had never heard more sarcasm squeezed into fewer words.

"The only footsteps I have heard are ours, Mr. Duncan."

"Shhh!" Duncan jumped up into a fighting stance, gasping with intense emotion, eyes wide, nostrils flared. He held the flat of both hands out at the sides of his ears, straining his hearing to the limit. "That! *That* is precisely what I am talking about, Mr. Nightingale. *That! That! That!*"

"Mr. Duncan, do you hear me, sir?" But Duncan was on the

move again. Shane stepped up the pace and easily fell in alongside of him.

"Look, Mr. Duncan, tell me what's going on. It's safe for you to speak."

"If that were true, we would not be out here."

"I've been checking ever since we left your room, Mr. Duncan, and I'm telling you, I really don't think that anybody is following."

"Did you not just hear—"

"No, sir! No. I don't hear a thing out here except for us, and I don't see a soul out here except for you and me. And I have to tell you, sir—"

"Shhh!" Duncan spun around, hands cupped to both ears, straining.

Shane felt a cold spike of dread when he realized the intensity of Duncan's fear. The man's sense of alert watchfulness was like nothing he had ever seen.

Shane stepped close to him and placed his arm around the man's shoulder. Duncan recoiled at the touch; all the muscles of his upper body were tensed as hard as iron. His focus remained fixed out in space, staring, straining to hear.

"Mr. Duncan, listen to me. Please try to listen." He had no idea if anything was coming across to him or not.

"You can't," J.D. muttered, still far away.

"I what?"

"Can't see him. Never see him. Maybe, maybe he isn't even real. I mean, he's real, all right, but not the kind of real that you can see, that's all."

J.D.'s gaze darted from shadow to shadow, ready to spy out an intruder at any turn. Shane sighed and shook his head. Could Duncan's abiding fear be the product of something so prosaic as a derelict father and an illegitimate son?

It made no sense. Duncan behaved like a man who believes he is being stalked by a demon, a fearsome thing dispatched to come for him and pull him down to Hell.

Shane remembered peering through the tiny slit between the top of the pantry door and the doorframe inside the Nightingale house. One thin split of vision was granted out into the kitchen, where the killer was working himself into a frenzy of murder that resembled nothing so much as a prolonged and hugely violent sexual climax. He held nothing back from his madness, and Shane had been forced to marinate in it for thirty-six hours without moving from the tiny space. The hiding place was only feet and sometimes inches away from the Nightingale family women while they ended their earthly existences in mindless pain and horror.

It was forces like that that called for the sort of dread that Duncan displayed. Not some unwanted son who turns up out of a dust storm. Even if the kid landed on Duncan's doorstep with his hand already out for contributions, that would hardly be the glimpse into Hell that Duncan's mannerisms implied.

Shane reached out with both hands and firmly took him by his tensed shoulders. He concentrated on getting through to him.

"I'd bet anything that he is your son, Mr. Duncan. Now, that in itself is none of my business. But sir, if he is the cause of the threat that you have been feeling, and feeling so strongly that you arranged for a police guard, then we have to talk this out."

Shane watched Duncan's eyes shift to meet his. They looked as if they were boiling under the surface. He thought that Duncan might be feeling a thin connection to him, but there was no way to be certain of it.

"Tell me, Mr. Duncan—that you haven't gotten yourself this worked up over having a son outside of marriage? Sir, in today's society, that's not necessarily—"

"Shhh!" Duncan clapped one hand over Shane's mouth and spun in a full circle, pulling Shane around with him until he realized what he was doing and let go. Shane yanked himself backward, gasping in surprise.

"Glass!" Duncan continued. "Did you hear it? I did. It's the elixir! Sharpens hearing! But it was glass, no doubt. A big piece, a long shard being picked up off the ground, maybe a piece of a broken window. You know that sound, eh? Like a broadsword slowly pulled from the scabbard. Faint, yes! So faint! But I heard it, plus I heard the first three echoes, plus I felt the next four that were too faint to hear. There's the elixir for you! Ha!"

"Mr. Duncan, that's it, now. I didn't hear any glass and I have not seen any long-lost sons."

Something triggered Duncan with the reference to long-lost sons. He turned to Shane. He could not speak or meet Shane's eyes, so he looked over his shoulder instead.

"Mr. Duncan, the man I saw is fully grown. Whatever kind of a life that he has, it's his own. He doesn't have to move into your life in any way that's harmful to you."

"I can't escape him. I was never going to be able to escape him. I only hoped that someone could slow him down long enough to give me time to finish my work." He gasped, as if something surprised him.

Still focusing over Shane's shoulder, he added, barely audible, "You can't escape him."

"I don't need to escape him, sir. Neither do you."

"It's too late for me."

With that, Duncan finally met Shane's gaze straight on. He spoke with a quiver in his voice that was so powerful, Shane could hardly understand him.

"And now you can't escape him, either."

A strong male arm whipped around Shane's face from behind while a knee slammed into his backbone with such force that it numbed his legs and turned them to rubber. The forceful grip tilted his face backward while the man's other arm slapped the edge of a long shard of glass up under Shane's chin. The man moved with such force that for an instant, it seemed a sure thing that the attacker was about to sever his neck.

CHAPTER TWENTY-FIVE

RANDALL BLACKBURN SAT BACKSTAGE, next to the huge and dish-shaped cyclorama at the back wall. He used the near-total darkness to help him think. There were a few faint sources of light bleeding into the theatre, but they were not enough to illuminate anything. They only defined the size of the darkened space as faint reference points. The purpose of the cyclorama's surface was to reflect sounds or light back toward the house, and it worked so well that an actor could whisper on center stage and be heard in the theatre's back row. In reverse, the concave surface acted like a giant ear, gathering tiny sounds and concentrating them. From Blackburn's position, the wall was an extension of his own ears, to the point that he clearly heard the building's ongoing language of creaks and pops. Darkness enhanced his imagination until he visualized the settling of badly reinforced walls and leaky steam pipes.

Don't kill me! cried the theatre voices, like the panicky whine of an aging actress.

He lit a wooden match and studied the flame.

Then he pulled out his pocket watch with his free hand and saw that seven minutes had passed since the last check: ten minutes after midnight. He blew out the match.

He had six more, all of them his favorite: the new red sulfur and white phosphorous tipped "strike-anywhere" matches. Miraculous little things. He kept them in a small silver match safe that fit the palm of his hand. Closed, it was watertight. The pure silver box was rounded at the edges and quickly warmed to the touch. He usually felt better when he carried it.

Tonight the matchbox brought him back to his orders, and the orders were clear: *Wait until after midnight, when everything is quiet. Then light it up. Let it burn 'til the place is done for. Run to the corner phone box. Call it in. If anybody gets to you before you get out of there, tell them you couldn't sleep, you went for a long walk, and thank God, you came by when you did—the neighborhood was saved. When it's time for the papers to interview you, smile and enjoy being a hero.*

His trusty little Ford would be back at the station house by the time he got there, none the worse. And as of the very next day, why, he could forget all about the ridiculous babysitting assignment to that theatre showman.

One match is all it takes, he thought. Maybe two. Set flame to a couple of good spots at once. The city government knew, and this was what they wanted. The insurance company knew, and this was what they wanted, too.

The owners were making themselves scarce, but were unlikely to object to the financial windfall that the insurers planned to shower upon them. Everybody was going to walk away fat and happy and in no mood to complain.

After all, the risk of humiliation that this place presented was apparent to him. The grand theatre was a disastrous creation of gorgeously bad work.

The plan was so simple. Blackburn noticed, however, that he had not yet started any fires. He was now ten minutes into the "go" period that began at midnight. But instead of lighting anything, what he did was sit in the darkness next to the giant ear, listening to the softly chattering architecture.

A sense of pure disgust balled up inside of him. It set off familiar words.

This is what they think of you.

Nineteen years, he had survived and endured the politics of the department, through an era of brazen corruption. A long string of arrests and solved cases were already under his belt, even before he met Shane. Afterward, he stood out even further because of having Shane's occasional help in looking at a crime's human puzzle.

And this is what they think of you.

After all these years, he still had no idea what had happened to Shane that had turned him into the fragile, hesitant, stammering boy he first met. Blackburn always came up against a granite wall with Shane when he tried to steer the conversation toward that question. Whatever the cause, it somehow left his adopted son with an almost supernatural insight into the darkest aspect of human nature.

But Shane's difficulties at forming any sort of social life with people his own age revealed that the mysterious experience had not left him with any special insights into the joys and the celebrations and the compassions in human nature. With those, Shane struggled along like any other young man.

Somebody—or some series of events—seemed to have taught Shane Nightingale all about the aspect of the Devil that was found in human nature. It had taken Blackburn a generation of time served in the human swamp to come to a similar understanding. What could have brought such a thing to a boy?

But even on top of all the extra help that had flowed to the department because of Shane, this was still what the department brass thought of Randall Blackburn.

He lit the first of the six matches.

The flare of light shrank his vision down to an orange glow no larger than the reach of his arms. He wondered if the people giving these orders had completely abandoned any notion of civic responsibility. It seemed for all the world that they had turned criminal themselves, and that they were ordering him to do their criminal work for them.

This is what they think of you.

And then there was the Big Question, the one nobody wanted to go near during their briefing session. In fact, their interest seemed to ricochet right off the topic at the moment he mentioned it. Nobody was interested but him.

What if an innocent bystander gets caught in it?

Was it any less a crime? There was an ironclad certainty that these upstanding fellows would abandon him in the wake of such a thing, and he realized that under the circumstances, it would be the right thing to do.

The match went out. Without hesitating, he flipped open the lid of the little match safe and took out a second one. He struck it along the sole of his boot and watched the satisfying flare. Ingeniously manufactured in an old munitions factory in upstate New York, the red phosphorous tip was thick enough to spark against any rough surface, and the white phosphorous head would then ignite and flare in anything less than a tropical downpour. Its three-inch wooden shaft was made of New England hardwood that burned in a slow and steady flame. The warm ball of light that it put out was good for twenty seconds, in still air. The match produced a moment of luxury that he could still afford, now with four matches left.

The canvas scenic flats leaned against the wall nearby, crying out for ignition. He had checked behind them earlier and discovered the buckets of paint thinner, ready to kick over. His bosses had thought of everything. The task had been accommodated as well as anyone could desire. He thought about how much he would have liked that sort of support back when he was pulling drunks and crazies and rampaging killers off the Barbary Coast and away from the public. The message about civic priorities only added to the night's grim picture.

The second match burned out.

He had already lit the third one before he stopped to wonder if that was actually a good idea. Then there was nothing to do but enjoy the fleeting moment. At least, he thought, he was still innocent. He had not done anything wrong yet. He was no criminal by anyone's definition.

In this fading bit of light, he still looked out at his world through the eyes of an honest man. During all his years as a beat-walking sergeant, doing street work so violent that he routinely lied to his own parents to conceal its dangers, he had never doubted that he was on the right side. He had grown up in an honest and hardworking household, and knew for a fact that such values were real and worth defending, even in the worst parts of a city. And because he had loving parents, he also knew that a loving household was a possible achievement. He knew from his experience at home that the key was to keep mutual respect within moments of anger.

Therefore he knew that there was a very real society of good and loving people out there who were deserving of protection. Their civilized and humane ways needed to be passed along as intact as possible.

Somebody had to help see to it. If not him, then someone else. And because his greater size and strength meant that he was almost always the most persuasive individual in any crowd, who else but him? He had always held to that. For all his flaws as a social animal, he held to it throughout his career.

And this is what they think of you.

The third match burned out. He was back in the familiar darkness of the big empty space.

He struck the fourth match. That left him with two good ones. Two was still enough to do the job, he figured, if he lit things carefully enough. He used the match light to move his straight-backed chair to the center of the stage, right down at the front edge. Here he was directly in the path of the cyclorama's focused sound. It functioned like a stethoscope; he could almost hear the building breathing, sighing, grumbling under its breath, trying to settle a bit more comfortably into its foundation.

It had already been pronounced a dying thing. The bastards were right about part of it; the whole place had to go. It had to go right now, before one more audience gathered inside it. San Francisco's prestige theatrical destination was booked with one kind of activity or another on most days of the year: weddings, revivals, traveling shows. But now he knew for a fact that the place had the integrity of a tired whore servicing an oversized army. All in all, it just needed to fall down and lie still.

What the hell. He could expend the last two matches in the course of less than sixty seconds and have the Pacific Majestic on its way to extinction before the next minute ticked on his pocket watch. He would read it by the light of the flames.

Timing was everything here. He had to gauge how long to let the place burn inside to guarantee that the place would be a lost cause, while still giving the department time to keep it away from the surrounding buildings. As for the timing, he could only guess. If he was wrong, if somebody was out there, working late, cleaning up, or curled in a back corner and sleeping one off—that was just a bad hand, yes?

He tried to remember the last time he saw somebody survive a major fire. It was rare, but it happened. The killer was the smoke. People who did manage to survive were always the ones who got out ahead of the smoke and fumes. The rest were dead before the flames ever touched them.

What if somebody gets caught up in it?

But the question was a piece of philosophy. The flat truth was that he had never possessed interest in much of anything other than being a detective.

He had no idea how to do anything else, had never even given it a serious thought, and now he was only one year away from a pension. He opened the little silver match safe with the last two matches. He pulled one out. For a while, he sat quiet and unmoving, with the match held between his thumb and forefinger.

⫶ CHAPTER TWENTY-SIX ⫶

IMMINENT DEATH CONCENTRATES THE MIND.

J.D. knew that the phenomenon was widely recognized, described in detail by those who had faced certain demise and somehow lived to tell about it. But until this very moment in his considerable life span, he had only known those words for the truth that they *seemed* to express. Their profundity did not register with him until the moment that his monster of a bastard son materialized out of the shadows.

The effect of seeing him could have easily triggered J.D.'s memory holes again. The godawful memory holes. And the shock of seeing a younger, stronger, faster, and many times crazier version of himself might have been enough to stop J.D.'s heart with the sheer power of the confrontation.

But just at that moment, none of those things were chemically possible. His unintentional overproduction of stomach acid matched his blast of mortal fear, and had quickly caused the very last of the wax coatings to dissolve, so that all six doses of methylenedioxymethamphetamine passed into his system at more or less the same time. His heart could not have stopped beating if he ripped it out and jumped on it.

An instant after the beginning of the attack, J.D. found that it completely altered time for him. He was able to slow down events to a syrupy pace, just by closing in on individual moments. It was as if he suddenly had the power to rush up very close to something or someone, and the closer he got, the slower everything moved.

If he mentally backed up, then things seemed to go by faster. A wave of primitive pleasure rushed through him from the bottom of his spine to the base of his skull, but the sensation was gone as quickly as it came. The evaporated euphoria left his point of view stripped raw, and because the imminence of death concentrated his mind so well, J.D. finally realized that in the material world of hard sidewalks and cold concrete walls, young Shane Nightingale was about to be killed by J.D.'s monster of a son.

He mentally moved closer to the picture of Nightingale being jerked backward under the effect of the sneak attack, and saw that a glass shard the size of a meat cleaver was poised to hack into Nightingale's throat.

The young man's legs had gone limp under the force of the blow to his spine, and now he sagged toward the ground, barely prevented from falling by the pressure of the glass blade on his neck. J.D. glanced at Nightingale's eyes and felt a hint of relief that he was still conscious; the kid would be no good to either of them if he went out.

He was about to think up a quick plan of action and begin the process of diverting their assailant's attention, when the first serious concentration of the elixir struck his brain, firing up every remaining receptor and kicking him like a draft horse.

He quickly sank into a deep and compelling hypnotic state. It happened on its own, propelled by the elixir.

Everything was suddenly effortless. He felt a vague sense of victory over whatever it was that was happening, because he knew that it was something that would ordinarily demand his attention. But instead, he was slipping away from the situation like water through a man's fingers. It was such a relief to be shed of whatever it was that had frightened him so badly back there.

He followed them, not much more than an arm's length or so away from the crumbled-legged young police fellow, who was being pulled backward at a surprisingly brisk pace by the younger man, who reminded J.D. a little of himself as a young man, and who had the angriest look on his face that J.D. had ever seen.

The elixir had closed down his ability to feel fear. It was the greatest moment of his long life. The sheer power of the massive dose destroyed his ability to remember much of anything, including his troubles and fears. It was wonderful, freeing, liberating beyond anything he had ever known. What did he need with memories? The pleasure they provided never matched the pain that they conveyed, anyway—eh?

Come and get me, you sons of bitches! He almost sang it out loud. He knew just enough to realize that he was supposed to care, really care about whatever it was that was going on in front of him. This time, the fact that he could not remember just what it was seemed so funny that for a passing second he nearly laughed in delight.

He felt only a passing interest when he noted that they had arrived at the Pacific Majestic Theatre. The theatre marquee cast a thick black shadow over the entranceway.

The door was unlocked and swung open to the touch. This seemed to cause the angry man concern. He tried to pepper J.D. with questions about the unlocked door, but J.D. only knew enough to realize that none of this crap had anything to do with him.

Their assailant struck a match and made them go inside, across the foyer and into the darkened house. J.D.'s senses were more stimulated than they had ever been before. It seemed that he was hearing sounds from blocks away, seeing deeper into the darkness than he ever had. Even his sense of smell felt many times more powerful than it would normally be. He detected a trace of smoke drifting through the theatre.

The basic function of smell easily captured his attention. He rode his nose down the darkened center aisle, carried along by his fascination over the origin of the smoke. There was not enough of a burned scent to the air to alert the others, yet, but J.D. could tell that they were moving toward the source of the smoke while they pushed deeper into the empty building.

The young man with the bleeding neck seemed to have calmed down and decided to play along, which J.D. admired. Thus the odd trio moved on down the center aisle, headed for the stage.

CHAPTER TWENTY-SEVEN

IMMEDIATELY FOLLOWING
ON THE DARKENED STREETS
OF SAN FRANCISCO

VIGNETTE WALKED SO FAST that she figured she would cover the distance in less than twenty minutes—all the way from the exposition's main gate, where she had just given her statement to the officer in command of the scene, to the City Hall Station, more than two miles away.

She was thankful that the officer had no idea that he was interviewing the young woman who had just penetrated the all-male police training school and kept up with the boys. The wig helped to protect her. Men see your hair and your tits. No doubt he would have seized upon the opportunity to make an example of her.

Fortunately, he seemed to be in a hurry to go off and deal with the crime scene itself rather than stay and talk to her. It never seemed to cross his mind to suspect a young lady like herself. She was the essence of respectability in her Gibson Girl disguise, a loyal civic volunteer who coddles and entertains the city's much-needed visitors. Truly, a good girl.

She was gone from there in a matter of minutes. The main gate's office was opened up for her while the guards used the telephone to call for a body wagon and to notify the precinct captain of this most inopportune crime. Vignette was amazed to see that just as she was walking away, two officers bearing a stretcher with a completely covered body emerged from the grounds. They carried it to a waiting flat wagon.

They're moving her already?

She decided it must be because this thing happened right on the exposition grounds, and so they were dealing with it at top speed. She was permitted to use the main gate's telephone to attempt her call, so she took out the slip of paper on which Randall had written out his "telephone exchange number." The term itself gave her a feel of nails across a blackboard. It was the occasion of her very first telephone call.

She got no answer—which perfectly summed up Vignette's opinion of telephones, right there. Here, she finally had a reason to call this contraption that was only in their house because it was so important that Randall be available for emergencies—and there was no answer. The whole idea of being able to reach him broke down, anytime he was not standing around waiting for the damned thing to start ringing.

Yet she could not deny the wonderful feeling of relief. She had made a fair attempt to reach him using the new technology, but been spared actually having to present him with the terrible news.

She had made the call in a trance of shock, with no real idea of what to tell Randall if he actually picked up his end of the thing. For all her terrible thoughts and dark wishes against the Eastern . . . against Miss Freshell, she knew that this idea of marriage was a big thing to him. The poor guy actually thought that this woman cared about making his life better.

Like any man, he was so busy trying to conquer the illusion that Miss Freshell set up for him that he never realized how she was maneuvering him into situations, putting him in harm's way. And it was all for a story, a book, and for whatever it was that she thought would come from that. It seemed clear to Vignette that the woman would have thrown Randall away, married or not, once she was done with him. But now she had gone and gotten herself tragically killed, and Randall's fancy illusion of romantic love was about to be cut to pieces before the truth of it revealed itself to him, as it would have eventually done. His image of her was now frozen in time, and he was about to suffer the loss of something far more precious than the real Janine Freshell. The fact that the one he was actually losing existed only in his imagination would do nothing to assuage the pain.

Vignette could feel nothing over Miss Freshell's death, other than the horror of the murder itself. And she knew that Randall would try to swallow the shock and the pain, try to be stoic. That, she thought, would be like walking on broken legs.

And so she at least had to be the one to reach him with this. There was nothing she could do to soften the news itself, but she could at least be there. It was unbearable to think of him suffering through it alone.

She paused at a street corner to let a horse-drawn milk wagon trundle past. A man also stood at the curb waiting, a few feet away, and he took the opportunity to smile at her. She gave him a curt smile in return, but just before she turned away again, he ogled her from head to toe and back up. Then he looked right back into her eyes and smiled again.

She did not say a word, but simply radiated her contempt. The fool receded into the shadows. Vignette kept going at a ground-covering stride.

Where was Shane? It would be better for him to be there with her when she told Randall. But he either was not home or he also planned to avoid answering the telephone. It only reaffirmed her distaste for the entire telephone system. Here they were in the Age of Miracles and she was back to *moving things around* by using nothing more than her feet.

The most likely place to find Randall, or at least to hear some news about where he was, would be the City Hall Station. Vignette pressed her walking pace until she was moving as fast as her clutched skirt and heeled boots would allow. There was enough cash in her pocket for a taxi, but she welcomed a chance to burn off the jitters that were overpowering her. She could hotfoot it down the wide sidewalks as fast as a taxi moved on the chaotic streets, anyway.

It was about five more minutes to the station house, she figured. But then what would she say to Randall? Dread caused a wave of nausea to nearly topple her. She paused and held on to the top of a metal fence, gasping for air. There was an image pasted across the front of her imagination, a picture of Randall being struck by this news.

If she revealed to him a few of the choice things that Miss Freshell told her, she might be able to stop him from pining away for her. But it would still do nothing to soften his grief. It would simply convert it from the shock of losing her into the grief of discovering that her love had been a concerted illusion.

She could feel worry carving itself into her muscle and her skin while she strode down Van Ness Avenue and neared the City Hall Station. In the course of that short distance she had already resolved one simple thing about this disaster of a night: She could never tell Randall the truth about, to hell with it, the Eastern Whore. It was too ugly.

She had to be the one to do this. Even if she found Shane beforehand, she could never throw the chore onto him. If he tried to break the news, he was likely to get rattled and start to stutter. In the meantime, Randall would be left sitting there with the suspense killing him. How in the hell could she put her boys through that?

No, she had to do it—which immediately confronted her with the question of exactly what *was* the best way to stab Randall Blackburn in the heart? The question swirled around her like bloody water circling a drain.

CHAPTER TWENTY-EIGHT

FROM THE MOMENT Shane felt the glass blade pressed into his skin, already cutting him, he was back inside his little converted sleeping space in the kitchen pantry. Once again he was a skinny twelve-year-old, frozen in abject terror while the monster outside the wooden pantry doors spent a day and a half killing his adoptive mother and two adoptive sisters. Every cell in his body sensed on some primal level that he possessed no strengths, no knowledge, no skills whatsoever to respond. He knew in his bones that he was helpless.

He felt himself pulled under a large, shaded area covered by an outdoor roof. When he glanced upward, he saw that they were under the marquee of the Pacific Majestic Theatre.

It was here that his sense of time and place began to return. That left him staring into the face of his attacker, who had spun him around to face him. Shane saw in that instant that he had been right about the man. It was the lone customer from the restaurant.

"Why's this place unlocked?" their attacker demanded in a whisper, hissing like a snake. "You two left it that way, didn't you? Out for a walk during a late rehearsal or something?"

Shane tried to answer him, but his lips felt as if they were asleep, tingling and numb, uncontrollable. So he responded by shaking his head, hating himself for not feeling any bravery at all. The paralyzing fear was all too familiar.

The attacker poked the glass blade at Duncan a few times, trying to get his attention. But by now, Duncan appeared to have no idea what was going on. He was off somewhere in a world nobody else could know.

Shane noticed that when he looked back and forth from the attacker to Duncan, there was more than a little similarity. The attacker looked for all the world like a younger version of Duncan. Maybe thirty, thirty-five years. Same large frame and naturally muscular mass. An impressive-looking individual.

The attacker had removed the blade from his throat, leaving only a shallow cut so far, and the sense of paralyzing fear finally began to leave him. He felt a flash of prayerful thanks that his pants were still dry.

Strength poured back into his muscles. It felt wonderful to feel his legs stabilize and to sense their power returning. The impression of being a little boy dissipated. In its place rose up the happy realization that this time, while he was not as strong as the attacker, Shane was almost certainly the smarter of the two. For the first time since the assault began, he felt a spark of hope.

The man had lifted a battery-powered electric torch from an usher's station and turned it on. Its beam was narrow, but strong enough to light their way along the floor.

They were near the bottom of the aisle at the foot of the stage when Duncan stopped, stiff as a pole, fully alert. He cocked his ears and stared hard into the darkness.

"What's that?" the showman murmured. "Did you see it? Who's out there?" he softly called.

Their tormentor ignored it and resumed driving them up onto the stage by jabbing the air with the blade and repeating, "Move, move, move!" Otherwise, he was telling them nothing.

Shane's eyes began adjusting to the faint ambient light coming through the upper draft windows; pitch black thinned to a translucent gray. He could see well enough to tell that the theatre was empty, but for them.

Duncan jumped again. "There!" He cupped his hand to his ear. "Someone's moving. You hear that?"

"That's good, Boss!" the attacker grinned. "You're starting to wake up! Here he is, ladies and gentlemen!"

Duncan did not react to him at all. He just kept staring into the darkness, straining to hear.

"Enough of that now!" the younger man bellowed. His voice took on a load of venom. "You haven't said hello to me, Boss." He turned to Shane with a sour grin and added, "I call him Boss around the theatre." He threw in a little wink, then turned back to Duncan.

"In fact, you haven't even looked at me, J.D. That's hardly common courtesy, is it?"

"Do you ever just call him 'Dad'?" Shane quietly asked.

The attacker stopped in his tracks. He spun to him, swinging the light onto his face. Shane winced when the narrow beam caught him straight on and flashed on the back of his eyes. He raised a flattened hand to his eyebrows.

"A *noticer*!"

The attacker turned to address the empty seats. "We got ourselves a *noticer*, ladies and gentlemen! What are the chances of that, in such a small group? This theatre only holds a thousand or so."

"Why wouldn't I notice you?"

It took the man a moment to register the question. "Why?" He lifted his arms. "Look!"

"What?"

"What do you mean, what? Look at me! I'm unnoticeable!" His face forced a dry sneer. "Or hadn't you noticed?"

"Actually, I think that you look sort of like a younger version of him," Shane replied, pointing to Duncan, the shadow watcher.

The attacker stared at Shane the way he would at a talking horse. He did not appear to know how to reply.

Shane advanced the conversation for him. "He never mentioned having a son."

The son whirled on him and shouted, "Stuff that! You stuff that right back down!"

"How long has it been since you've seen each other?"

"I said stuff it! You don't know what you're talking about!"

"I think that this is your father, standing here. It's a natural question to wonder when you last saw each other."

Now the son stood quiet for moment, studying him through a suspicious squint. When he finally spoke up, he sounded, for the first time, like a rational man.

"Who the hell are you?"

Shane made a conscious effort to keep his voice full and strong. "My name is Shane Nightingale."

"All right, Mr. Nightingale, what do you do?"

"I wait on tables at The Sea Mist restaurant down the street."

The son burst out laughing. "Well, J.D. always did like to hobnob with the big shots!"

He turned to J.D. with a sneer. "Maybe you should be the one to tell Mr. Nightingale why I don't call you 'Daddy.' Eh, Boss?"

J.D. gave no indication of hearing anything they said. He remained fixed in the shadows, wide-eyed, muttering under his breath while he studied the darkness. "Gone now. Whoever it was."

Shane wondered what would beguile the man's attention away into darkened corners, with the immediate threat just a few feet from him. The son had the same relentless stare that Shane had been forced to learn so well in the Nightingale house, to the point that all these years hence, he could not help seeing all of the various levels of that same energy. He found it in most every set of eyes that he had looked into, since that day. In the nine years since the Nightingale murders, he had absorbed the habit of meeting people's eyes for a moment upon greeting them, but then keeping his gaze on neutral things as much as possible after that. It was his primary social handicap.

Now, a single glance into the son's eyes was enough to justify despair. Whatever was on his mind had murder at its core. The quality of his energy could not lead anywhere else.

And at that moment, the details of this man's objections no longer made any difference at all. The story would be revealed, or it would not, and it would have a cause, as all things do. None of that helped him with the maniac in front of him.

The unhappy son poked at them and gestured toward the stage. When Duncan did not respond, his son shoved him into motion. Shane joined in. They would be up on the stage in twenty seconds, but Shane saw no rational reason for going up there at all. It made no difference what purpose their captor thought he had in mind for them. By now Shane had regained as much of his strength as he was going to get back, under the circumstances. He was slowly losing blood.

His adrenaline-soaked senses caught the faintest tinge of wood smoke. It was familiar enough, in an age not yet electrified. Distinct from the oily odor of lamp smoke, the bitter dust of coal heat, or the acrid smell of electrical fire—none of these were in the aroma. He was glad for that much; any of them was a sure sign of disaster.

Wood smoke: The trace smell reminded him of wooden matches. Such a distinct scent could hang in the air for half an hour. It did not necessarily mean trouble, but there was the question of its origin.

And so the time picked him. Shane slowed his pace to a shuffle, turned to Duncan, and went to work. He pretended to be speaking to the showman, but when he shouted at the top of his voice, using every ounce of his vocal power, the intent of every word was aimed at the big man with the glass sword.

"My father didn't even bother to kill me! He just rubbed me out of his life! He walked away like a mongrel walks away from its own puke."

That put the brakes on. Their assailant stopped along with Shane, while Duncan stopped with the lack of momentum. And initially, at least, the younger version of Duncan did not protest. His attention was not engaged, yet, but his expression showed annoyed impatience. That meant that a door was open, no matter how small, or for how brief a time. If Shane could sink a hook into the opening before it slammed shut again, he could possibly drive the man to an hysterical explosion—one in which his own emotions might provide enough distraction to create an opportunity to finish him off.

He pressed on, without giving the brief flicker of interest a chance to fade from the attacker's eyes.

"He wasn't just famous!" Shane shouted to Duncan while watching Duncan's twisted progeny from the corner of his eye. "The man had to *feel* famous! He had to be the biggest news in the room, no matter what, no matter where!"

He felt it more than saw it; a slight wave of confused disinterest passed over the son—that shot had missed. Shane tried again, throwing one out that could catch his opponent on either the literal or symbolic level.

"He never even knew I was alive! And the day he finally saw that I was alive, was the day he decided to *wipe me out*!"

Shane saw the brief facial spasm that flashed across their assailant's face. Bull's-eye.

"Why don't you tell me something I don't already know?" he snarled at Shane, even while his eyes shifted to Duncan. For an instant, Shane disappointed himself by dropping his concentration long enough to notice that the smell of smoke was getting stronger.

One thing at a time, the words went through him, just the way Randall always said it. He threw his focus back onto their unstable host.

"He made you the garbage bucket!" Shane hollered back, and

this time it was directly to him, ignoring Duncan. "He soaked up everything good and left you with nothing but the dregs."

No reaction.

"He's only your father the way a dog in the alley is a father!"

That one set off a little spark of the son's interest. Shane drilled into it, taking a risk with facts.

"He never even gave you his *name,* for God's sake!" That one hit the son like a spike. Shane caught an involuntarily swallow.

A bastard, then, with the expected load of a bastard's resentment. He noted the younger Duncan's terrible teeth, his mottled skin, his yellowish, rheumy eyes. There was a range of sore points to explore.

"You grew up on your own, from when you were small. On the street. You didn't know anything about a showman named James Duncan."

"J.D.!" the son corrected him, with a strange grin popping onto his face. "You have to call him 'J.D.'! Very important!" He gave up a malevolent chuckle.

"Unless you call him 'Boss,' " the son went on. "He doesn't mind that one at all." Just as abruptly, he dropped the grin and raised the glass edge. "Now keep moving. We've got a show to attend."

The attacker was only a few inches taller than Shane, and a good sixty pounds heavier. He stank of criminal intent: the sour smell of fear, the animal musk of unwashed skin, rotting teeth, and mouth blowing death breath for two yards in every direction. His body appeared to have been street-hardened into a piece of walking pig iron. One glance was enough to convince Shane that a direct attack would leave him badly the worse.

He had to hold silent for a moment and let J.D.'s progeny feel his power, here. Feed him an easy win. Watch for any sign that it might cause him to lower his guard.

After all, something had been gained already. The emotion in the younger Duncan's reply had hinted of some good pay dirt.

Shane was getting closer. It was like navigating blind, following a smell. And with the thought of smell, there was the smell of smoke, back again, tapping at his attention a bit harder now.

There was too much of it not to notice, but not enough to see. Shane had no idea whether it figured into young Duncan's plan, but the bastard son appeared to be completely unaware of the unmistakable tinge to the air.

Shane hoped that this meant he was severely distracted by whatever roiled his mind at that moment. Shane could look for a way to use that to his advantage.

Now he could feel that he would be able to shove his fear far enough down inside of himself to put forth a convincing façade of confidence. The illusion was all he needed; Shane's twenty-one years of life had already been enough to convince him that all bullies were cowards. Therefore, he did not need to die fighting this one; he only needed to convince him that he was quite *willing* to die—so long as Sonny Boy died with him.

When a bully realizes that you are actually prepared to die fighting him, he can be counted on to fill his pants, scream random accusations of unfairness, and vacate the premises. Randall had often claimed, laughing, that half his ability to survive years of walking a rough beat lay in that sole piece of knowledge.

The thought of Shane's adoptive father flushed enough guilt through him to push away the rest of his fear. The effect was immediate. Anger rushed in to fill the void. He could almost feel himself stepping out of the huddled little body back in that kitchen pantry, facing the attacker today on far better terms.

They were up on the stage by then, the three of them, front and center. Shane did not know that he was smack in the middle of the focal point of the giant bowl-shaped cyclorama on the back wall. But he noticed that he could clearly hear the breathing of both the other men. His own breathing suddenly seemed abnormally loud and clear. It was a sensation he had never experienced before, and it only added to the aura of unreality that hovered over everything.

And then there was the smoke itself. Things were still spiraling out of control. He had to go back to work now, whether Sonny was ready to play or not. "Hey!" he shouted. "Am I the only one who smells smoke in here?"

In response, the bastard stepped directly to him and swung his thick right arm in an overhead hammer blow that exploded against the right side of Shane's head. He felt something hit him hard on both of his knees, and then vaguely realized that he had just rammed them into the floor in the process of falling. Instinct twisted his torso to the left, away from the direction of impact, just enough so that the left side of his body, shoulder, and arm took most of the force of the fall before his head banged on the ground.

The shock wave blasted through him so hard that he immediately forgot where he was and lost track of his senses. His vision crumbled into flashes of light and shadow. The insistent ringing in his head drowned out everything else, even the well-focused sounds from the cyclorama.

Half-baked orders from his brain caused his muscles to raise his arms in self-defense, strike back with his fists, kick with his feet, and run away, all at the same time. The result was that he lay twitching on the floor, half conscious. A tiny part of him was aware of the sound of hysterical laughter. He was clear enough to realize that his attacker was enjoying Shane's convulsions and savoring his victory. There was no way to fight back. His brain was caught in a lightning storm and his spasmodic limbs were otherwise engaged.

CHAPTER TWENTY-NINE

J.D.'S FIRST CLEAR CLUE was the smell of smoke. His second was the sudden and sharp awareness that the smoke was coming up from the floor beneath him. His third was the realization that he and Shane Nightingale were in the midst of a pointless and fully preventable confrontation that he would have already concluded by now, if he had been playing with anything more than half of a deck before this moment.

This moment! What just happened?

Like electrical lights that suddenly flare up to illumination, full awareness returned to James "J.D." Duncan, Master Mesmerist. It arrived without warning, and it was exactly as Dr. Alzheimer had cautioned him: a sudden reappearance of his full, true, and sterling self. It could not have been more of a shock if he had looked into a mirror and seen his own young face.

He knew, with clear recall of the doctor's words, tone of voice, facial expressions, and the small gravy stain smeared on the man's lab coat, that the effect was temporary. It was rare, utterly mysterious, and seemed to have no other purpose than to taunt the victim with all the differences between their normal selves and the impaired imitations of themselves that they had become.

In that brightly shining moment, J.D. saw with complete acuity that this nightmare of a disease had been pulling him deep into its grip for some time. It was only now that he could comprehend the difference. He could not imagine a better gift. He leaped at the chance to drink as deeply as possible of his magically restored ability to perceive and comprehend.

Since there was no way to know how long it would last, he knew that there were actions to be taken, and they had to happen soon. If not, what sort of evil would the bastard have committed by the time J.D. spontaneously got his clarity back again?

If he ever did.

He took a deep breath, making it a point not to reveal that he realized the deranged unfortunate in front of him was his own monstrous creation. J.D. would no longer give even a tiny gesture of affirmation to that destroyer of helpless women. What could his mother have ever done to him, if she caused his madness? And if she had not, how many insufferable and useless nights had she paced the floor over this abomination before he finally ran off and disappeared from her life?

To J.D., his demon seed existed in this world to haunt him for every sin that he had ever committed. So it seemed. And now of course it was clear that the bastard had not ceased shadowing him as he had promised to do, after the last big payment.

The feeling of sickness and insanity that circled around the bastard was powerful. J.D. knew that there must be a trail of bodies leading to this night.

When the bastard had first hunted him down, common sense would have had J.D. hand the lad some cash and send him on his way. But no. He was the all-powerful mesmerist who would fix the damaged orphan with a job and an income. This was going to compensate him for a life of existing on garbage.

In truth, he had plainly seen the rage on that too-familiar face. If he had been honest with himself, he would have realized that so much compacted anger could not go without an explosion. He pretended to stare into space and was glad not to have to look at the ruined hulk speaking to him. He pretended not to hear, not to understand, and waited for this curse of consciousness to deliver him to a workable moment of attack.

He ordered himself to shut up and wait for something to happen. To his genuine surprise, instead of doing that, he noticed himself standing up quite without thinking about it, and he heard his voice declare, "By God, I look at you and pray to be forgiven!"

J.D. was taken aback by his own outburst. Fear shot into him and lodged like a freezing bullet. It lay defrosting inside of him, radiating its icy message—he was not in control. There was no denying it. Even his reclaimed clarity was unable to stop him from shouting things that he had not planned to say.

And yet . . . his rejuvenated mental powers combined with the youthful speed of his thoughts and allowed him to grasp effortlessly the depth of the troubles to which he had been abandoned by his own less capable self.

After doing nothing more than appearing in J.D.'s life and asking for a handout—the bastard repaid him by using his new job as a cover for murder. They said that his first known victim was "only an alcoholic prostitute," and for no better reason than that, he had been sentenced to the imminently escapable prison hospital. Nothing good ever came from anything that the bastard put into motion.

Time slowed down another level. J.D. was astounded to realize that he was now thinking so fast and comprehending so powerfully, the others nearly appeared to be standing still.

He glanced over at young Shane Nightingale, who looked as if he might get his legs back if he could just recuperate for a minute. In the same instant, it became clear that J.D. had to take control of the situation and stall the bastard until Shane came around enough to pitch in and help.

He stood up to his full height and turned to face him full on, keeping his chin up so that it would not quiver and betray him. "Do you intend to explain what you are doing?" he demanded. "Explain why you were following me?"

"Boss! Good morning! Nice to see you all shiny-faced! Are you surprised to see me?"

"Frankly, yes. If you are alive, it almost certainly means that others are not, because of you."

J.D.'s bastard son leaped onto Shane Nightingale while he was still down, slipped the glass to his neck, and carved in a second long cut. This one was shallow enough, but it was a second source of bleeding.

"You show me one of your patented sneers and I will slice his head right off his body!"

J.D. met his stare and held it. "I believe you."

"Good." He stood up again. "What did you do, work out some kind of cheap after-hours rehearsal arrangement with the management?"

"I was summoned here."

"I'm *asking* if that's why you two were here! I imagine you were taking a break, stretching the legs, when I found you, eh?"

"We haven't been in here at all, tonight. We just came down the hill from the Fairmont Hotel."

"The door was already open, here!"

"Yes. I assume you saw us coming, ran ahead to jimmy the lock, then back to ambush us."

"Fine idea, Boss, if I'd thought of it. But I followed you all the way down Nob Hill, so I guess it was just Fate that had me stake out your hotel."

J.D. snorted. "Fate got you to *this* point? You need a new invisible force."

The bastard's face darkened. "I'm improvising here, Boss! Improvising! Latching on to whatever the circumstances may be and dancing along! I learned it from you!"

"You learned nothing from me."

"Then maybe it was Fate after all, that left the door open for us, eh, Boss?"

"I never told you to call me that."

"Liar!" The bastard's face went purple again. "I finally track you down—you give me a job, following you around?"

"An opportunity that you squandered. Ruined your reputation there and mine for knowing you."

"Knowing me? God damn you to Hell! Say my name. You never say my name. Sure I call you Boss. You never say my name!"

"And never will again, you miserable excuse for a man."

The bastard froze at that and stared at J.D. for one densely packed second. His posture shifted. His face went dead of expression.

The overall effect made it look as though he simply dropped one persona and became another, except for the eyes, which did not change at all. They remained emotionless, predatory perceivers. J.D. realized then that the change in the bastard was not a real change at all. It was merely the dropping of a mask in favor of a more bluntly truthful expression of the cruelty waiting behind those eyes.

J.D. felt the predatory gaze. It radiated a fundamental truth more subtle than waves of body heat: Any trace of willpower would be seized as a provocation.

Another tick of the second hand passed. Years of habit propelled him to take control. "Did you follow me here from New York?"

The bastard laughed. Even his voice came out as a flattened version of itself. It was not there to help him to express himself; it was merely a function of delivering information with the minimum necessary effort. "Nah. I got here weeks before you. To get things ready."

"It took you weeks to get things ready? What things? You followed me in the dark."

"Hey!" the bastard bellowed, purple veins mapping his face. "*I! Am! Improvising!*" He turned toward Shane and saw that he was just climbing back to unsteady feet. So he stepped close enough to menace him with the blade and shouted at the younger man, "Your head's still ringing pretty bad, eh? Can't get your balance back into the legs, right? I don't care if I have to kill you, but you really ought to see this. Just stand right there. You'll be a witness to career history for the Great Mesmerist!"

He gestured to J.D. and added, "Duncan here is going to give us a show. He's going to tell the entire audience why he had me arrested and stuck inside of a little brick box, a place for . . . I thought I'd never get out."

"You broke out. There's no show to be made of that," J.D. replied. Try as he might, he could not keep the disgust from his voice. "The answer is too short to make a show out of it: I called them because you don't belong anywhere else."

In the next instant, J.D.'s olfactory nerves finally got their message to his beleaguered brain. He visualized thin wisps of smoke that his eyes could not see—warning ghosts rising up around his pant cuffs.

The bastard must have been here. He broke in when he saw them coming this way. He had set the fire going. Started it small, to give him time. *No wonder he wanted us all up here.*

The fire had been artificially restrained, so far—the stage had no good air source below it. It would burn without great flames, more like fast-moving rust, until it heated everything under the stage to the combustion point. Then it would require nothing more than the chance to take one good, deep inhale. It would scream flames into the air.

J.D. was beginning to hate his crisp senses and crystal-clear thoughts. *This* was what he had been fighting so hard to preserve? Why? It had seemed so important to regain it all. Yet he had awakened into a situation that perfectly demonstrated one undeniable fact—consciousness was hardly worth the trouble. All it really did was make you aware of an ever-growing list of dangers and threats.

He saw a flash in Shane's eyes and realized that the skinny kid was finally coming around after having *his* brain rattled, fighting off a plague of doughnut holes where *his* memory was supposed to be.

Young Nightingale had saved J.D.'s life, but it cost the kid a real skull-buster of a head blow and a quick trip to the floor.

J.D. was cheered to think that after all this was over, they would be able to sit down together and he could tell him all about his memory struggles, knowing that Shane would understand him perfectly well. Maybe the two of them could work something into the act, since Shane and Blackburn were going to be around backstage anyway.

In the next heartbeat, he was struck by the absurdity of thinking about a future, a reflex that could not help him now. He ran his gaze across the center stage area, knowing what had to be there, and spotted the telltale small iron ring lying flat in a carved-out circle that allowed it to lie flush with the floor. He could barely make them out, in the semidarkness, but there were the clean lines of the large rectangle cut into the floor. This one was well done, invisible from the audience perspective.

He had used trapdoors for trick entrances and exits a thousand times, sometimes assisted by smoke, but sometimes daring to use them even when he was covered by nothing more than shifts of light to distract the eye. This trap was a good size, maybe four feet long and three feet wide, lifting up on the upstage end and hinged on the downstage side.

The bastard's back was to Shane, so that he did not yet realize that Shane was again among them. He leaped in shock when Shane called out, "No matter how many I kill, it never comes out right!"

The bastard spun to Shane, confused about hearing his own thoughts narrated to him. Shane hurried on without giving him the chance to interrupt.

"They don't act the way they're supposed to! I need them there, I need them to watch me kill them. But they die out from under me before they do anything right!"

J.D. was so close to being telepathic in that moment that he could practically converse with Shane over the plan. He knew that Shane had just bought him a few precious seconds, and that he would have to act inside that small margin.

He bent forward and grabbed on to the recessed iron ring, then pulled hard. The trapdoor smoothly rose on well-oiled hinges until it stood perpendicular to the stage.

The bastard let out a scream of frustrated rage and crouched to leap at Shane, except that in the next instant J.D. had him from behind with his arms pinned back.

It was during the third blink of an eye that the air flowing in through the open trapdoor reached the starving fire down below. And with the deafening sound of a hundred banners snapping in the wind, orange and yellow sheets shot up through the trap.

J.D.'s personal clarity was bright and alive inside of him. He saw without any burden of doubt that jumping into a Hell pit and dragging his life's greatest mistake along with him was going to be the perfect way to begin the long atonement that he expected to serve for having set this monster loose upon the world.

The fourth instant passed, and he felt the younger man's mortal fear kick in. The bastard was about to begin fighting for his life and J.D. knew that he could never prevail over him.

It had to end right away. There was not even time to explain it to himself any further than that. The edge of the hole was about four feet away, the closest part being just to his left. He crouched and leaped, throwing all of his body weight toward the left side of the open pit.

The bastard stumbled toward the hole under the force of J.D.'s impact. But there was not enough momentum to pitch them over the edge. There would be no opportunity for a second chance. So when they toppled sideways together, he forcefully contracted his legs and shoved his knees forward, throwing his body weight into their forward momentum. When they landed on the floor next to the edge, that momentum was just enough to keep them moving toward the hole.

There was no time for either man to do more than grunt with the physical shock of the impact with the floor. They went over the ring of fire and dropped into the artificial volcano.

· · ·

The moment that J.D.'s son landed on the blazing basement floor, he reflexively gasped and took in a lungful of the superheated air. It instantly seared his airways and vocal chords so badly that he could produce no other sound but a frenzied gurgling. It did not carry against the roar of the flames.

After that, his arms and legs did the talking for him. His limbs flailed in spasms that described a frenzied dance with his own agonies. It went on for instants that were too prolonged to measure, until pain overwhelmed his consciousness and chased him out of his body. The carcass continued twitching before, during, and after he died, so that it was impossible to tell when his actual moment came.

When J.D. landed, the bill for all of his backstage stomping on cracks finally came due; he broke his lower back and instantly lost all power of movement and all feeling below the waist. However, in clutching on to the bastard during the fall, he had clenched his upper torso muscles with a level of power that only a poisonous overdose of the miracle medicine could enable him to do. When he hit the floor, his contracted muscles helped him avoid the impulse to gasp in a lungful of air. Thus he remained fully conscious and alert after the impact.

His lumbar vertebrae had shot slivers into his spinal cord, but he was not going to be needing his legs anymore. The loss of sensation in the lower half of his body was merciful; his right leg was resting directly on a burning beam and he felt nothing.

Still, he was the sole visitor in that place, and there was really nothing else for him to do there but roast. So when the heat overtook his willpower and the inevitable attempts to scream unlocked his chest muscles, he opened up with a tremendous inhale.

It was as if a giant blast torch was shoved into his mouth and fired directly down his throat. The delicate flesh of his vocal cords and airways instantly scorched over with a black crust. The resulting blackened tube channeled the killing fire straight down inside.

Meanwhile, J.D.'s highly trained mind, capable of such tremendous feats of concentration, remained self-aware and conscious of what was happening to him. His grasp of the incoming flow of sensory information was just as insistent as the blowtorch firing down his throat and the blazing heat peeling away his flesh.

J.D.'s awareness had already continued for several eternal seconds longer than his crisping and curling accidental son. That was to the credit of the elixir, just as his professional survival over the past few declining years had been.

As for his current condition, he clearly recalled that the German scientists made it a point to inform him about the mysterious power of their discovery: that an overdose could flush his glands of their powerful influences and send them all raging into his bloodstream at the same time.

He was at that rare place now.

His pain response was practically wiped out by the stuff. Even though he was suffering, his sensors were dulled to a shadow of themselves. An honest experience of what he would be feeling without the elixir would be enough to snuff the life from him. It would happen as easily as the wind puffs away a flame.

The elixir's gift of clarity denied him the comfort of oblivion. Instead, it claimed its ugly price for all the days and nights that it had pulled him through meetings, interviews, and even something so simple as a pleasurable day browsing in a quiet library. The price came home to him by the elixir simply continuing to do what it did so well, long after there was any need. Straight pins may as well have been jabbed through his eyelids, holding them wide open and forcing him to witness the flaming of his clothing, of his skin.

Even when his eyeball fluids predictably exploded, the plunge into blindness went unnoticed, for the raging visions in his mind's eye. And even still, the relentless curse of consciousness did not release him.

The oil in his body fat reached its natural ignition point and his flesh itself caught fire. Still his crystalline mental clarity remained spring day perfect; he was still quite unable to stop himself from noticing that his blackened flesh was actually not the problem of the moment.

He had absolutely no power to prevent himself from recalling, with photographic clarity, the specific page of the medical text wherein he had once learned that human nerves stop firing once heat turns them black. There is no message of pain to be conveyed by destroyed flesh. When part of someone is burned to blackness, that is actually the merciful part of the injury. It is the advancing burn that carries the Devil's pitchfork. The *living* nerves die off just slowly enough to trigger their loudest messages of what their host will recognize as mortal agony, before they burst open and sizzle away.

J.D.'s final revelation concerning life in this world was that it was possible for the flow of time to melt into nothingness. An instant or an eon, now. They were the same for him.

For one brief flicker of that eternity, overheating brain cells fired and died in miniature convulsions that broke off chemical shards of memory and spewed them into his awareness. He wondered whether he would be able to use any of this new knowledge in his act. It would be a great addition.

Now, with his own body burning, this other part of J.D. ignored his mortal state and imagined himself perched center stage and bellowing to a packed house of enthralled audience members. Everyone who had ever mattered, for reasons good or bad, filled the house and occupied the best seats for clear sight lines and optimum sound. His agent was there, all the way from Manhattan in the great New York City, and the soulless bloodsucker was finally fulfilling his promise to bring along those new clients with the new chain of theatres. The men were ready to invest in James "J.D." Duncan because they had wisely decided that these new motion picture devices were a fad that would dry up and wither.

As for the general audience, every eyeball in that sea of up-turned faces was privileged to see him spew the depths of his rage before them. He bellowed like King Lear over the egregious seeping theft of his mind. The folks out there in the darkened theatre stared back up at him, spellbound one and all, clearly feeling oh-so-sorry for having failed to appreciate him as much as he deserved, in this nasty old trick of a world.

This eternal second took place in what would be termed the very briefest of moments, by anyone whose flesh oils had not ignited.

CHAPTER THIRTY

THE RAIN AFTER MIDNIGHT was persistent and came with ground-level clouds, so the creeping fog rendered even the newest electric streetlamps useless. As for the older gas flame models, their dim light receded into pale ghosts that hovered overhead. Vignette found that the bleak surroundings perfectly mirrored her drizzling mental state. She paced the streets back and forth in front of City Hall Station, keeping her eye on the front door so she would spot him in time to get to him first, no matter what direction he came from.

It was the third hour of her vigil. All she knew was that there was no one at home; Randall would pick up the thing right away, and she was sure that Shane would even answer it. His curiosity would get him. But neither one had answered the useless thing.

She prayed that they were at least together out there in the chilly rainfall. So far, the long vigil had done nothing more than assure her that none of the cops knew where their Detective Blackburn was. If so, there would have been talk of his reaction to learning about his fiancée's murder.

There had not been time for Vignette to risk taking an hour to get home and change and then return. She remained in her ridiculously fashion-correct costume with its stiff button shoes and blouse of regulation white: high-necked, form-fitting, and long-sleeved. The clownish, puffy-sleeved waist jacket that capped the outfit made her feel ridiculous. The whole picture was one more reason for men to speak to women with sneering disrespect.

In weather like this, the clunky shoes did her feet no good and the thin waist jacket repelled rain for around two minutes before soaking through. After that, its wet weight only added to the cold.

She knew that it would be foolish to simply go in and ask. There would be a scene if any of the policemen recognized her. No one in that place was going to tell her anything. Likewise, she could hardly stop the officers who were passing in and out of the station and expect them to give up their rumors or suspicions to her.

It was necessary to call upon old espionage skills, of the kind that she had picked up way back there at St. Adrian's Home for Delinquents and Orphans. The skills came more from the delinquent side of the premises, but they had proved handy on nearly every day of her life since that time.

So she held up her handbag over her head as if to protect her hair, but used her bent arms to cover her face. Then she fell in behind any small group of two or three men who exited the station. She followed closely enough to eavesdrop until she determined that they weren't talking about Randall. The repetitive and time-consuming work took her the better part of an hour, just to confirm that the murder victim up at the exposition grounds was officially identified as that New York author, the one engaged to Detective Blackburn. And that he had not been located yet.

These were the leading topics of gossip for anyone who had been inside the station within recent hours, but no one spoke about suspecting him of committing the crime. It was obvious from the tone of their voices that Randall was going to have a large and rapt audience for his story as soon as he turned up back at the station.

She thought that there was far too much eager anticipation in the voices of the men who were talking about this case, and precious few expressions of support. She had to get to him first, no mistakes, no excuses. Break it to him gently enough to give him time to get a grasp on some sort of a social face, before he had to sit for their blundering questions.

She felt a bolt of fear over the way Randall might react to thoughtless provocation from routine questions while he was under the shock of Janine Freshell's death. Over the years there had been those rare occasions when Vignette had cause to witness him in the more brutal aspects of his line of work. She dreaded seeing him snap. If the idiots at the station casually employed their usual manly cruelty in telling him about the murder—and then questioning him, as the victim's fiancé—he would probably hospitalize a few before they subdued him.

The underlying sense of physical power that he carried had always been a puzzle to her, because of the quiet and gentle manner he consistently used with her and Shane. He also was a gentleman in the company of other adults, as far as she ever saw.

She knew, though, that he could turn into somebody unrecognizable. At the drop of a dime. Sometimes he came home with terrible bruises, and seldom mentioned where they came from. But she had heard other cops laughing about the wrecked condition of Randall's opponents.

There was no way to abandon her vigil long enough to get home for dry clothing, for food, for shoes that did not insult the foot. The terrible events of that night had already convinced her that she, Shane, and Randall were in the middle of a very bad trend. It felt as if their lives had begun swirling around a whirlpool and were being pulled toward the bottom, when the Eastern Whore . . . when Miss Freshell first came sniffing around. And unless their luck had already turned with her passing, then the moment Vignette dared to turn her back and flee home, of course Randall would return to the station just then, possibly even with Shane in tow.

There was no way to call home again from this portion of the streets, but she knew that if Shane had been at home, somebody would have reached him in calling for Randall, and would have told him about Miss Freshell. He would head straight for the station if he heard that.

She realized that this was yet another problem with these telephone voice devices; they would just as easily deliver a message to one person as to another. The potential for people to be betrayed by gossip traveling at such speed was enormous. It was plain to her that the public would soon realize that, and reject the jingling things altogether.

She remained stuck outdoors in a drizzle that felt more like liquid ice than falling water. The only good news so far was that at least she no longer needed to traipse along behind people, trying to listen in. Now she could move at top speed, so she rebuilt her body heat by pacing to the end of the block and back, over and over.

It was a costly effort. Already she sensed the rag doll weakness seeping into her. The woolen skirt was heavy with water, and the rotten thing tugged at her legs with every step. For Vignette, the sensation of that was a grating reminder of the pointless social impotence that her sex bestowed upon her. She had never felt the weight of that miserable yoke more than on this violent night.

Shane saw Duncan and his attacker go over the edge of the stage trap, but it happened too fast to stop them or even utter a sound. They had to have been killed right away. There would have been no saving them if he had been ready with a team of men and water hoses. Two lives blinked out before he could do anything more than witness it and stand amazed.

His neck wounds had spared his arteries and windpipe, meaning that he and Duncan could have eventually dominated this fellow. Shane had managed to stall off the attacker long enough to give Duncan the chance to fight back. But somehow, Duncan's need to exterminate this troubled progeny once and for all was so strong that he had thrown away his own life, just to guarantee that his unclaimed son would at least die with him.

Shane could not begin to imagine what Duncan suspected of his son—or what he might have already known about him—that would drive him to use this means of apologizing to the world for creating such a life.

And now Shane needed to get the hell out. The rush of air into the trap had so vastly accelerated the fire that the entire stage was smoldering, about to burst into flame. He began thinking about the fastest way to sound the alarm, once he got back onto the street. But within moments he was astonished to hear the unmistakable sounds of fire sirens, the big steam engines, and rubber tires squealing to a halt, just outside the front of the building.

They know?

There was no way for the fire to be visible from outside the theatre. Not yet.

How?

He had only managed to take two steps back into the offstage wings when the entire stage floor burst into flame. The explosion of air pressure knocked him against a big rack of scenery flats. By the time he regained his bearings, a wall of flame blocked him from the front of the house. He looked around for the rear fire escape, remembering its position from before, and quickly spotted it through the rolling black smoke. His legs were already in motion before he decided to run for it.

The backstage exit did not have any sort of special release handle for emergencies, but that barely slowed him down. He slammed into the heavy wooden door, simultaneously yanked back the draw bolt and untwisted the knob lock, turned the handle, kicked the door open, and hurled himself into the alley before he had time to think about any of it. Within a few more heartbeats, Shane was safely away, running in the opposite direction of the arriving fire units.

The wet night air thickened into a rolling overhead spray. Before he traveled another full block, it swelled to a persistent drizzle. Good news for the firemen. The miraculous firemen. The speedy fellows who could not have arrived so soon unless they were tipped by whoever started it.

As soon as he reached the point where the alley emerged into the street, he stepped onto the sidewalk, turned east, and walked away down Market Street and toward the bay. He never looked back at the firefighters while they deployed into action. It felt as if someone might catch his eye and shout for him to return.

Shane was grateful that he never heard their attacker's name before he was wiped off the planet by the Last Will and Testament of James "J.D." Duncan. It made it easier to trust that Duncan did the right thing. Action far louder than words. It left no room for lawyering.

The fire department's response was shaping up to be big. Fortunately for the arriving crews, there was no interference from traffic and the streets were mostly empty at that hour. However, the few morning workers who were already out and about had all turned and headed toward the theatre, curious about the action.

That was the only reason that Shane noticed Randall Blackburn moving along, on the opposite side of the wide commercial boulevard. They were the only two people out there who were heading in the opposite direction.

On any other day, Shane would have immediately been concerned over Randall's presence, ready with a dozen questions. Now he only thought of how good it was to see him after this bizarre and terrible turn of events. Shane moved at a brisk trot across the wide street, jumping the emerging puddles and the melting horse piles. Once he was finally across, he avoided calling attention to himself by moving up behind Randall at an easy pace.

He was only a few paces away when the first twinge of awkwardness sank in. He could not think of how to greet him, under the circumstances. Instead, he just silently fell in beside him and walked along, an arm's length away. For the first few steps he did not meet Randall's gaze, as if they were just coincidentally walking along there and unaware of each other.

"Son of a bitch! Shane?" Randall nearly whispered it.

Shane turned and saw Randall's eyes boring into him. He immediately felt a wave of dread roll through him. Shane saw that the flesh of Randall's face was sunken, making his eyes seem to bulge. His color was pale ash.

"Hi. Well. This is something. I was just inside the theatre. Mr. Duncan and I were dragged in there by this street thief, but there was a fire. And Randall, Duncan grabbed him and pulled him into the stage pit. They both died down there. I saw it."

Randall stopped walking, at that. He turned and looked him in the eyes with more pain than Shane had ever seen on his face.

Shane went on. "I, ah, guess you're headed to the station?"

Randall looked off in the distance and a dry smile slowly spread over his face. He turned back to Shane and nodded. And with that, resumed walking.

"Where's the car?"

"The car. The car is at the station."

"Why did you leave it?"

"I didn't. I parked outside the theatre, right out front. The captain had his men tow it back to the station to hold on to, until I did my job. Something about using it to help frame me if I didn't."

"So. Now, ah, now you can retrieve it?"

"That was the deal."

"Why are they going to be willing to release the car now? You know, as opposed to before?"

"Because I did what they asked."

"Ah-hah. What, uh . . ."

"I set the Pacific Majestic Theatre on fire." He said it simply, without looking at Shane, and kept walking at a brisk pace.

Shane kept up with him, but he was already panting. His old stutter returned, the way it still tended to do when things went bad in a hurry.

"N-no—no. You didn't seh-seh-set that fire. It was the guy who has been after Duncan all along. There really was a sssstalker, the way, the way, the way that Duncan feared!"

Shane ran around in front of Randall and stood in his way so that he had to stop. He stared into his eyes and pushed all of his will into his words.

"Randall, *the stalker* lit the fire."

Blackburn held Shane's gaze with a sad smile. "I appreciate what you're doing, Shane. But I lit the fire. You know those new matches I like, you can strike them on any rough surface?" He pulled out little silver box. "I saved two matches out of this little match safe here. Janine gave it to me. Pure silver. Two fires at each end of the basement. Paint thinner, canvas sets."

Blackburn resumed walking. "I used a call box on the street to get the fire department rolling as soon as I left."

"Oh," Shane replied, trying to digest what he was hearing. "So . . . you're the reason that they got there early? You saved the place then, right? You called it in early to make sure that it didn't spread? So without you—"

"Without me, there wouldn't have been a fire! I set it."

"Oh you set it. I see. And now . . . you can get the car back, and have everything be all right with the department, *because* you set the theatre on fire?"

Blackburn said nothing. They kept walking.

The mist became a steady horizontal spray, worse than the most aggressive fog. The silence between them would have been awkward, but it was relieved by the watery drone of the wind. The distance to the new City Hall was only a few blocks. They covered it in minutes.

Shane could sense the depth of Blackburn's turmoil, but he was having a hard time picturing what he had been told. It made no sense at all. He tried to think of anything else that could have an effect like this on Randall, who was in most ways the strongest man he had ever met.

Nothing came to mind. He could see that the story of whatever Randall had done and whatever reasons he had for doing it would have to unfold on its own. They finished the short walk in silence.

CHAPTER THIRTY-ONE

LONG AFTER MIDNIGHT
THE CITY HALL STATION

VIGNETTE SHIVERED UNCONTROLLABLY BENEATH a hellish drizzle. She had expended the last of her core body warmth, and so her remaining wisps of energy could only move her limbs in clumsy, jerky motions.

By this point she was so frustrated and angry that she would have screamed for the sheer release of the emotions, if her body were in any condition to accommodate her. Every terrible scenario she had ever overheard during nine years of living in the home of a police officer leaped to the front of her imagination and tormented her.

After the long night, those images of disaster gradually metamorphosed into tragic scenes that she ought to have prevented, but did not. Jumbled bits of voices and images fractured, mixed, and re-formed into artificial memories based on her worst fears.

It was her fault. The Eastern Whore had only managed to get herself selected for murder because Vignette had left her alone, shirking her duty in the public bathroom. It did not console her to know that her presence at that moment might have done nothing more than provide the attacker with another victim. The voices in her new false memories continued to feed fatigue-borne fears.

She could have prevented it, somehow. The fact that she was Randall Blackburn's adopted daughter meant that she should know more about such things than the average young woman her age. She could have demonstrated some of that knowledge, but she had not. Therefore, she had not only failed Janine Freshell, but also failed Randall yet once again.

Because of her, he was going to go for another swim in the sewer for the pleasure of his commanding officers. No one had spoken a word out loud to her but she was already damned sick and tired of the accusations bellowing in her imagination.

Yes! Vignette wanted to bellow it. *Yes, I hated her!* She wanted to throw every ounce of her energy into her throat and cause everybody within half a mile to stop and listen.

Yes, I left the room to avoid her! And no, hell no, *I had no desire to risk my life for her. Are you insane? Why would I do that, for a woman like her?*

"It would be obscene!" she hissed under her breath, without realizing that she spoke out loud.

Her inner turmoil rolled with such power that she could not imagine where its energy came from. She remained alone in the rain-deepened darkness, but inside felt as if she were being torn apart by dogs.

She could see everyone accusing her this time, and not just the police officers. She could see Shane staring at her in disgust, shaking his head, turning his back. She saw Randall, losing his temper and getting violent with her at last, the way she had always known he would do someday—like any other male human of that size. Men did it because they could.

Why would he not rage at her, now? Why not do her harm? What was there, really, preventing him from snatching her away and dragging her home and assaulting her behind closed doors, just the way that the Helpers did back at St. Adrian's?

He called himself their "father." But really, what would stop him from doing whatever he wanted to punish her, to hurt her in the deepest way he could? The question hung there.

Nevertheless, it disappeared completely when she turned at the corner and started back toward the station; she was just in time to see Randall and Shane emerge from the fog just a few yards away from her. They were coming right up the street and heading for the station. Neither one had seen her yet.

So they were alive, moving under their own power, and apparently not injured. Only an instant had passed, but this much was already cause for celebration. Vignette felt it right away. Muscles that she did not even realize she had been clamping down on suddenly relaxed and stretched out. A huge inhalation came upon her, inflating her lungs on its own power. She gave a deep sigh of relief.

However, they were only going to be "all right" for another few seconds, before one of the emerging officers spotted them and ran to them with the news. They both looked tired, nearly beaten.

A movement caught the corner of her eye, and she turned to see that another pair of cops was just walking out the main entrance and heading down the steps. Their path would take them so close to Randall that they were sure to recognize him.

She called out to them, but the wind gusts blew her voice away like a dry leaf. She stepped up her pace, running as fast as her exhausted body and her cramping muscles and her chilled temperature and her damned rain-soaked skirt would allow.

"Randall!" she cried out again. Her voice remained tiny against the wind. She called again, then again, rushing toward them.

The two cops were getting closer, although they did not seem to have noticed her or Randall, yet. They were too close.

"Shaaannne!" she screamed, feeling her legs give out. Her foot caught in the hem of her skirt. Her body pitched forward into the sidewalk on her forward momentum. The crash to the ground was hard.

But she ignored the pain, because Shane spotted her just as she was falling. By the time she looked up again, he and Randall were already hurrying toward her.

She rose to all fours and tried to stand, but her legs immediately buckled again. Now the pain and frustration took control of her, quickly replaced by near hysteria.

Randall reached her, and she latched her arms around his neck, wailing, out of control. When he realized that she was soaked through and shivering, he started to lift her and carry her into the station, orders or not.

She cried louder, got him to put her down, and stood with her arms around his neck and her feet barely touching the ground. The sobs tore through her and she had no power at all to stop them. She cried for the pain coming his way, and for having to be the one to deliver the news. She cried for fear of losing his love for her, and for her sense of guilt over hating Miss Freshell the way that she had.

And right there in that lousy freezing rain, she struggled her way through what she had to tell him. She could tell that she was doing a miserable job, sobbing and breaking down, probably slowing up the story more than Shane would have done.

But as it happened, she helped him as much as anyone could have, because her great distress focused his mind on the difficulty of getting the story out of her in bits and pieces. It slowed the flow of information and padded its impact. Instead of taking a blow to the chin from a bare-knuckle fist, he got one wrapped in a boxing glove.

He remained calm enough to gather her up and take the three of them home in a taxi. His silence was deep throughout the ride, but Vignette could not help but notice that at least he had not struck out at her yet. So far, she had not spotted that crazy mad look that men get in their eyes when they are going to hurt you.

She knew that it was bad, to be worried about her own relationship with Randall at such a terrible time. It was selfish. But she was also nurturing a tiny spark of hope so beautiful and so thrilling that she did not even want to think about it. She just wanted that secret hope to be left alone long enough to grow into a reality, and for the reality to be that somehow Randall would find it in himself not to turn his back on her because his fiancée had died in her company. It felt like wishing for the moon.

CHAPTER THIRTY-TWO

SINCE IT WAS SATURDAY morning, Shane took over making the coffee and breakfast, letting the big man sleep in. He knew that Randall had returned to the station the night before, for questioning in the murder case. He had finally arrived back home in the wee hours. Shane would have been happy to let him sleep through until Sunday. He set things up so that Randall could eat if and when he wanted to, putting out bowls of fruit and cheese while he brewed the coffee and made up a pot of oatmeal.

Vignette came downstairs at the first aroma of breakfast. She and Shane met eyes long enough to acknowledge each other's presence, then she silently took a seat at the kitchen table while Shane moved around her.

He realized that there was actually some comfort, on this strange morning, in her usual morning role as the brat who has already learned how to dismantle and reassemble the engine of the Ford, but who refuses to learn how to cook. Shane's usual disapproving annoyance at her felt good to him now. That sense of easy familiarity was like fresh air.

The case of the Freshell murder was no mystery to him; he witnessed the son stalking Duncan at the restaurant. Clearly, the raging man had also seen Duncan with Freshell. So no matter what sort of thoughts the killer had in his mind at the time, he had initially turned his focus onto Miss Freshell simply because of her proximity to Duncan.

No one had asked Shane's opinion, but to him it seemed clear that she had set in motion the very chain of events that ended with her death. But now, fresh out of bed, it was all too much to talk about.

Everyone in the house drank coffee or tea with breakfast and usually did little else until that first cup. Shane and Vignette had not finished theirs yet, but the weight of the unasked questions and their useless answers was already tiresome.

After nine years of mornings together, their connection was nearly telepathic. And so from the mere silence and the fact that neither one glared at the other, along with the fact that they both remained in the kitchen instead of leaving, they both silently realized that neither wanted to fight.

Shane was glad for Vignette's gentle side, for that rarely visible side of her that behaved as if she had actually been raised somewhere within a real civilization. The silence between them felt eloquent to him because of that, more so than words.

By then he knew that he and Vignette would be able to get through the morning together. Randall could sleep for as long as he needed to.

Upstairs in Randall's large bedroom, his smoldering internal condition was nothing at all like sleep. He sat in a stuffed chair in front of the doorway to his screened balcony, staring into the view without seeing anything.

He had built that balcony himself, years before. It was done in anticipation of sleeping out there during summer nights. There had just never seemed to be a reason to actually do that. When it was used at all, it was his place to enjoy the rare feeling of thinking without interruption.

There was no respite in that today. The same words that had tormented him the evening before, while he sat below the stage and
waited for the instructed hour, came back to haunt him now.

This is what they think of you.

He failed to walk away from the task. Even while he was putting
each match's flame to the canvas flats, he saw that he had foolishly
allowed their coercions to work on him. It all came down to the loss
of his career, a falsely shamed reputation, an arranged arrest and
conviction, effectively destroying his life from the ground up. It
would obliterate his little family at a time when it seemed to him
that they needed one another as much as ever.

Shane and Vignette were both young adults now, but he could
not imagine them doing well on their own, not yet. With just a few
more years to grow into themselves, to finish casting off the worst
effects of the brutal experiences of their early years, they might
each grow into fine lives.

Of course none of that would matter anymore if he went to
prison. An even deeper burn came from the knowledge that his
sanity would never survive a false imprisonment and the destruction of his family.

Still, it was not the burning of the building under orders and en-
couragement from above that held him tied in knots, now. The poisonous element was that for the rest of his days, he would never
escape the knowledge that he had taken a chance with the life or
the lives of innocent people—no matter how remote that chance
may have been. The only thing that would have been necessary for
a real tragedy to ensue was for some unexpected person to be in the
area.

Then Detective Randall Blackburn would have been a killer, a
common murderer. Nobody at the station house showed any interest in that during the hours of his debriefing. His lieutenant-level
tormentors repeatedly assured him that he nearly ruined everything
with his "safety" tactics. Officers outside in the hall who caught
snips of conversation probably assumed that he was in there ex-

plaining the details of how he spotted the fire. Instead, he spent every moment fighting to control his anger until the lieutenants' sneering disrespect was replaced by that of his captain. The captain was so angry over the risk that Blackburn had taken with his tactics that he threatened to retract his prior offer and have him arrested anyway.

Blackburn's last-minute concession to his conscience had been to set the fire down beneath the stage, instead of the backstage area. Down there, he trusted that the lesser air supply would slow down the fire's advance. Then he sneaked out and hurried to one of the new police call boxes to report the fire. It would be hard for him to explain, if somebody on the fire department questioned how it was that the fire got reported before it was visible from outside. He would have to make up something. Tell them he smelled smoke.

He successfully minimized the fire, which was easily extinguished. But the smoke damage was barely enough to justify sealing the building. It would provide a plausible rationalization for declaring the entire place condemned, but just barely. No thanks to Blackburn, it would be quietly slated for demolition in what would be advertised as an abundance of caution against undetected fire damage.

The fishy circumstances would quickly wash away amid the public excitement over the exposition. The news representatives were not going to print anything that could not be explained. Key players had all been rewarded or threatened into silence.

And so this challenging incident of civic corruption was guaranteed to pass undetected. There were, after all, other things screaming for priority in the public attention span. The city was trying to hold an international party while a great war was spreading all through Europe, threatening to pull the United States into the mess along with everybody else. The civic authorities counted on the fact that people had a lot of other things to think about.

Fortunately for Blackburn, the captain reminded him, his tracks were being efficiently covered by the authorities in spite of his cautious performance.

Except that he felt as if he were the one who had fallen into the fire. He was burned and blackened in ways that he could not escape. At the worst of the damage points, he felt nothing, like the burn victim whose flesh is charred black. There was only ash remaining in the places where he had always found pride in his life. He was used to the feeling of living his life as a good man. All of that was in ashes.

A soft knock came from outside his bedroom door. He tried to respond and found that his vocal cords felt as if they were asleep. He resented any intrusion at this moment, and the feeling was heightened by his frustration at not being able to come up with some decent way of keeping either of them from coming in.

It did not matter what he might have said, because it was Vignette knocking. She took advantage of his brief silence to test the doorknob, discover that it was unlocked, and walk into his room without waiting for an invitation.

He turned to look at her with a small sigh and tried to make a smile of some kind, but was not sure what it must have looked like. She suddenly smiled so large, so quickly, that he realized it was in reaction to her own thoughts and not to whatever facial expression he had just tried to imitate.

She kept a bit of distance, the way she always did, and leaned against the edge of the tall bookshelf next to the doorway. She spoke to him in a near whisper that he recognized as her most tender tone of voice. She used it on frightened stray animals. Her voice already told him that she grasped his condition.

"I knew that she wouldn't want me to let you sit here alone like this, without knowing."

He raised his eyes to meet hers for a moment, but it hurt too much and he had to pull them away.

"I finally had to accept that she loved you. The last thing we talked about was her plans for your marriage, and she sounded so wonderfully happy." Vignette snickered and added, "She talked about you like you are the finest man ever born and she couldn't believe her luck in finding you. I told her I've been driving the women away ever since we all moved in, and she laughed and thanked me!" She shook her head and laughed a little, just to think of it.

Blackburn was instantly caught up and so completely mesmerized by the pictures she was painting in his imagination that he did not speak. He felt their eyes connect again and a wave of the girl's love washed over him. It broke his heart and spared the rest of him. Tears rolled down his face without stopping. His masculine habits barely restrained his facial muscles. They prevented his sobs by pushing them back down where a man was expected to keep those things.

Vignette grew serious and gazed directly at him. "I want you to know that I don't think I could have helped her. I really don't, Randall. I've thought it all out."

He found his voice. "All right, you listen to me. I'm thankful that you weren't around. I know this was the same guy who went after Duncan. And Duncan knew all about him. He was just so ashamed of him that he never gave us the real information that we could have used to keep him safe."

He stood up, feeling about a hundred years old while he walked over to her. She flinched the way she always did when he hugged her, but then she relaxed a little.

He whispered, "You were never going to take down a man like that. Don't you worry about any of that other nonsense. I'm glad you weren't there, Vignette. That's all. I love you too much to ever want you to risk yourself like that."

He felt Vignette take in a long breath. For once she didn't try to push away. She stood and returned his hug.

"It gets lonely downstairs." Shane spoke from the doorway. Blackburn grinned and motioned him in. He released Vignette and went back to the stuffed chair. His energy was spent by that small exertion.

"I was just telling Randall about the fine things that Miss Freshell was saying about him," Vignette announced.

Shane glanced at her in a flash of surprise, but he immediately erased it. He kept quiet and listened while she went on.

"Her book was using James Duncan for the main character, because he was famous and all, but she was going to make Randall the real hero. You know, as if to say that the fancy guy was just the one who had to be protected, but it was Randall who was the one who really does things. In the story. Not that it was finished yet. These were her ideas. Sketches of ideas. Apparently that's how you write those romance novels. You sketch things out in advance. Or that's how she does. Did. She just admired you so much, that frankly, it was something to see. She was besotted. That's the word! 'Besotted' with love over Randall Blackburn!"

"Not that we can understand why," Shane added, grinning.

Vignette laughed at that and quickly added, "Of course not. It's a mystery!" They both turned to Randall to see if he was catching the wave.

He could not get there with them. His insides were charred. He did not know how to pretend.

"Listen to me, both of you." He spoke softly, but his tone was strong, resolute. "What would you have done, if they had hauled me away today?"

"Why the hell would they do that?" Vignette interrupted.

"Later. Right now, just tell me. What would you do? Those little inheritance payouts might keep body and soul together, if nothing goes wrong with the economy, what with all of this war talk. But how long will that be enough? You get old enough, people don't want to give you chances anymore. You can't get started. Nobody wants to give you a break, because they figure that if you haven't done things right by then, maybe you've got something wrong with you. That way, no matter how well you approach them, they're going to look at you and see trouble. How would you two keep yourselves from coming to that?"

"Well, Randall," Shane began, "I don't see why anybody needs to come over here and arrest *you*, so I—"

"Forget about why they do it. Just say they do, for any reason."

"All right, then. I *have* been working at The Sea Mist for almost a year."

"That's fine for a young guy. But what if arthritis starts to settle in your hands, your wrists, your leg joints? What are you going to do then? If you don't have working skills?"

"Randall," Vignette interrupted, "I don't see what any of this has to do with Miss Freshell."

"It doesn't. It has to do with me realizing you both need a livelihood that lets you be yourselves, that doesn't force you into some kind of a mold."

"You're just now realizing that?"

"Vignette . . ."

"Sorry."

"Tell me, does either one of you think that if something happened to me, I could rely on any help from the department for you?"

Vignette started to answer, but her throat seized up. She put her hands on her hips and stared at the floor.

"Shane, I'm proud of you for taking on an honest job. It's just that, to me, your temperament does not seem suited to restaurant work. I think that in order to make it through a shift, you have to become like a sleepwalker, and not feel anything."

"Jesus, Randall . . ." Shane muttered.

"No, come on now, I'm not saying this to rub your nose in it. I'm telling you that yesterday might have been the worst day of my life, but it forced me to ask hard questions.

"You both need to get out of the traps you're in, just like I do."

"What 'trap' are you in?" Shane asked.

"In one more year, I get a twenty-year pension. Good for life. And it's a stupid goal to throw away your soul for."

"Randall," Vignette began, "what are you getting on about?"

"You just look at the kind of danger both of you were in, yesterday, because of my line of work."

"We never said that we—"

"Each of you came close to getting killed, for no reason but for me being a police detective."

"So what? That wasn't your fault. You always wanted to be a detective. It's why you walked that beat all those years," Shane said.

"Here's what would be my fault: If I let you two go on out into the world without being better prepared for it than you are."

"Oh, well then. You'll put in a good word for us at City Hall?" Vignette sweetly asked.

"Too late," Shane said with a grin.

Randall stood up and took a deep breath. "No, right now I'm going on in to the station." He picked up his boots, sat in a chair, and pulled them on. Shane and Vignette watched in puzzled silence. He opened the closet and took out a topcoat and a heavy felt hat. "I won't be gone too long."

"Who's in, today?" Shane asked.

"I don't know. Doesn't matter." He put his coat on.

"You mean you're not going in to see somebody in particular?" Vignette asked.

Randall stood holding his hat and looked her straight in the face. "I have a letter of resignation in my pocket, here. Actually, a note. There are three lines. I only needed one. So I'll give it to the desk sergeant. Doesn't matter who's on the desk. Long as I turn it in, that makes it official."

"Randall," said Shane, "I have a bad feeling that you're still in shock. You shouldn't be making this kind of a decision. Not now, anyway."

"Yeah. I'm in shock, all right. But waiting around isn't going to change anything." He turned to go.

Shane grabbed his arm and turned him back around to them. "Wait, I mean it. Please. Just wait."

Vignette jumped in, saying, "Wait *ten minutes*! You can always do it after ten minutes, can't you? You can wait ten minutes, right?"

He gave them a tired smile, and did not start for the door. "What will change in the next ten minutes?"

"Nothing, maybe," Vignette replied. "But you might find that after you more or less count to ten, things start to look different."

"Nothing will look different. I already wrote the letter. I even used so much tact that it took up three lines. Did I mention that I could have done it in one?"

"Randall," Shane used his most serious tone, "you also just mentioned your twenty-year pension. If you quit—"

"I know."

Vignette spoke though a pensive frown. "I've known you all this time, Randall, and I don't ever remember hearing you talk about anything with the kind of enthusiasm that you always show. I mean, when you talk about figuring out crimes and outsmarting bad guys. Doing your work."

"Playing their game better than they do," Shane added.

Randall stood looking at both of them, overwhelmed by their attempts on his behalf. They meant the best, but they also had no idea.

"Because of my *job,* you two. It would have been amazingly easy for them to blow us apart. Look how close they came."

"Hey," Shane protested, "we are not children! I'm not so sure what it is that you're afraid of, with us."

Blackburn quietly regarded Shane while answers flashed through his mind. He had no doubt that both of these young people were capable of having fine lives, if they could keep using the special individual skills that they each possessed while they learned to compensate for social skills they lacked. Without such a chance—without some sort of protective place where they could finish developing fundamental things that they needed—he could hold out little hope for them in a society like theirs, so quick to judge and quicker to condemn.

Shane's awkward social behavior kept him isolated. And Blackburn thought of Vignette's strange need to reject any attempt to treat her as a feminine creature, her constant state of battle with the world. They would both be lucky to scrape by and keep out of jail.

The world itself was a slaughterhouse, for them, even when it was safe and serene for others. Its terrible mechanisms would be activated by their eccentricities, the process powered by the inevitable hostility that would eventually corner each of them, visiting destruction in any of countless ways.

He took out his weathered silver pocket watch and flipped open the case. The crystal was cracked again—for, what was this, the seventh time? He dropped it back into his pocket.

"Makes sense," he said. "Time for a new watch."

Because the flow of time was not on his side. Ten minutes, ten days, or ten years, there would be no fixing this one through the mere passage of time, unless he found a way to fix it himself.

He put his hat on. It helped make the point to them—and to himself—that it was time for him to leave and get this thing done now, no matter how many minutes it had been.

‖ EPILOGUE ‖

THE ROUTINE DETAILS WENT by in the fashion of final rituals: the wrap-up on Miss Freshell's murder by James "J.D." Duncan's maniacal bastard son, the burial of Miss Freshell's remains. When they were done, Shane went back to working at the restaurant. Vignette went back to burying herself in her books. Randall spent a good deal of time outside, taking long walks. His legs had spent so many years walking a beat that they demanded regular use.

Over on the exposition grounds, the water in the dead space behind the life-sized Cave Dwellers exhibit never rose high enough to spill out and repel the visitors. Not that the problem went away; rather, the further crumbling of the hastily man-made six hundred and twenty-five acres of land allowed the leaks to spread throughout the landfill. The phenomenon distributed the water load so well that it would conceal the problem until the next major earthquake, at which point the land would liquefy and swallow large homes up to the second floor within a matter of seconds.

The rest of the exposition was thus able to play itself out for the full ten months without the embarrassment of a spontaneous geyser in the middle of the fairgrounds—and without the embarrassment of a collapsed balcony at the Pacific Majestic Theatre.

The minor fire story played for a couple of days, but since nobody died, it faded like a spent match.

Blackburn especially enjoyed the experience of having Captain Merced show up at their home in an attempt to dissuade him from leaving the force. Shane and Vignette hung in the background to eavesdrop. The men were behind closed doors, but it became clear to them that Blackburn was continuing to refuse Merced's offer, while the captain's voice grew louder.

When Captain Merced finally opened the office door and stomped out, he shouted that Blackburn was finished at the department. He marched to the front door, stopped just long enough to announce that there would be no second chances, then glared at Shane and Vignette with disdain and slammed the door as he left.

Shane and Vignette sat without moving. They both wanted to know how Randall was taking this, but neither was going to be the first to interrupt him.

Their caution paid off. He walked out of the study a few seconds later wearing a broad smile, and made no mention of the captain at all. Instead he cheerfully offered to take them out somewhere fancy for dinner. They both lunged at the chance to get back to normal footing.

After everyone got into their going-out-to-dinner clothes, he opened a closet and produced a small package wrapped in brown paper. He refused to tell them anything about it until later in the evening.

They all hopped into the Model T, with Vignette enthusiastically piloting them on the journey between the other motorized vehicles, the horse-drawn wagons, countless random pedestrians, and the ubiquitous piles of fresh horse flop. The destination that Blackburn navigated her toward turned out to be an upper-class seafood restaurant on Fisherman's Wharf. The place was so overpriced that the locals generally avoided it, but he insisted that it was a good choice for a special celebration.

It was only after they went in and got their table, placed their orders, and sat enjoying their dinners that he pulled out the package and placed it on the table.

"What's that?" Shane asked.

"I guess one of you better open it. Either one. It's for both of you." He smiled and softly added, "And for me."

Shane shot Vignette a puzzled look, but she gave him a hurry-up push, so he grinned and went ahead and tore off the paper. When he pulled it back, it revealed a carved wooden sign. The sign was about eighteen inches long and a foot high. It was just the right size to mount on the exterior door of an office.

"Blackburn & Nightingales—Private Investigation."

"You're ready to learn a detective's skills, Shane. You just don't need to be a policeman first."

He saw the confusion on their faces, and added, "I don't need to be a policeman anymore, either."

"It says Nightingales, plural," Vignette pointed out.

"It does. Hell, Vignette, you've already got most of the skills of an undercover investigator, anyway. So now you'll formally learn a trade that you can use anywhere in the world."

"Hey! If I get good enough," she enthused, "maybe we'll make it Blackburn & Nightingale & Nightingale. Or Blackburn and the Two Nightingales. We need some kind of an emblem to stand for us. A crest, or something. Do we have to wear uniforms?"

One thing at a time, Blackburn reminded himself.

He had made it his credo for a long time. It delivered him to this place. What mattered was that Shane and Vignette had both caught on to the idea. He spotted the recognition in their eyes; they saw that this could be a way for each of them to continue in this highly impractical little family. Their enthusiasm for it was a tonic for him. He felt as if he had just gained back ten years and lost fifteen pounds.

"Do we carry guns?" Shane asked. "You know, I can't honestly say whether I care to or not. Maybe I could try it both ways. There ought to be other sorts of weapons that—"

Vignette leaned in front of him to interrupt. "Do we really have to have a telephone, though? If we do, I'm not going to answer it. Would I have to answer it? Do we even need one?"

"One thing at a time!" Randall grinned and raised both hands. "Right now, all we can do is have dinner. After that, dinner will be over but the answer stays the same."

"We agree on what we're doing and we're going after it," Shane said, raising his glass.

"I like the sound of that," Randall responded.

Vignette nodded, raised her glass, and added, "One thing at a time."

THE END

DOSSIER

The Hidden Man

ANTHONY FLACCO

THE MORE THINGS CHANGE

FANS OF HISTORICAL FICTION tend to be eclectic people. That egalitarian quality may also be found in their tendency to value a wide breadth of experience in life, just as they do within the pages of a book. The hobbies of such a person, for example, are often counterintuitive to what an observer would be likely to guess from their appearance. While that does not necessarily mean that readers of historical fiction can be expected to be stunt skydivers, they are nevertheless people who value a thoroughly rounded combination of choices within their daily existence. I will generally predict that the range of that person's choices will be wide, from one to another, whether their specific interests are many or few.

It will not matter if a fan of historical fiction is a world traveler or is someone unable to leave their home, hospital, or prison cell. In any case, there is a particular kind of satisfaction being sought out by that person whenever they open a book. That search and the needs that drive it will tend to set this reader apart from other sorts of readers, by virtue of specific things that resonate so deeply that the reader becomes passionate over the story. Such a reader lives with a quiet and ongoing search that automatically activates whenever they enter a bookstore. The internal alarm bell goes off at the moment that their attention is captured by a specific book.

From that point on, we fans of historical fiction know how the pattern plays: We pick up a book because we have heard good things about the story or the author. Maybe we just pick it up because we've been grabbed by the title or by the cover art. No matter, this is only the opening salvo.

In searching for that elusive Good Read, we may not always insist that a novel be set in a distant past, but we certainly want to feel that the book will deliver the particular sort of good stuff that we get from historical fiction.

The good stuff is whatever can catch *your* eye and then hold *your* attention.

We've all been there, by design or by chance: that moment when we suddenly realize that we've just picked up a real one. Such a book will have an initial presentation so compelling that we feel obligated to investigate. We open it, we scan, we skip around, then finally pick a passage and actually *read* it, slowly, carefully drinking it in. On a lucky day, we find ourselves hesitant to believe but soon pleased to discover that there is real content there, so effective that it transports us straight to the checkout line. This scenario begs the question: What elements must a contemporary novel have, then, to satisfy the true fan of historical fiction?

Pssst . . . don't look at me while I talk, just listen: Everybody in the book world would love to know the answer to that. Everybody. From those crazy kids in the mailroom to the proverbial cigar-sucking CEO lounging aboard a cash-laden yacht while using satellite communications to keep a sharp eye out for the next megabestseller. Everybody.

So why ask? What possible function can such a question have, other than to unnecessarily harsh one's literary mellow?

All right, none. But even though nobody has the entire answer, there are four definite clues to its attributes, along with one absolute must-have for any written story:

1. We Don't Trust the Scenery—Let's begin by agreeing *not* to assume that the trappings of the past are enough to capture a reader's interest, no matter how fresh, exotic, or original the distant setting may be. If that were so, publishers would burn up the presses to keep up with the demand for travel tomes and history textbooks.

2. We Do Trust the Subtext—Historical fiction offers its readers the potential delight of discovering familiar human problems in disparate times and places. There is an innate magnetism between a reader and any character that arises when the character displays aspects of personality that remain essentially the same across spans of time and space. In some instances, the thoughts, feelings, and reactions experienced by these characters can so profoundly resonate with our own that there is a comforting familiarity even in the midst of a setting's overt strangeness. That "so near but so far" aspect of a story sets up a natural dramatic tension.

And such things are either present in a book or they are not. We can verify the answer with a thorough online peek or bookstore skim.

3. Dialogue Binds Us All—We want good dialogue in historical fiction, perhaps more so than with other novels, because dialogue is so effective at communicating the core meanings of archaic phrases and mannerisms. To expand on the earlier point: The foreignness communicated by historical books creates flashes of tension within us, whether conscious or unconscious. And yet in the next instant, the familiarity of the *behavior* evoked by those same foreign words or phrases releases this tension by removing its sense of otherness.

Therefore when we read engaging historical fiction, a silent thrill ride takes place in the back of our minds, speeding along a track made out of lines of text. This ride affects us even if it occurs on an unconscious level.

Example: Fans of historical fiction are always pleased when an author employs terms or phrases that may be outside the modern lexicon, but are nevertheless perfectly clear to the reader by virtue of artful application. Thus when good dialogue is strange to the ear but familiar to the heart, it does a valuable service by entertaining and educating within the same pages.

Any story that accomplishes this without resorting to overt preaching has a touch o' the old magic, does it not? It's the stuff that all of us who love historical fiction come sniffing around the library stacks to find—ditto our favorite bricks-and-mortar bookstore or favorite online bookseller.

THE FAMILY CONNECTION

Our one and only must-have is the Family Connection.

There is a deep and abiding sense of *belonging* that we as a species continue to prove that we need. Issues and questions about a character's family are always compelling forces, no matter what time period the story uses. Furthermore, they will be there whether the author consciously deals with them or whether they simply take the form of a deafening silence when carelessly ignored.

Today's reading audience knows that insights into any character's true personality will come across best in the form of specific answers to the question of how they were raised. And especially how they reacted to those events and circumstances, as well as to how well they handle them, or not, today.

The family is older than any form of literature and as ancient as humanity itself. Not only is it largely responsible for the survival of the race, but as a phenomenon it is so successful that most mammals live in a family structure. Some may alternatively live within a herd structure, but that is a form of traveling extended family.

Individuals who cleave to neither one must be expected to do poorly, unless they are truly exceptional specimens. This is true in the wilds of the jungle or the terrors of the company meeting room.

We tend to call the human examples "loners," with a hint of condescension. The attitude provides the added bonus of sparing us the effort of applying our judgment or empathy to any strenuous degree, since it is in the nature of condescension that the receiver is regarded as unworthy of a better effort. Some people employ the downward gaze at any "loner" whether or not that particular loner has a criminal state of mind, or is merely an eccentric who lives by a recognizable ethos, and who is going to do the right thing according to that ethos whether or not the popular crowd plays along.

Loner is only one letter away from *loser.* People seem to sense that unhappy fact, even if they don't play out the spelling. A modern author of either gender can create a male hero, but giving him mere "loner" status no longer confers the mystique that it once did. And while changing the character to a woman might make her seem slightly more distinctive (if the plot is male-dominated), the same problem arises as soon as the novelty wears off.

A genuine loner today, however, could also be that rare and yet certainly extant enlightened solo female who neither seeks nor avoids pairing. At her core, this character knows that she will be all right, either way, *so long as her heart is otherwise open.* We know it along with her. Readers may rightly expect to come across women like her inside the pages of today's fiction, whether the story's setting is historical or not.

Moreover, nowadays our pale rider may elect to avoid any sort of "showdown" altogether—and sneak in, instead. Many readers today would applaud that pragmatic choice. I would. Especially if I were next in line to walk the dangerous point.

Sure, sure. Some will disagree: random contrarians, Internet flamers. But I say that today's democracy of readership will respond less to a "guns and guts" approach because we as a society have been forced by experience to learn an appreciation for stealth over bluster.

All of this brings us to the truncated adage employed in the title. We can read stories set in any exotic time and place, and so long as a story involves human beings, "the more things change," the more the writer is confronted with the challenge of what to do about a given character's family.

It makes no difference if the family members themselves never make an appearance and have no direct connection to the plot. There was a life lived inside that character's family walls, and it will be part and parcel of the character's background, hence also part of any decision or reaction that this character makes.

This circle will not be broken. Regardless of the wailing and gnashing of teeth that our public representatives frequently perform to convince us that the family is failing, both the potentially positive influence of the family and the negative consequences of toxic families are everywhere to be seen.

What's failing in our time is the white picket fence image of "family," like the one born in the United States during the first half of the twentieth century and lasted until approximately the time that the oil began to run out. Plenty of people who were around at the time never saw it themselves. For one reason or another they were never able to buy into an arbitrary ideal invented by advertisers to sell real estate.

Suburban, one-job, two-parent nuclear families were simply one of the countless ways that humans have grouped over the ages. Of course, modern suburban life also ushered in the age of young men with stomach ulcers, three-martini-lunch alcoholics, and a leap in the national divorce rates.

There are no great stories of domestic bliss that have come to the fore among those who were able to buy in and live the dream for the handful of decades that it lasted. Now, the shifts of economics and public policy that have put most parents back to work, full-time, chipping away at family togetherness, are cited for their destructive effect upon the family.

Upon one picture of the family, yes. But every day, the sheer volume of phone calls, e-mails, and instant messages that get traded reminds us that the family drive is perennial. People trying to describe a deep sense of bonding shared by those who are not physically related will often refer to the group as "family."

We can separate people from one another in any manner possible, but they will immediately begin to reassert clandestine connections. They will do this in the face of whatever outrageous stresses that events can place upon human existence. They are continuing to do it despite media campaigns designed to distort the world's image of "family" into a salable corporate commodity.

Therefore, in any story—no matter what era—if a child character has no parents, he or she will nonetheless have *parental figures*. So who are they, then? And are they real or imaginary? They must absolutely be present as influential forces in the daily planning and decision-making process that this personality goes through.

Of course, the dark side of today's shifting picture of what constitutes a family is that in the absence of positive and healthy versions of family connections and loyalties, the drive for family will still assert itself. And we all know that the substitute families who fill in the vacuum go on to account for the rise of violent gangs and major crimes upon individuals.

The depth of the brutality is often carried out in the name of a twisted loyalty to a group that may represent the only family connection that the perpetrator has ever known. Even in that extreme case, the distorted family and its poisonous effects (such as the demands placed in return for membership) will define and outline that individual's personality. Every writer has to look for it; every reader will be let down if they don't find it.

So we see the beauty of the full title to this dossier. The adage begins with what sounds almost like a warning, *"The more things change,"* but then comes the comforting conclusion: *"the more they stay the same."*

The settings found in historical fiction are grand pageants, flickering parades of fascination devices. They conceal a simple truth.

ANTHONY FLACCO is a 1990 graduate of the American Film Institute, where he won their Paramount Studios Award for Writing. Immediately upon leaving the A.F.I., he was hired as a feature screenwriter by the Walt Disney Studios. He later published his first of several books, *A Checklist for Murder* (Dell Books), in 1995. He has since done other books, including the internationally acclaimed *Tiny Dancer,* known in Italy as *La Danzatrice Bambina.* This is his second novel about Shane Nightingale and Randall Blackburn.

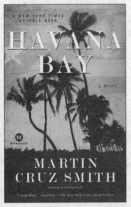
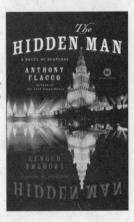